THE SHAMAN TREE

ALSO BY RICHARD ABSHIRE AND WILLIAM CLAIR
Gants

AND BY RICHARD ABSHIRE
The Dallas Drop
Turnaround Jack

THE SHAMAN TREE

Richard Abshire and William Clair

ST. MARTIN'S PRESS / NEW YORK

Design by Robert Bull Design

Library of Congress Cataloging-in-Publication Data

Abshire, Richard.
    The shaman tree / Richard Abshire and William Clair.
      p.   cm.
    "A Thomas Dunne book."
    ISBN 0–312–03426–1
    I. Clair, William R. II. Title.
  PS3551.B84S5   1989
  813′.54—dc20   89–34932

First edition

10 9 8 7 6 5 4 3 2 1

To:
Carol, my wife and
my first fan.

—Richard

To:
The three women in
my life: Gina, April,
and Sher.

—Bill

PROLOGUE

MIDNIGHT. The lake lay waiting, dark and still. Moonlight like a shimmering bridge. A light cool breeze stirred the woods as though to cheer the long-suffering oaks and pines after the heat of the August day.

Upon the lip of the patient lake stood a woman, her face turned back over her shoulder the way she had come, toward the towering oak and the house beyond. She poised there for a moment like an elegant bird, her weight on one leg. The leaves in the top of the massive oak, so far above her that they were lost among the stars that seemed so near, whispered in the breeze a secret the old tree had to tell her.

She was alone, as if she were the first ever to be there. Only the wind in the trees and the lapping of waves at her feet. The frogs who had hushed and jumped in with tiny splashes at her intrusion chirruped again, farther off.

The woman stepped out of her shoes and untied her sash, careful that her robe did not trail in the mud as she laid it upon a handy bush. The water was cold at first as she waded through the clearing between cattails toward the deep water. She shuddered with delight as she bent at the waist and pushed off; the water closed around her, lecherous and brusque over her naked breasts, tumultuous between her thighs. She escaped the compost smell and clinging moss of the shallows with sure unhurried strokes, her legs scissoring in time as she delighted in the secret embrace of the lake.

Moving smoothly toward the moonlight bridge that seemed to span the lake, she swam as though expected toward her certain spot. Halfway there, she turned on her back and swam that way, the lake now slithering with her progress between her cheeks and frothing at her cunt, which glistened silver instead of gold in the cool moonlight as she pulled herself evenly, effortlessly, across the band of light and was swallowed again in darkness. Swimming on her back, she could see the

1

big oak tree waiting for her on shore, but not the house she knew was just the other side of it. As always when she saw the tree at night, thoughts of it flitted through her mind. Quick and unbidden, flickering by without her considering them except to know they were old and hers and familiar, the thoughts of the tree meant nothing, just reflex, like the hardening of her nipples in the cold water.

She turned back onto her belly when she reached her spot and bobbed there, her arms and legs working just enough to keep her perched upon the surface without tiring. She had already adjusted to the water and it was not cold anymore. With three preparatory huffs and puffs, she filled her lungs and disappeared beneath the surface, the smooth and silvery halves of her backside, her trim and shapely legs ending in pointed toes the last of her until all the waves and signs of her having been there were gone and the lake was still again, and then she finally broke the surface, gasping for air. She had not made it all the way to the bottom this time, but the cooler water, the layer deep and still, had invigorated her. She dived twice more before she gave up on making the bottom and contented herself with floating while she thought of Charlie Gants.

She would have told him about the tree, she thought, and all the rest of it. But she had frightened him. Poor man. It was in his eyes, something that had been done with him that he could not let happen again. She mused about poor Charlie, and regretted having troubled him. But she had to do something. There had to be someone.

Reluctantly, she started back, swimming more slowly now than on her way out. Gliding the last few yards on her kick alone, she judged where the swallows began and in a graceful turn spread her arms wide and righted herself, her legs curling down beneath her until her foot sank into the mossy mud. She sloshed ashore with her arms spread wide for balance, her hips rolling with the lithe sinewy grace of an athlete. Now the water felt warm and the night breeze cold, and she shivered when she paused, the water at her knees, to push back her long blond hair with both hands. She wrapped her arms together over her flanks so that her breasts lay upon her wrists and she shivered again and took her next step. Her right foot sank ahead of her in the mud but her left would not follow somehow. A branch or root of some kind beneath the surface rubbed against her left ankle and she swore as she tried to tug herself

2

free. She pulled as hard as she could with her left leg, her whole body, but could not bring her foot free. She had stepped into the fork of a root, she thought, and jammed her ankle tight. She stepped back and pulled, with no better luck. She looked up at the big oak and laughed aloud.

"Is this your doing?" she asked the tree. "I'll bet this is one of your roots I've gotten tangled up with."

As she bent down and groped with both hands to find the root and free herself, she shivered with the chill of the breeze and muttered something about "old dead Indians" and "medicine man."

It was a root all right. She felt it with both hands. It was snug all the way around her ankle and she wondered how she had managed to wedge her foot in so tightly.

With a sudden jerk that took her breath away and toppled her over into the shallow water and wrenched her ankle so badly she thought it might be broken, the root moved. She did not scream, but cursed again and righted herself, and then it moved again. This time it did not stop. The root moved steadily away from the shore and the big oak tree, toward the middle of the lake where the channel ran between drowned trees half as big as the oak itself. She fought and struggled and tried to swim, and thought at first that she was making headway. But she was only going out, away from the shore toward the deep cold water of the channel.

At last, when it was too late and her strength was spent, she tried to scream. But there was no sound except the splashing of her struggle, like a fish on a line. There was no air left when she tried to scream, only the ingushing water and then the cold, cold darkness.

Within moments the lake was still again, calm settling over the patient water. The frogs who had left when the woman came returned and made their night song again as if she had never been.

3

CHAPTER ONE

"**MAKE YOURSELF COMFORTABLE,** Mister Gants," the young intern said, smiling.

He was in his late twenties, rumpled and bored, and sat on one side of a small table, the side nearest the door, thumbing through a collection of printed forms and handwritten notes on a silver clipboard, the kind with a hinged top. He drummed on the table with the ballpoint pen in his right hand.

Across the table sat the patient, a fortyish man with thinning sandy brown hair, slumped in a cheap straightbacked chair, wearing jogging togs. The patient returned the intern's quick smile.

"This is just a routine case review, Mister Gants. We want to update your file."

The patient smiled again and nodded.

"Since this is the first time you and I have spoken, I'd like to start at the top and go through everything, just sort of skim through, hit the highlights. Is that all right with you, Mister Gants?"

"Charlie," the patient said.

"Okay, Charlie. And I'm Doctor Bledsoe."

You're an intern, Charlie thought. How many does this make? An even dozen?

"Now, Charlie, I understand that you're a policeman. A homicide detective, is that right?"

"I was a homicide investigator, but I'm not anymore."

"Oh? Tell me about that."

"Simple. I've been here so long my sick leave ran out. I used up all my benefits. So the department sent me my last pay check and I don't work there any more."

"I'm not sure I understand. I was under the impression that your condition . . . that your being here was job-related."

4

"So was I. But downtown they don't see it that way. They're not sure I lost my mind in the line of duty. I'm still trying, though."

"Trying?"

"Appealing. Trying to get a pension."

"Oh. Well, I certainly hope it works out for you."

"Thanks."

"Tell me about it, will you, Charlie?"

"Sure. I've had plenty of practice."

"I know you've gone through all this a number of times before, but I'd like to hear it from you, all right?"

Charlie knew the kid wanted to put him through it again to compare this version with the earlier ones. He wanted to see if Charlie was what they called making progress. Charlie had been at the Institute long enough to know what they wanted to hear.

"All right. Where shall I start?"

"There was a murder, wasn't there?"

"There were a lot of them. A couple hundred a year."

"One in particular though, yes?"

"Yes."

"A retired police detective?"

"Captain Jonas."

"That one affected you particularly, didn't it? Can you tell me why?"

Damned right, Charlie thought. But I won't.

"It being a policeman, of course. And it looked like a suicide at first."

"But it wasn't a suicide, was it, Charlie?"

"No. It was murder, all right."

"I understand it bothered you so much that you began to have dreams about it, is that right?"

No, Charlie thought, not dreams. The old dead sonofabitch crept into my head, into my life, he haunted me every day and every night until . . .

"Yes, I had several bad dreams."

"About the dead captain?"

"Yes."

"How do you explain that, Charlie?"

The old man wouldn't give up, wouldn't let go until the whole thing was cleared up, all the accounts settled, and he picked me for the job. He haunted me from the grave until it was all settled, he picked me to catch the lightning and he didn't care if I got burned in the process, burned up like a paper match, the goddamned . . .

"I think I overidentified with the victim. It's not unusual. Every once in a while a case comes along that gets to you, you take it home with you, you know? That's what happened to me on this one, I think. I took it personal for some reason, and brooded over it too much. It happens."

"I see," said the intern, chewing his lip and thumbing back and forth through the papers on his shiny clipboard. "Why was that, do you think?"

"I beg your pardon?"

"Why this case? Why did you obsess on this particular case, Charlie?"

"Well, like I said, Jonas was a policeman, so I guess I identified with him on that score. And something else I've given a lot of thought to . . . I think he reminded me a little of my father."

"Your father?"

"Yes. My father had passed away not too long before this, and I think that was on my mind."

"Anything else?"

"Yeah, I'd gone through a divorce not too long before, also, and my daughter . . . she was on my mind a lot. I was pretty depressed already, brooding a little over being separated from her."

"That's . . . Elizabeth?" the intern asked, having found her name somewhere in his forms.

"Yes. Bit. That's my pet name for her."

"I see. And where is she now?"

"In Houston with her mom. She—her mom—remarried."

"I see. Have you seen your daughter lately?"

"Some. Her mother used to bring her to visit, but only twice since they moved. It's been a few weeks. She writes, sends me pictures, stuff like that."

"I guess you're pretty eager to get out of here so you can see her more often."

Damned right, Charlie thought.

"My first priority is to get well. I want to get myself straightened out first. There'll be time enough for everything else after that."

"Good, good," the intern mumbled, making a note. When he had finished, he looked up again at Charlie. "You solved the murder, didn't you?"

Not really, Charlie thought. Jonas did that. He lived inside my head and gnawed at me like a rat until I couldn't sleep, couldn't think of anything else. I went where he sent me, and finally it was over. I hope to God it's over.

"Yes," Charlie said, nodding. "It was a pretty complicated business, but we finally cleared it up."

"I would say more than pretty complicated, Charlie. During this time, there was a serial murderer on the loose. I remember that well enough. The 'East Dallas Slasher,' the media called him. Only it wasn't a man at all, was it?"

No, not at all. It was the most beautiful girl you've ever seen, doc. Charlie remembered her, the eyes, the long coal black hair. Face like an angel.

"No, as a matter of fact, it was Captain Jonas's granddaughter."

"Fascinating."

Yeah, Charlie thought. Bloody fascinating.

"And your partner was involved in the whole thing in some way, wasn't he?"

"Yeah. He was in love with the girl. He'd known her since she was a kid. He knew how mixed-up she was, but he'd fallen in love with her."

"And he went to enormous lengths to protect her, didn't he?"

I would say so, Charlie thought. He put a pistol to old Jonas's head and blew his brains all over his pillow, all over the dingy little bed with the noisy springs in the old man's little end-of-the-line hotel room. He was going to kill me, too, and he would have if the girl's mother hadn't killed him first. Either of them would have killed me if it hadn't been for the old captain . . .

"Considerable lengths, I'd say. He murdered Jonas. Tried to make it look like a suicide."

"Why?"

"The old man had stumbled onto things. He knew about the girl, wanted her to turn herself in, or he would blow the whistle on her. But Braverman stopped him."

"Braverman? Your partner?"

"Yeah."

"How did that make you feel?"

What an ignorant goddamned stupid shrink-ass question! Charlie thought, keeping his face a thoughtful mask.

"Betrayed, I think."

"Betrayed?"

"Yes, I think that would be fair to say. I felt a little betrayed by the whole thing."

"Hmmmm." The intern made more notes. "And what is this reference in your charts to hallucinogenics?"

Charlie was still thinking about Wes Braverman and how he felt, about how it had felt to look up at Wes's smiling face as he stood over Charlie with the gun in his hand and talked about how sorry he was it had come to this.

"I'm sorry?"

"According to your charts a complication of your condition when you were admitted to the Institute was your having ingested hallucinogens. Can you tell me about it?"

"Mrs. Copeland slipped me something in the coffee."

"Mrs. Copeland?"

"Captain Jonas's daughter, the mother of the girl Braverman was in love with. Like I said, it all got pretty complicated."

"And she was married to Miles Copeland, wasn't she?"

"Yeah."

"Jeez, just one of the richest guys in the country, huh? Imagine!"

I don't have to imagine, you dumb shit!

"Yeah, imagine."

"But I'm not clear on that. Why did she drug you?"

"So I wouldn't get in her way. Wes and I went out to see her after her daughter died. She slipped me the stuff and then she killed Wes."

"God. And then what happened?"

And then she killed me, you pencil neck cocksucker.

8

"I managed to get away from her. She was using a razor. I locked myself in a bathroom, and when the cops came she was outside the door. Dead."

"A suicide?"

Not exactly. Charlie remembered the voices on the other side of the door in the big house, the woman's and the old man's. The dead captain's voice. He killed her, Charlie thought, Jonas killed her and took her to be with him, leaving no trace on earth that he had ever lived.

"Yes."

"Jeez," the intern almost whistled. "What an ordeal for you."

"It was pretty rough, but I feel that I'm getting a handle on things now."

"Can you explain that for me, Charlie?"

"Well, I've come to terms with the dynamics of it. I was pretty vulnerable, you know, with the divorce and losing my father and all, and then this case comes along, an old cop and everything. And the thing with Wes, well, what can I say? He was my best friend, and then things turn out the way they did . . . I can look at it all now and see that it was quite a shock, and it's taken time to come to terms with all those issues that contributed to the effect. I feel fortunate that the Institute was here for me. The counseling and everything, it has really helped me to see the whole thing with some perspective."

"Hmmm," again. More notetaking.

But mostly, Charlie thought, I've learned to bullshit with the best of them. The reason I feel better is because the dead captain has left me alone, he's gone wherever the hell you're supposed to go when you die and he has no more use for me. And I think whatever it was that Julia Copeland slipped me in the coffee is out of my system by now, although God knows it ain't easy to tell, with all the dope you people keep giving me to keep me quiet.

"Well, I think it's a good sign that you view your experience here at the Institute in such a positive light. I see by your chart that you've gotten some very good attention. Dr. Cartwright and the Director himself both took personal interest in your case. I think that speaks for itself, don't you?"

"Absolutely."

Charlie thought of Dr. Cartwright. Samantha. Sam. Only he did not think of her in her doctor's white frock. Hardly. When he thought of Sam, it was of the one time they had made love. But that was another story.

"You've had quite a lot of press, haven't you?"

"I suppose so."

"I've read a number of articles. Local papers, even a few magazines. Do you know what they call you?"

"What do you mean, Doctor?" Charlie asked, upset with himself that he had neglected to call the twit "doctor" before. He knew how much the interns liked that.

" 'Charlie Gants, Psychic Detective.' Have you seen that? Have you heard that before?"

"Somebody brought it up, I think. To tell you the truth, I'm not a big newspaper reader, never have been. I don't pay it any attention."

"But what about that? Do you see yourself as a psychic detective?"

"I don't even see myself as a detective anymore, Doctor. I know that if you gave me a clean bill of health today I could never get my job back. There's no way they could chance taking me back. The flashback thing with the hallucinogenics alone would be too big a risk."

"I see. But about the psychic part of it . . . how do you feel about that?"

Like I'd rather be a goddamned leper, Charlie thought. One ghost in a lifetime is more than enough, thank you.

"I'll put it this way, Doctor. You folks have given me every test in the book here at the Institute. What do you think?"

"Hmmm," said the young intern. "But I understand you had a visitor last week. A Miss McKendrick. Yes?"

"Yes."

"What was she here to see you about?"

None of your goddamned business.

"She's not a relative, is she?"

"No. I guess she reads the papers, too. She wanted me to help her with something."

"As a psychic?"

"Or a detective, I'm not sure. I told her I wasn't interested and that was it."

"I see."

10

The intern sat looking at Charlie without saying anything for a while. Charlie did not like that. He preferred counterpunching.

"That was it, Doctor. I promise you I haven't taken out ads or anything."

It was meant to be funny, Charlie having forgotten for the moment that these people had no sense of humor.

"How did you feel about that, about her coming here?"

Charlie tried to hide his sigh of relief. They were back on the bullshit trail again, and he knew his way.

CHAPTER TWO ▮▬▬▬▬▬▬▬▬▬▬▬▬▬▬

CHARLIE GANTS ROUNDED THE LAST CURVE ON THE jogging track, his eyes fixed on the rise ahead, the last obstacle on the course. After that there was just the downhill slope to the pond and then home, back to his room. Calvin Rakestraw, the attendant who had taken a special interest in Charlie, was a few yards ahead of him, and Charlie was closing on him.

Calvin was chiding him.

"Run, Charlie. Dammit, at least trot! Jog, do something!"

Charlie was not intimidated by the taunts of the sadistically con- scientious attendant, who was smiling at him, jogging backward.

" 'Run two miles a day,' the doctor said. Not walk. How are you going to get well walking?" Calvin demanded.

"Screw the doctor," Charlie muttered, conserving his wind and thinking that Samantha Cartwright did screw the doctor. "Screw you."

"Okay, okay," Calvin said, relenting. He slowed to a halt beside the trail before they came into sight of the others. "Take five, man. I don't want you to work yourself to death."

Charlie muttered something about Calvin petering out on him, then joined him on the ground beside the track. He took the cigarette Calvin offered him and they shared a match.

"You're going to get me fired. You know that, don't you?" Calvin said. "If they find me furnishing you cigarettes. We both know that's against the rules."

"Screw the rules," Charlie snarled. "It wasn't smoking that got me here. I guess it would be all right if I smoked a pipe like the Great White Headshrinker."

"And aren't we in a lovely mood this morning," Calvin noted. "Again. What is this, five, six days in a row?"

"I'm in a wonderful mood, considering."

"Right."

"I am, considering. Considering my ex-wife has remarried and hauled her ass off to Houston with my little girl, Samantha Cartwright thinks I'm a headcase that she's just about through playing with, and she's still sleeping with the Great White, 'tops in his field,' and I'm about to get bounced out of this dump like yesterday's news and I don't have a clue where I'm supposed to go or what I'm supposed to live on. Considering all that, I would say I'm in a tip-top mood, screw you very much."

"All that's bullshit and you know it, Charlie. It's been like that for a long time, and you were dealing with it. If you're still biting your lip waiting for Dr. Cartwright to remember the good times you two had, you deserve to be blue. Your daughter moved a couple of months ago, and you know as well as I do that you would like nothing better than to get thrown out of here. As for what you're going to live on, you're probably going to have to get a job, like everybody else. So don't hand me any of that. It's that girl that came to see you last week, and we both know it."

"It is not."

"Damned sure is."

"Is not."

It could have gone on like that while both men finished second smokes, but over the hill came another patient and attendant. It was Miss Shapely, a misnomer come to life, puffing and slobbering along at a full gallop. Miss Shapely was lowing like a Holstein, which was her custom, and trailed her attendant in her wake.

"Somebody to see you, Charlie," Miss Shapely's attendant said as she trotted by, pointing over her shoulder toward the clinic with her thumb. "Been waiting a while."

"Yeah, I've been on the track longer today," Charlie answered as the woman trailed Miss Shapely down the trail. "Went around twice."

"Liar," Calvin spat, returning his cigarettes and matchbook to his sock and smoothing his trouser leg down to make sure they did not show. The no-smoking rule applied to everyone.

Charlie and Calvin argued all the way over the hill and down the slope past the pond and into the clinic about the girl who had come to see Charlie last week. She had been his first visitor in almost two months. His friends from the police department did not come around anymore, and his daughter was gone.

Across the patio where the chief of police had given Charlie his medal while Charlie sat like a vegetable thinking the whole thing was his funeral, Calvin paced his charge, then put on a dash at the very last to beat Charlie inside.

"Cheater," Charlie said, following Calvin through the sliding glass door with two dozen plastic daisy decals spread everywhere there was glass so patients would know when the door was closed and finding himself face to face with Samantha Cartwright, who appeared to be on her way outside, her ever-present clipboard in hand. "Oh," Charlie said, checking himself short of a collision. "Hi."

"Good morning, Charlie," Sam replied, cheery and oblivious to him as anything more than one of the patients. "You were on the track quite a while today, weren't you?"

"Yes, ma'am," Charlie replied, nodding like a dunce. "Went around twice."

Sam cocked an eyebrow at Calvin.

"Certainly did, Doctor Cartwright. The man's a running machine."

"Well, that's good, Charlie. Keep it up."

"I will, thank you."

"Oh, by the way," Sam added, already out the door. "There's a man waiting to see you in the lounge. And don't forget, we'll be taking a look at your test results this afternoon."

"Right. Thank you," Charlie answered, almost touching two fingers of his right hand to the bill of his team softball cap, the one with "Branville Research Institute" in white letters on the front, before he caught himself. "Bitch," he said instead, when the door was shut behind her and only Calvin could hear.

"Good man," Calvin encouraged him. "Keep working on that attitude."

The two men walked off toward the lounge together, and Calvin added, "Next thing you know, you'll have the nerve to say it to her face."

"Screw you."

The man waiting for Charlie had the lounge to himself. They did not get many visitors at the Institute Monday mornings. Charlie had no idea who the man could be, and that bothered him. No visitors for two months, then a stranger last week and this guy today. Charlie did not believe in coincidences, and he had a delicate feel for them, a delicacy he made a point of not mentioning to the doctors, who might think of it more in terms of paranoia.

"I'm Charlie Gants," he said, walking toward the man with his hand extended. He hoped the guy was some kind of a salesman, insurance maybe. Lost track of you, Mister Gants, but you're still in the old data bank, that kind of thing. It occurred to him along with a dozen other thoughts flying past him as he covered the ten or twelve feet across the lineoleum. The whole place was tacky, as far as Charlie was concerned. "Are you here to see me?"

"Leighton Childress, Mister Gants. Good morning. And yes, I am here to see you."

The man turned out to be tall when he stood, and well dressed. His nails were immaculate and polished to a high gloss. His hair was fluffy clean, his shoes patent leather shiny but the real thing. He was so well turned-out he reminded Charlie of a stiff. Ready for the family. Charlie thought to himself that this guy was trouble.

"Is there somewhere we can talk?" Mister Childress wondered.

"Right here," Charlie answered, raising his hands to indicate the lounge. As he said it, Charlie looked to Calvin to see if that would be all right. Calvin nodded. "Good a place as any."

"I thought," Mister Childress said softly, careful of offending, "that perhaps we could talk in private. Your room, perhaps?"

"If you want privacy, that'd be the last place to look," Charlie laughed. "It's me and a couple of other guys. One of 'em won't stop trying to eat all the porcelain, and I'll tell you, I think the other one's crazy."

"You don't have a private room, you mean?" Childress seemed shocked.

"Not anymore. When I first came here I had a room to myself, but I guess I'm not a star anymore."

"I see."

"But enough about me. Seriously, this is as good a spot as any around here. What is it you want to see me about?"

Childress cleared his throat and took a seat, settling his briefcase across his skinny knees. Charlie sat beside him because the seats were bolted to the floor and there were no chairs he could move to sit facing the man. This was for the same reason there was no silverware in the dining room.

Calvin would have left Charlie and the stranger to their business if it had been up to him, but he and Charlie knew he was on orders not to leave Charlie unattended. He was not even sure Charlie wanted to be unattended. Settling for a kind of discreet compromise, Calvin took up a stand near the door that opened from the lounge into the front desk area, the foyer as they liked to call it at the Institute. There was nowhere for Charlie to go, not even through one of the two big picture windows through which you could watch the traffic pass by. The windows were Plexiglas, not glass, and they had not even bothered to put any of the plastic flowers on them. There was no need.

It occurred to Charlie as Childress twirled the combination lock on his briefcase that maybe this was good news. What the hell, he told himself, look on the bright side for a change. Maybe the man is from the pension fund. That could be it. The city had turned down Charlie's original request for a disability pension because he could not prove he had lost his mind in the line of duty. He thought the letters from the pension board made it sound like carelessness on his part, like he put his mind somewhere and then just could not remember where, as if he went to work one day and forgot and left his mind at home and when he remembered and went back for it somebody had thrown it out. It had not been like that, and he had expected more consideration from the board. There was the thing about the drugs, but that had not been his idea or his fault. Julia Copeland, the late Julia, had done that, slipped the stuff in his coffee. Now there was all that about flashbacks and how they could not risk giving back his gun. He had tried to explain to them in his letters that he had not lost his mind over the drugs, that had not been it at all. That was over and done with. The mind thing was from the stress of the whole business, the dead captain, the dreams, and . . .

Charlie noticed that Mister Childress was looking at him, and he surmised that there had been a question he had missed. Childress looked at him with raised brows, waiting.

"I beg your pardon?" Charlie said, leaning toward Childress and raising his eyebrows in return.

"I said, this is about Miss Amber McKendrick."

Charlie heard it that time, but the name did not register. He made a note to pay closer attention. He did not want any bad reports getting back to the doctors. But he was at a loss and it must have shown on his face, because Childress explained.

"Amber McKendrick. She came to see you the first of last week, I believe. I have the letter you wrote her."

"You do?" Charlie asked and Childress showed it to him. Writing the damned thing had not broken any rules, but Childress was pointing it at Charlie like it was evidence. "Why? What are you doing with it?"

"I am here to learn exactly what it was that she wanted you to do. In your letter, you write that you cannot do what she has asked of you, but there is no mention of specifics. I would like you to explain."

"Look," Charlie began, his mind clanging like a rusty engine as he tried to kick it into life. "I don't know who you are or what's going on here, but a nice young lady came to see me and we talked. I wrote her a letter, and that's it. I haven't done anything or said anything that would be a problem for anybody. And if you want to know any more than that, I think you should ask the young lady. And by the way, I remember now, she did say her name was Amber. The McKendrick part, I'm not positive."

"I would very much like to ask her, Mister Gants, but I'm afraid I can't. In point of fact, if I could, then there would be no reason for my coming here at all."

"What do you mean?"

"My card."

Childress plucked a flat gold case out of an inside pocket with two thin, pampered fingers. Charlie took the card and began to understand. G. LEIGHTON CHILDRESS, ESQ., the card read in gold letters that stood up like the walls of a house with no roof. Below that, ATTORNEY AT LAW and a phone number with a prefix Charlie could not place.

"Oh." Charlie sighed, casting a reassuring glance at Calvin to let him know things were clearing up. Calvin did not appear to be paying any attention to Charlie or the lawyer. "This explains it."

"It does," Childress wondered. "Explains what?"

"You know," Charlie answered, spreading his hands and shrugging his shoulders. "The general feel of it. You and the manicure and everything, a guy like you in a place like this talking to me. You know, the . . ." He could not think of a better word and meant no offense. "The smell of it, like day-old fish. The heartburn. That's what it is, you're a lawyer. I was having a perfectly natural reaction. You must get it all the time."

"As a matter of fact . . ." Childress began, his head bobbing forward on his scrawny neck like a bull calf, and then he stopped. His eyes left Charlie and rolled up as if he were remembering something. His head raised to its more or less normal position, allowing for the hump between his shoulders from too much time spent hunched over law books, or something. "As a matter of fact, Mister Gants, I do get a lot of that. I really do. Huh."

Charlie's eyes went to the card in his hand, to the letter Childress was holding, and as far into the open briefcase as he could manage without being obvious.

Finished considering this little insight Charlie had provided, Childress cleared his throat and was all business again. Before he could speak, Charlie beat him to the punch.

"What do you mean about you can't ask her and if you could you wouldn't be here? What happened, is she gone or something?"

But Childress was a cautious man. He reached into his case and produced a photograph, an unposed snapshot of a very good-looking blonde in her twenties with blue eyes that looked out at Charlie as if there was nothing to be afraid of. She was wearing shorts, horsing around with a hotsy-totsy pose that showed off her legs as well as if she had been serious. It must have been a picnic, Charlie thought, with the tables behind her loaded with food and people milling around in the background. Behind her, beyond the milling people, there was something so big and blackish that it not only took up the center third of the frame, it would have drawn your eyes to it before the girl if she had not been so good-looking. Charlie remembered her eyes especially, and then for the first time admitted that the girl in the photo looked a lot like Doctor Cartwright. When she was younger, he added venomously to himself.

"Amber is dead, Charlie," Childress said, and the words fell like sandbags dropped on the concrete slab beneath the linoleum at Charlie's feet from way up in the backstage rigging somewhere, from somewhere a lot higher than the roof of the one-story Institute. "May I call you Charlie?"

"Yeah," Charlie told him, looking at the picture of the girl in his right hand while his left hand pressed itself against his chest to keep the heartburn from starting. "Why not? How?"

Childress was looking for something in his briefcase and this time he did not hear Charlie.

"I beg your pardon?" he said.

"How did it happen? How did she die?"

"It was her then, Charlie? It was the girl in the picture."

"Yeah, it was her. Why wouldn't it be? You know her, don't you? I mean, you know Amber and you found my letter to her, why wouldn't it be her? Isn't this Amber in the picture?"

"Of course it is. Don't upset yourself. We're all in shock about it."

"Who's in shock?"

"The family, of course, her parents, brothers and sisters, all her friends, everyone who knew her."

"How did Amber die?"

"She drowned, accidentally."

"You mean as opposed to on purpose?"

"Of course not, Charlie. Suicide is out of the question. Anyone who knew Amber knows that."

"Anyone who looked in her eyes knows it," Charlie said. "I didn't mean to imply that she committed suicide, I meant exactly what happened, exactly what are you saying. No foul play, absolutely?"

"Absolutely, as far as I know personally. The sheriff was called out. And the fire department too, for that matter. They found her. Drag

18

lines were no help because of the way the bottom is. They had to use divers. Poppa McKendrick wouldn't let them quit till they found her."

"That's her father?"

"Yes. Fine man."

"So?"

"So what, Charlie?"

"So what did they find? They recovered the body, what else? Do they have autopsy results yet? What about marks, wounds, that's what."

"Professional suspicion, or do you know something, Charlie?"

Charlie did not miss the change in the tone of the lawyer's voice. He was paying attention to everything now, and he caught the change, in Childress's voice and in his eyes. The man was even sitting straighter. This was not the way he had been sounding, stiff and a little silly, a little clerkish. This guy was real, Charlie told himself. Watch your step, Charlie, he said to himself. Test the wind.

"I know she came to me wanting help. There was trouble at home. I'm not sure exactly what kind of trouble, and I don't think she knew either. Said there had been a rash of accidents, like a streak of bad luck only she thought there was something or someone behind it. There was something she tapdanced around about like she thought I would think she was crazy or something. I thought that was funny, I would think she was crazy, right? I didn't probe it, but something about a family curse."

"Did you think her crazy?"

"If I did, I wouldn't hold it against her. I've been crazy a little over three months now. Some of my best friends . . . you know."

"Did you take her seriously about the curse? Or, I should say, would you have if you had probed?"

"I spent a rough couple of weeks not long ago walking around with a ghost at my elbow, a brainshot old man who didn't know when to call it quits." Charlie stopped to catch his breath and wished to God he had a cigarette. He darted a look at Calvin but Calvin was chatting up the new girl on the floor and could not be bothered. "Childress, I'm being a little flip about it right now, but the point is that I know exactly what it is to see what nobody else sees and butt your head against a wall trying to make somebody understand. So, no, if she had said she believed there was a curse, I would not have written her off."

"I know about the police captain and the other murders, Charlie. I found these among Amber's things, along with your letter."

Childress showed the newspaper clippings Charlie had seen before but had not kept. They were all there, one original and the rest photocopies. That told Charlie that Amber had come across one article, the original, and had dug up the rest of them in somebody's back-copy file and copied them.

"I'm afraid I wasn't as open-minded about it as you, Charlie. Amber and I talked about this, about all the accidents, the rumors and the business about the Shaman Tree. But I don't hold with the mumbo-jumbo side of things. There'll be time enough for magic when all the evil of simple greed is done with."

"The what? What kind of tree?"

"The Shaman Tree. That's it in the picture, in the background."

"This is a tree?" Charlie wondered, looking at the photo again. "She said she was from Paris. Outside of Paris, Lamar County."

"Yes."

"Well, I'm from that part of the country myself, Sulphur Springs, and I've never seen a tree this size anywhere around there."

Charlie remembered that he and the girl had laughed about Paris, about telling people she was from Paris and sometimes they thought she meant France. Of course, she meant Paris, Texas. "Freak of nature. It's a damned big tree, I'll grant you, for what it's worth. An oak. I understand people used to come from miles around to gawk at it. Of course that was in the old days, before television. There weren't many diversions then, and I guess a damned big tree was news. But let's do this in order. The answers to your questions first: no autopsy, because it's seldom done in Lamar County and no one saw a need for it; marks and bruises, there were dozens, she'd been in the water seventeen, eighteen hours; pronounced lacerations, though, on her left ankle. Probably wedged in a tree branch or something. That lake was not meant for swimming, not that far out. It's just a creek dammed up to water the stock. Out in the channel where they found Amber there are hundreds of submerged trees that used to line the creek bed, plus whatever has washed down downstream and settled in the last fifty or sixty years. That's why the drag lines were useless, too much for them to tangle on in the water. A man couldn't find divers willing to go down there for money. The men from the fire department did it for Poppa. Everybody thinks a lot of him. They didn't want him to have to wait until . . ."

Until she decomposed and her entrails congealed and made gas to give her enough buoyancy to work loose from the snag and rise to the surface. Charlie knew what the lawyer meant and raised his hand to say so, so he wouldn't have to listen to it.

Neither of them spoke for a while, sitting side by side in the tacky lounge considering their respective horrors. From down the hall around the corner somewhere Charlie heard Miss Shapely coming in from her run, bawling like a hungry calf.

"What else?" Charlie asked at last.

"Nothing more about Amber. I'm afraid that's all there is."

"It's going to be an accident, then. Officially."

"Unless somebody comes up with something. Poppa is resigned to it. He knows Amber thought herself a good swimmer, he'd asked her not to swim alone in the lake at night, offered to have a pool put in if she wanted one. But she was headstrong. Maybe you saw that."

"Maybe." More than a little, Charlie said to himself. Which was why he had not been able to make her settle for no face-to-face. The least she would accept was a promise to think on it. He had told her no the next day in a letter, the letter the lawyer had now, along with the rest of her effects. *Effect.* Charlie thought not for the first time that was an odd thing to call a dead person's stuff. "That's it, then. The sheriff buys it, Pops buys it. Case closed."

"Not yet," Childress said, his voice dead flat and earnest.

"What does that mean?" Charlie asked.

"It means I don't buy it, not yet."

"What do you have to do with it?"

"I represent Amber. If she was murdered, I want to know it. And I want whoever did it."

"Good. Which leaves me."

"Exactly. I have an offer for you, if you're up to it."

"I don't take dares, counselor. And they're holding a staff meeting somewhere right now trying to figure out what I'm up to."

"I've spoke with Dr. Branville. Good man," Childress assured him.

21

"Yeah, tops . . ." Charlie mumbled.

"I beg your pardon?"

"Screw Branville," Charlie whispered.

"I'm sorry?"

"Never mind, clearing my throat. You say you talked to Branville?"

"Yes. He thinks you've made good progress."

"That's what they said about the roommate I had before when he started pissing in the flower pot instead of the trash can. Progress is a relative term around here, counselor."

"I can imagine. Relatively speaking, then, Branville thinks you're probably ready to leave the Institute."

"Probably? What is it with you doctors and lawyers? You get a course in weasel words at school, or what? What color is that wall over there, basically more or less greenish? Give me a break."

The wall was an unqualified green, like an operating room. All the walls at the Institute were green because it was supposed to be a restful color.

"The bottom line is it's up to you, Charlie. Has been all along. Yours is a voluntary commitment here. There's nothing holding you."

The hell you say, Charlie thought, the list of reasons for not leaving spinning by in his mind's eye like screen credits. Among them was the threat, he could not remember if it had been made aloud or only intimated or even just imagined, that it would be a simple matter for the doctors, Branville and Cartwright, to arrange a mandatory commitment for a man in his condition. Or to have it extended, for that matter.

"So," Charlie said aloud. "What I hear you saying is that the free ride's about over. They're ready to toss me out of this little cabaña by the duckpond, is that it?"

"Talk to them, Charlie. I won't meddle. But if you are up to it, and I understand you are, I'd like you to listen to my proposition."

"Go ahead."

"As Amber's executor and legal representative, I am empowered to discharge her estate and see to her last wishes. One of those wishes was that you would come to the McKendrick ranch and find out what is going on there. I am within my authority to engage you to do that. She

22

left a sizable estate. I've no idea what your financial situation is and it's none of my business, but . . ."

For all his bitching to Calvin and his very real horror of leaving the Institute and starving to death a bum, Charlie did have a little money. For three months he had had no expenses except child support so most of his salary had gone to his mother's bank in Sulphur Springs. There was something in his payroll deduction savings account at the credit union and his vested interest in the pension fund if the board said no to his appeal, a pension for life if they said yes. The lawyer was calling his bluff with his offer of money. Nothing to stop you now, Charlie. He interrupted Childress.

"No, it's not your business. But let's understand what my business is, if you want to call it that. I'm not some frigging ghostbuster who makes haunted house calls, and I'm not . . . I'm not anything in particular. I'm just what's left after a couple of weeks being chased all over town by a ghost and then ninety days in this dump. I told her that, and I'm telling you. If you want somebody to ride into town with a Ouija board and an ectoplasm detector, don't waste your time with me. I tried to make her understand that, but she wouldn't take no for an answer. All I am is . . . a burned-out cop. Ex-cop. And if my luck finally turns good, which I don't dare to hope, my dream will come true and I will be a retired cop. With honors. Which I would gladly refund if I could take back the last few months."

Childress took his time answering, so Charlie wouldn't think there was an argument, wouldn't feel Childress gently convincing him of something.

"What you are, Charlie, is an experienced homicide investigator with a good record until your last case. The last thing in the world I want on Poppa's ranch is a spook hunter, a clairvoyant. I didn't do enough for Amber and now she's dead. There it is. I feel responsible and I want to do whatever I can so I can feel better about it. She thought you were the man for the job and that's enough for me. I don't think it was an accident, Charlie, any more than you do. Amber was too . . . she wasn't a person that kind of accident happens to. She'd swum in that lake all her life. She was strong and smart and she didn't lose her head."

"I know," Charlie said. He thought those things about her too, although he'd only spent an hour with her.

"There's more to it than a big tree, Charlie. I don't know what Amber told you, but she might have failed to mention how rich they are. Poppa's estate is in the millions. Nobody knows what the land alone is worth. Big stakes, and people who could stand watching. I'm not looking for a ghostbuster, Charlie, I need a good detective."

"How do you see it? If the old man . . ."

"He's resigned himself it was an accident. But I've told him everything I've just told you. If you agree, Poppa will go along with us. He'll provide a cover for you with the rest of the family. Only he and I will know. If there's a chance of foul play, he wants to know."

"I see."

"What do you say, Charlie?"

"I'll think it over and get back to you."

"That's what you said to Amber."

"That's right, and I can spot a guilt trip a mile away. I haven't just been sitting around this dump enjoying the sitz baths. If you think you let her down, that's your business. Leave me out of that. I've got enough reasons of my own to keep straight."

"You're right, Charlie." Childress closed his briefcase and stood. When Charlie offered the photograph of Amber he shook his head. He wanted Charlie to keep it. Charlie knew what that was, too, but he didn't call it. He didn't mind keeping the picture. "You have my card. The office can get in touch with me any time."

Childress offered his hand and Charlie took it. Charlie walked him out toward the desk and the front door. Toward them. Calvin could not let him go beyond the line where the linoleum stopped and the carpet started. So Charlie stopped there. As the lawyer said good-bye, Charlie was looking down at their feet, the lawyer's shiny oxfords on the carpet, his sneakers on the linoleum.

"One more thing, Charlie." Childress turned in the door he held open with one hand so that Charlie could see the world beyond him. "If you decide to help me with this, I'll look into that pension business for you, pro bono. Call it a bonus. No guarantees, of course, but it's hardly corporate mergers, is it?"

Childress did not say good-bye, he just pushed the door all the way back against the stop and he was gone, and Charlie stood at the line this side of the desk and watched the pneumatic arm at the top of the door collapse on itself like an elbow, swinging the door ever so slowly shut.

CHAPTER THREE ▰

"**COME IN,** Charlie. Make yourself comfortable."

Samantha Cartwright held the door open with one hand and with the other invited Charlie into the office.

Charlie stepped across the threshold onto the plush beige carpet. He had been paying a lot of attention to floor coverings lately, he admitted to himself, wondering what that meant. Carpet meant a lot in this place.

It was a corner office, with big windows along one side and behind the desk with its high-backed leather chair. Branville's office. Charlie settled into one of the two armless straight chairs with chrome legs that faced the desk. He did not think the arrangement of chairs was any accident either, any more than the thick carpet. When the doctor was in, he could lean back with his desk in front of him like a judge and he could see the door that opened into the corridor. Sitting in either of the straight chairs facing him, you could not lean back or swivel or anything. You just sat there, with the door behind you. If someone opened the door to show the doctor something or to signal him somehow, you could not see it without turning around or standing up. All you could do was look at the doctor behind his desk or look out the big windows onto the grounds behind the Institute, at the pond or the patio, the jogging track. If the day was pretty enough to be a distraction, the doctor would close the drapes and then you could only look at him. Charlie knew enough about interrogation to know there were reasons for everything in the room, for the way things were arranged.

"I have the results of your tests," Sam said, after she had closed the door and retrieved Charlie's file from the desk. "How are you feeling today, Charlie?"

"You tell me," Charlie answered, sounding a little bitter without meaning to. Sam reproached him gently with a look and he added, "Fine. I mean, I feel fine. Really good."

25

"I'm glad to hear it."

She settled onto a corner of the desk facing Charlie, her hip resting beside Branville's desk set, her leg dangling. She kicked her foot absently as she looked through Charlie's file.

Charlie did not ask her any of the questions he wanted to ask or say anything to distract her, to remind her that he was there. He contented himself with looking at her from the safe voyeurism of having been forgotten by her.

He wondered at it, the way she seemed untouched by him, by what had happened between them. As if he expected his having once made love to her to show somehow, he searched her face for some sign of it. But she was unmarked, untouched by him, the way the ocean after a shipwreck carries no sign of the passion and struggle of a sunken ship. That notion having appeared to him, he thought again of the photo in his pocket, the face of the pretty blonde. She reminded him of Sam, although he had not realized or admitted it until the lawyer showed him the picture. Drowned. And the lake where she had died closed over her like the sea, with no sign of her struggle. Like Sam, unmarked by his struggling.

Charlie was remembering his ex-wife, how he and the silly cuddling girl he married had become someone else, until he could not remember their having been in love. He thought that the last time he had seen her it had been as if their being in love, making love, had never happened or had happened to someone else. It is amazing how people change, he thought, or is it something else?

"Doctor Branville will be joining us in a moment, Charlie."

"What's the occasion?"

"Meaning what? Why do you say that, Charlie?"

"I don't know. I haven't seen much of him, that's all."

"I hear resentment."

"No," Charlie lied. "It's just that he doesn't meet with patients personally very often. I'm just wondering if this is something special."

"Do you feel special? Do you feel that this is a special occasion in some way?"

"I don't know." Charlie was sick of it, the way everyone in this place answered questions with questions. It must be the first thing they learn in school, he thought. "How did I do on the tests? What do you think?"

"I think you're coming along very well. You've made a lot of progress since you've been here. Your tests are all very encouraging."

"So I'm well?"

"Don't be simplistic, Charlie. You're more intelligent than that, and you've been in treatment long enough to know how things are."

Her eyes swept up and her face brightened as she rose from the desk and smiled. Charlie knew without looking that it was Branville.

"Good afternoon, everyone."

Branville's voice was so good you knew he had worked on it. He could have made a living narrating documentaries on public television. He swept into the room and Sam cocked her head to one side, smiling, for all the world like a dog wanting to be petted.

Branville rounded his desk and Sam, who pivoted to stand beside his chair, snuggled Charlie's file to her breasts. Branville took no particular notice of her as he slipped off his tweed jacket and hung it on a rack in the corner between the two big windows. The drapes were open today, and Charlie looked past the two of them at the grounds.

The good doctor's pipe, and expensive briar caked and worn with use, dangled from a corner of his mouth. The room was quiet, waiting for him to settle in. Charlie looked behind him and of course the door was closed.

"Worst part of all of this," Branville was saying. "The money part. Lunch with the ladies. Well-meaning old crones, millions their late husbands left in funds to do good or ease their consciences. Haven't a clue what our work is about, all they want is entertainment and stroking. 'Doing the good work,' I tell them. They all like giving their money to museums better. They can see the bloody paintings."

"How did it go?" Sam asked.

"Well enough, I suppose. We'll see."

He plopped into his chair and swiveled toward Sam to take Charlie's file from her. He opened it and raised the first few pages as his brow furrowed, which Charlie had long ago decided was an affectation the doctor intended to impress you that he was deep in thought about your case. Charlie thought that Branville was never very deep in thought about anything except funding. That was what these people called money, funding.

Branville worked his swivel chair in a slow circle away from Charlie toward the window and then all the way back again until he sat facing his desk. He dropped the file upon the desk and rummaged through a drawer until he found a book of matches.

Sam and Charlie waited patiently while Branville struck his match. Clamping the gnawed stem of his pipe with his teeth, he cupped the match between his thumb and forefinger and was absorbed for what seemed too long in setting fire to what was left in the bowl. When he was satisfied it was stoked and burning properly, he finally raised his eyes to Charlie and smiled.

Leaning forward on his elbows on the desk, Branville studied Charlie for a moment before he spoke. Charlie returned his gaze as amiably as he could, not wanting to either challenge the doctor with a glare or to avoid his eyes.

"So, Charlie," Branville began. "We have your test results here."

Charlie nodded but did not offer anything.

"Everything looks . . . satisfactory. Good, I would say. Don't you think so, Sam?"

"Yes. Very good," Sam agreed, looking at Branville, not at Charlie.

"Well, 'very good,' I'm not sure I'd go quite that far," Branville cautioned. "We don't want to paint too rosy a picture, do we?"

That was another thing about this place that was driving Charlie crazy, besides the way everybody answered questions with questions. There was never anything clear or permanent. Everything was a matter of opinion. They had the results of his latest tests right there in his file. If they were real doctors, the results were one thing or another, good or bad. The leg was broken or it was not. Period. But these people interpreted everything.

"I feel pretty good," Charlie offered, as much to side with Sam as to explain how he felt.

"Good, good," Branville said, preoccupied with tamping his pipe with a little chrome tool he had taken from his shirt pocket, as if that was more important than how Charlie felt. "And how long have you been with us now, Charlie?"

28

"Three months, give or take."

"Yes. I remember you were not in very good shape when you came here. Yes?"

That was another thing, the way Branville said something and then added that little "yes?" at the end of it, like a villain in a war movie, the Nazi doctors interrogating the hero. "You vill tell us everyzing, yes?" It was not hard to find things he did not like about Branville. Of course, Sam was the main thing.

"Pretty bad, I'd say," Charlie agreed, trying not to let them see that any of it bothered him.

"Well, you had been through an ordeal." Branville thumbed through the pages in Charlie's file as if to refresh his memory as to exactly what Charlie had been through. "A fascinating case. And a bloody mess." He turned pages. "Highly publicized."

Branville showed Charlie several pages of photocopied newspaper stories, some of them the same stories the dead girl's lawyer had shown him. Charlie could make out some of the headlines: HAUNTED DETECTIVE SOLVES FAMILY MURDERS, PSYCHIC COP? Charlie looked at the second one twice, thinking at first that it said "psycho cop." Charlie knew that the publicity had been part of what attracted Branville in the first case. High-profile patients attract funding. But he had not panned out for the good doctor. Because he was not haunted anymore. Or his dreams had stopped, depending on your point of view.

"It was your dreams that most interested us, of course," Branville went on. "The notion that you were somehow especially sensitive to some kind of . . . psychic disturbances . . ." Branville did not finish, his voice trailing off as he lost himself in something theoretical.

Charlie had long ago given up trying to convince anyone that the ghost who had driven him mad had not been a dream at all, that it had been as real as moonlight. That was what he had learned at the Institute, he had learned not to insist.

"But your dreams have stopped, yes?" Branville rejoined them.

"Yes."

"And your test results are unremarkable."

"Indicating that you've made good progress," Samantha put in, seeming not to want Charlie to feel dismissed as unremarkable. Feeling

29

Branville's cocked-eyebrow look, she added, "That you've basically gotten over a very trying experience."

"Indicating that there's precious little more we can do for you here, Charlie. Except perhaps to tell you this: You mustn't live the rest of your life as if it were merely a sequel to the case that brought you here. Your life from this point on has its own meaning. Do you understand?"

"I think so."

"And don't believe your own press, 'Psychic Cop' and all that. You're no psychic and you're not a cop anymore, either. And that is just as well. You were probably too . . . delicate for that sort of a life anyway. Don't look back, Charlie. Take charge of your life and get on with it, that's what I'm saying. Sam, where are we on medication here?"

Sam and Branville huddled to murmur about what they had been giving Charlie, pills, injections, and all the rest. Charlie tuned out the talk about cc's and Thorazine and all of it, and watched how Sam's hand lay upon Branville's shoulder as they conferred, the graceful way her fingers curled.

"Well, that's certainly progress," Branville announced. "Sleeping through the night without sedatives. You are making good progress with your physical therapy, according to Mister Rakestraw's reports."

"Running my butt off," Charlie smiled, happy that Calvin had lied to them about the jogging. "And I seem to have more energy."

"Endorphines," Branville said, without bothering to explain. But Charlie had read the magazines in the lounge, the stuff about running making your body crank out enzymes that got you high and all of that. He could play their game.

"Your physical looks good. Everything well within normal ranges. I think we've put you back in pretty good shape, if I do say so myself."

"Well, I feel good."

Branville sat back in his chair and went almost cross-eyed staring into his pipe bowl as they all heard the gurgling sputtering sounds that meant he would have to reload the thing. With a harrumph he took the pipe out of his mouth and laid it aside on his desk. Still leaning back, his legs crossed, he studied Charlie for a long moment before he spoke again.

"Good enough to leave?" he asked.

"I beg your pardon?"

"Do you feel good enough to bid us adieu, go back out into the world?"

"You're the doctor. I mean, I feel pretty good . . ."

"Are you afraid?"

"Yeah. A little, I guess."

"Perfectly normal. I'd be concerned if you weren't."

Charlie lost focus then, not wanting to think about leaving. He had been thinking about it since the lawyer left that morning, thinking about it and the girl in the photo in his pocket. But he did not like the idea that it was here now, the part where he only had to say so and it would be over. He did not want to leave them alone, Sam and Branville. It made no sense, he knew. His being there had not kept anything from happening between them, but he had the notion that leaving meant something more, meant saying it really was over. He had imagined that she would come back to him if he waited long enough, if . . . They were huddling again, talking about him as if he was not there. Charlie watched them, and he knew that Sam cared more for Branville than he did for her. Why couldn't she see that? There was more to it, he knew. He could have understood if she loved Branville. He knew about loving someone. But it was not that. She did not love him, only needed him and all the rest was only what she had to do to have him. But Branville did not need her, and he used her. Serves her right, Charlie told himself. Turnabout's fair play. As the two of them talked about him, Charlie imagined that they were making love and he was watching them. Branville's big hands up her skirt, her thighs parting as he pressed her back upon the desktop. The silk blouse opening, her breasts rising out of the blue chemise Charlie remembered from the time he had made love to her. Branville's lips playing over her throat, his tobacco-stained teeth biting her here and there as she squealed and whispered his name. His gray-streaked beard disappearing between her breasts, her legs closing around his back as he . . .

"Charlie?" Sam said, her eyebrows arched to mean that she was repeating herself.

"I beg your pardon?" Charlie shifted in his straight-backed chair and crossed his legs to hide from them the effect his daydream had had on him. He looked from her to Branville and realized that by crossing his legs he had mirrored the way Branville was sitting. He wondered if Branville was hiding an erection too.

"I was saying, you've had a pair of visitors," Branville said, with a smirk that left Charlie wondering if his mind was being read. "First the young lady, Miss McKendrick. And Mister Childress this morning. I spoke with Childress yesterday, you know."

"He told me. I hope you gave me a good reference."

"Have you thought about his proposition, Charlie?" Branville asked, not bothering to tell Charlie what kind of a reference he had given.

"Yes."

"Well? What have you decided?"

"To wait and see what the two of you had to say about my test results. What do you say?"

"We've already told you," Sam put in impatiently. "You're doing well. Your tests are normal."

"It's up to you, Charlie," Branville added, with a look at Sam that Charlie knew meant he had not liked her saying anything so unambiguous as "normal." "If you feel up to it, there's no reason you can't accept Mister Childress's offer."

"Oh, good . . . I guess."

"You're ambivalent," Branville informed him. It was not news to Charlie.

"And a little surprised. I thought you two would be against it. You know, what Childress is talking about is a little . . . I mean, a family curse, that kind of thing. It's a little close to home, don't you think? Aren't you worried I might have a relapse or something? I know I am."

"That's understandable," Branville assured him. "But as I look at it, this is a promising opportunity for you. You've spent ninety days with us calming down, quieting yourself. Naturally, you can continue this after you leave here if you wish. But in a sense you may never know how far you've come if you never confront your feelings. It's a therapeutic technique . . ."

"Confrontational therapy. I've heard of it before," Charlie interjected. Sam had explained it to him that time so long ago when he had been afraid of a song. She had made him listen to it, and he had slept and the ghost had . . . Yeah, he thought, I know about that approach.

"There are significant differences, too. If you choose to accept Childress's offer, you can maintain the option to withdraw. If things get too rough, you can always quit. It won't be like your experience before, compulsive."

"And we will be here for you," Sam offered. "A phone call away, if you need us."

"Sounds like you two are throwing me out."

"Not at all . . ." Sam began, and then Branville cut her off.

"Exactly. Throwing you out, the way a bird nudges a fledgling out of the nest when it's time for him to try his wings. We'd be doing you no favor to let you hide from the world here forever."

"You're saying it's time for me to go. If I don't go for Childress's deal, then I'm still out. I just have to find myself a place on my own."

"Not quite so cut and dried, Charlie," Sam said. "We think if you don't want to take the job Childress offered you, it would still be best that you take a step. We would still see you, as an outpatient. It's just that you've progressed to that point. It's time to make a move."

"I see." Charlie put his hands together like church steeples and brought his fingers to his lips, resting his chin on his thumbs, as if he was deep in thought. What he was really thinking was that he did not believe in coincidence. What he was really going over in his mind he would never say to Sam or Branville, not with the way they liked to talk about paranoia. But he was not buying it for a moment. The girl last week, the lawyer today, and now this. It was too neat by half.

"And if you find we've been too optimistic, you can always come back to us, re-admit yourself."

Branville meant that to be reassuring, but it was anything but. He was pressing, Charlie thought, trying to sell me on the idea. There was nothing in Branville, body or soul, that would let him admit he had made a mistake. It was that part about being too optimistic, as if Branville wanted Charlie to believe that the Great White Shrink would ever admit error that sealed the deal for Charlie. There was something going on, he knew. And there was only one way he could think of to get at it. But he did not want to go along too easily.

"But what about your research, Doctor Branville? The paper you're going to do on me? Do you have enough for that?"

Sam and Branville exchanged glances and Charlie wondered if she had said too much back at the first of it, or had he surprised her by remembering?

"Don't concern yourself, Charlie. You're my primary concern here." Branville began reloading his pipe. "The patient before the paper, you know."

"I see."

Branville fidgeted with his pipe and Sam stood silent, her weight shifted onto the hip nearest her lover, her eyes on the doctor's busy hands. They waited for Charlie to speak.

"Okay," Charlie said at last. "I think you're right. I'll call Childress and see what I can do for him."

"You have his number?" Sam asked.

"Yes, he gave me his card."

"You can use the phone in the day room if you like," she said.

"Thanks. I'll make it collect." They all smiled at that, but Charlie did not think any of them meant it. "And then what? Do I just walk out of here?"

"You're voluntary, Charlie," Sam reminded him. "We're not holding you here, we never have been. It's up to you. Just speak to Miss Cowpers in the office. There will be papers for you to sign. You can be on your way this evening."

"I see." Charlie stood. "Well, it all seems pretty sudden. Thanks. Thanks for everything."

He did not shake Sam's hand, only smiled at her. She returned his smile and put a hand on his shoulder. It was only there for an instant and might have been just a gentle push toward the door. Charlie stood his ground long enough to reach across the desk and offer his hand to Branville, who did not rise from his chair but did lean forward enough to shake hands with him.

"Remember," Branville called out to him as Charlie reached the door. "We're here if you need us. A phone call away."

Charlie smiled again and nodded, then rolled his hand at them to wave good-bye.

Calvin sat waiting in one of the half dozen chairs outside Branville's office. He looked up as Charlie stepped through the door and eyed him critically.

"You don't look any worse for wear," Calvin stage-whispered.

Before Charlie could answer, Sam called from behind him.

"Mister Rakestraw, would you come here for a moment?"

Calvin rose and started in, then paused to let Charlie re-enter ahead of him. Charlie stood holding the door.

"That's all right, Mister Rakestraw. Charlie will wait for you outside. We won't be a minute, Charlie. Do you mind?"

Charlie shook his head no and smiled at Calvin. This was irregular, for Charlie to be left unattended. Calvin mugged with his lips and eyes to show Charlie he was impressed, then went inside and Sam asked him to close the door.

When the door closed, Charlie found himself alone for the first time in longer than he could remember. As Branville would say, he felt "ambivalent" about it. Calvin was a good man, and Charlie had grown accustomed to him. He settled into the chair where Calvin had waited and hoped a nurse or orderly would come along to challenge him. He wanted a chance to tell someone he was leaving, a chance to hear himself say it so he could see how it made him feel.

CHAPTER FOUR ▉════════════════════════

CHARLIE WAS LOST IN THOUGHT WHEN CALVIN CAME out of the office, but not so lost that he did not have the feeling that he had been in with Sam and Great White a pretty long time. He could not be sure about how long it had been, or of anything else about time, though. He was not allowed his watch and there were no clocks on the walls of the Institute. There were reasons, of course, but he had never puzzled it out, except that it was a way of not being in control. They were the timekeepers here.

"Well, well, well," Calvin smiled down at him. "Big day, huh?"

"Yeah, I guess so."

"Try to clamp a lid on your enthusiasm, will you? I hate it when you gush like that."

"I guess I just don't realize it yet."

"Yeah, it can take a while. Bound to make you happy though, the way you're always bitching about this place."

"Yeah, it's a good move. I'll come around."

"Doc says you have a phone call to make."

"Yeah. A job."

"That's my guy. Don't waste any time."

Charlie rose and started down the hall toward the office where Miss Cowpers presided over the files and the patients' personal property and who knew what else.

"You coming?" Charlie asked as Calvin fell in step beside him.

"Might as well. It'll save you having to convince people you don't need a keeper anymore."

Charlie took the lawyer's card out of his pocket, but left the picture of the girl there.

"I guess you'll be getting a new patient now."

"Nah, not right away. I'll probably take my vacation first. I like a break between nuts."

"Sounds sensible. Got any plans?"

"Get out of town, somewhere away from there. That's all."

"Cancun, Acapulco?"

"Get serious, on my salary? Antlers, Oklahoma, maybe."

"What's in Antlers?"

"Aunt Bess and her third husband. They've been after me to visit."

"Sounds exciting."

"Woman's a good cook, and it's free room and board. Don't knock it."

Calvin vouched for him to Miss Cowpers and Charlie made his call. Childress was not in his office but his secretary had been told to expect to hear from Charlie. She gave him directions to Childress's office after Charlie assured her he knew the way to Paris. Childress would be expecting him at noon tomorrow.

That done, Charlie went to his room to pack and say good-bye.

Of course, there was not much to pack. A shaving kit with everything in it except a razor, two sets of pajamas, and a couple of watercolors he had done in the dayroom with the rest of the patients, under the direction of an intensely helpful young volunteer. They were not very good, one with zebras at the zoo and a couple of murky figures meant to be him and his little girl, Elizabeth, the other so bad he could only claim it was abstract. The abstract went in the trash, the other he tucked under his arm. That was it. He was wearing his warm-ups and the robe on the hook in the closet belonged to the Institute.

There was not much to saying good-bye, either. One of his roommates was gone in the literal sense, off doing something wholesome. The other was away from his body at the moment, his mind far away. Charlie gave him a pat on the shoulder and that was that.

By the time Charlie and Calvin got back to the office, Miss Cowpers were ready for them. There was a canvas bag standing open on the floor beside her desk, and on the desk in front of her she had arranged all of Charlie's property. There was just over a hundred dollars in cash, the balance of the last check his mother had sent from the account that she was minding for him, the one where his salary checks had been forwarded. No wallet, just his worn black badge case, the badge removed and the plastic window empty where his police ID card had been. The clothes he had been wearing when someone first brought him to the Institute, a cheap suit with a shirt and tie. It had all been drycleaned, and he could hardly tell where the bloodstains had been. Socks and a pair of shoes. That was it. They had taken his revolver at the hospital, long before they brought him here. Not much in the way of worldly possessions, he thought.

Charlie rolled up his suit and took his driver's license out of the badge case before putting the case and the suit into the canvas bag. The shoes went in last, which was probably backward but he did not bother to redo it. He folded the money and tucked his license inside the folded bills, then stuffed them into the hip pocket of his jogging suit, the one with the zipper.

Miss Cowpers put the paper in front of him and handed him a ballpoint, pointing with the pen to show him where to sign. She did not say anything, but he thought it upset her that he read the form before he signed it.

It was a waiver, as far as he could tell. There was a typed paragraph that read like a lawyer had made it up, with everything said two or three times so there was no way to get around it. He was leaving voluntarily, it said, the same way he had come, and the Institute was held harmless

37

and not liable and on and on like that. He signed it and Miss Cowpers took the pen. She gave it to Calvin and he signed as a witness. Then Miss Cowpers filled in the bottom part and carefully squeezed the whole thing with her notary public's stamp and it was official. She tore off one copy and gave it to Charlie. Have a nice day.

All of that did not mean anything to Charlie, he had done so many things they had told him to do at the Institute. But when he and Calvin walked past the desk to the front door, it suddenly hit him that he was leaving. Just like that, as if it were the most normal thing in the world, he and Calvin crossed the line from the tacky linoleum onto the carpet, Calvin showing the receptionist at the desk with a wave of his hand that it was all right, that Charlie was leaving legally and not escaping. Charlie balked at the door and Calvin pushed it open for him. It was real, there it was, the world. He was out.

"Now what, Mister Gants?" Calvin asked.

"The Childress job. You know that. Why?"

"First lesson for living on the outside. Childress is tomorrow at noon in Paris. 'Now what?' means right now, between now and then. Like, where are you going right now?"

"I hadn't thought about it." Charlie laughed, blushing. "I guess I thought it was all a trick, you were going to stop me at the door and yell April Fool or something."

"It ain't April, Charlie. It's August. Watch that. Not knowing what month it is can get you back in here."

"I was . . ."

"Joking, I know. But people who know where you've been won't be sure when you're joking and when you're not, so take it easy. What about tonight, you have a place to stay?"

"I thought I'd take a room at a hotel," Charlie lied. If he had thought about it at all, he had imagined he would go home. He knew his apartment was not his anymore, had not been for weeks. He did not have a home. He knew that, but it had not connected. It was like he thought that since he was out again the last three months had not happened, he would go back to things the way they were. He knew better, it just had not clicked.

"A hotel is good. You can get room service there, and everything. Not too big an adjustment from this place. You don't have anybody to put you up?"

"No." They were all gone, Charlie thought. Dead or moved away or too busy.

"Okay, then. Hotel's the next best thing. And transportation?"

"I'll take a cab."

"Right. I'll have Miss Cowpers call one for you. How are you getting to Paris tomorrow?"

Charlie started to say he felt up to driving, but he remembered in time that Uncle Jim had come down with Mom the last time she was here and he had driven Charlie's car home to Sulphur Springs for safekeeping.

"Bus."

"Good."

They stood on the porch and Charlie watched the traffic in front of the Institute as he worked things through his mind, making sure he did know what he was doing. Calvin looked out toward the traffic too, waiting to see if there was anything more. There did not seem to be.

"Okay, I guess that's it," Calvin said. "I'll tell Miss Cowpers to call you a cab. It'll pick you up here in front."

"Thanks."

"Yeah. Good luck."

Calvin and Charlie shook hands, and it was the first thing Charlie had felt sure of all day.

"Take care of yourself, Charlie."

"I will. Thanks."

Calvin went inside and Charlie breathed deeply, impressed with himself in the double newness of being alone and outside.

The cab came in a few minutes and the driver tried not to stare at Charlie or his canvas bag. Charlie got in and was ready. He had been thinking and had decided which hotel. He told the driver to take him to the downtown Holiday Inn because it was within walking distance of the bus stations. As the cab backed around in a circle in the gravel lot to head back out the long drive to the street, Charlie heard Calvin calling his name. He asked the driver to wait.

"What?" Charlie asked, leaning out the window of the car.

"Listen," Calvin said. Charlie thought the man looked embarrassed, as if he were about to confide a secret. "Why don't I run you up to Paris tomorrow?"

"You don't have to do that."

"I know. But I just started my vacation, and it's on my way going to Antlers. Why not?"

"I'll be fine," Charlie assured him, knowing that was what was embarrassing Calvin, that he was worried, that he cared about Charlie. "Don't worry about me."

"If I was worried about you, I'd put you up at my place for the night. It's not that I can't live without your smiling face, either, it's just we're both going the same way and there's no point . . ."

"Okay, if you're sure it's no trouble."

"Okay then. Where're you staying?"

Charlie told him and they agreed on a time to meet in front of the hotel. After rush hour. Calvin was starting his vacation and he did not want to get up early or fight traffic.

As the cab reached the end of the drive and stood poised to join the stream of traffic, Charlie could not help looking back at the place where he had spent the last three months. He was surprised that it looked so small from the street. He looked for the windows he knew were the lounge and the day room, hoping he would see Sam in one of them, watching him leave.

He might have only thought he saw her, or it might have been someone else, but as his cab bolted out into the street he believed that he did see her, in the lounge window, watching him through the curtains she held slightly parted.

CHAPTER FIVE

CHARLIE PAID CASH AND CARRIED HIS OWN BAG UP TO his room. It was nice, carpet everywhere except in the bath, twin beds, a color television. He wasted no time turning the television on, and he switched from channel to channel like a kid with a toy. At the Institute, there was one television, in the day room. You voted on what you watched, and the other patients preferred soap operas, day and night. Charlie was convinced the nurses cheated on the vote count because they were the ones who liked the soaps. Half of the patients did not know when the TV was on.

It was early evening, and Charlie had his choice of news shows. The local coverage was a little confusing, because he was at a loss on current events. It did not seem he had missed much. It was still the schools, DART, and politics. He thought that the Dallas Area Rapid Transit thing was a good idea, but it occurred to him that people would take it more seriously if they didn't call the people who ran it the "DART Board." The name did not inspire confidence about the decisions being made.

Some of the local news went on for an hour but Channel 4, the CBS affiliate, still contented itself with a half hour of news and ran "Wheel of Fortune" in the second half hour, just before the network programming took over. Charlie sat watching the game show, wondering why the geeks with the wheel kept guessing letters when it was obvious what the secret message was. One of them, a woman who leaped and screamed for no apparent reason, even bought a vowel, which convinced Charlie that either she belonged in the Institute or maybe he just did not appreciate the nuances of the game. The hostess reminded Charlie of Sam, but then everyone did who was blond and beautiful.

He convinced himself he could afford the charge and switched on the cable channels. There was a movie about teenagers chasing each other across a desert in Japanese imports, running over every roadside produce stand in sight. On another channel, a guy with a badge on his belt was shooting up the central business district of a city Charlie did not recognize with a pair of Israeli submachine guns. He switched the set off and went for a walk.

If Charlie was behind on the local news, he was really out of step with what the developers had been up to. Walking west from his hotel, he stumbled into a new world the signs posted here and there were calling "The West End." A dozen restaurants and bars were nestled among the old buildings that had been vacant the last time he remembered being there. He could have been away three years instead of three months, the way Dallas changed downtown. Maybe all this was here before, he thought, and I just did not notice.

He cut across Dealey Plaza alongside the old red courthouse, past John Neely Bryan's log cabin and the Kennedy memorial to Commerce Street, thinking he would drop by the Commerce Street Newsstand for a paper or two. He told himself it should not be a surprise when he found the newsstand and Sol's Turf Bar next door had disappeared. There was valet parking where they had been, for Nieman Marcus customers.

Back at the Holiday Inn, Charlie bought a pint of scotch and had dinner in his room.

After dinner he found the ice and poured himself a drink. The first in a long time. He remembered what Sam had told him once, but did not dwell on it, that business about drinking. It could be trouble, she had warned him. All life's a gamble, he announced aloud, and made himself another.

With his second drink in hand, Charlie looked into his bag and found the envelope with his daughter's address on it. She had sent him a picture she had drawn and colored with crayons, a bright and colorful thing with an enormous yellow sun and red and purple flowers, to cheer him up. His ex-wife had written out the address of the Institute on the front and stuck a return address label in the corner of the envelope, with her new married name and their new address in Houston. She had not enclosed a note of her own. Charlie got an outside line and dialed the directory assistance number for the Houston area code. But the operator could only tell him that the number was unlisted. He thanked her and finished his drink. Then he poured another and wrote his daughter Elizabeth a letter on the hotel stationery with the hotel's ballpoint.

"Dear Little Bit" he wrote. What else? "I don't think I'm crazy anymore and they've let me out. Love Dad." So why aren't you on your way to Houston to see the kid? Charlie asked himself. Then he wrote: "I'm feeling better. I'm not in the hospital anymore. I have a job to do . . ." After looking at his reflection in the mirror across the room, he added: "so I can be sure I am really well. As soon as my job is over, I would like to come see you. Please ask Mom if that would be all right with her." He knew his ex-wife would read it. He added that he loved her very much and signed it "Daddy." It occurred to him that he did not know what Bit called her stepfather, and hoped that would not cause any trouble. But what the hell, he had been Daddy first. He sealed the letter

42

in the envelope and leaned it against the bedside lamp so he would not forget to mail it.

He finished his third scotch and put the cap back on the bottle and turned in early, the television picture on without the sound. It was like the Institute in a way, people moving in the corridor and in the room beside him, the place never really asleep. He would be all right, he decided. He was ready. He had talked himself into a full head of confidence, and his time at the Institute had already begun to fade into memory when he realized that he was lying in the bed waiting to fall asleep with all the lights on in the room. He was waiting for lights out.

■

By nine-thirty the next morning Charlie and Calvin were on their way. Charlie had insisted on buying their breakfast at the Denny's on Thornton Freeway at Jim Miller Road. It was a place where Charlie had brought his little girl a hundred times for Sunday breakfast so they could be alone and his wife could sleep late. The house where he had lived was within a mile, over a hill the other side of the little school.

Calvin was chipper and his car, an old but clean Mercury, was running smoothly. They crossed Lake Ray Hubbard and Charlie did not bother to mention how much building had been done since his last time out this way. By eleven, they were in Greenville, then off the interstate onto the two-lane at the sign that said COMMERCE, EAST TEXAS STATE UNIVERSITY.

By the time they had to stop at the light in Commerce where the college kids jogged across from the dorms on the west side of the road to the campus on the east, Charlie had told Calvin everything he knew about G. Leighton Childress, Amber McKendrick, and the job he had agreed to do. He showed him Amber's picture and Calvin whistled and said something about it being a terrible waste.

Charlie was pleased to find that Calvin was what he would call a good driver. He kept his speed within five miles per hour of the limit and did not crowd anybody. It was twenty to twelve when they crossed over the Paris loop and moments later passed the big cemetery on their right.

"Evergreen," Charlie said. "Nice name for a cemetery."

Calvin smiled and shook his head but did not say anything.

For all the city fathers had done to complicate things with one-way streets and arrows and traffic buttons, Paris was not a hard place to find your way around in. They found the offices of Childress and Hampton, Attorneys at Law, with time to spare. It was a big old house converted into an office, on Lamar Avenue a mile or so east of the plaza that marked the center of town.

"Before we go in here, there's something I want to ask you," Calvin announced when he had parked at the curb in front of the lawyer's office.

"What?"

"Do you think the McKendricks would have a place for me? Some place to put me up?"

"What are you talking about?"

"They're rich, you said. Big ranch. They ought to have a place I could stay. A bunkhouse or something."

"What the hell are you saying?"

"A bunkhouse. You know, like on Roy Rogers. They always have a bunkhouse, don't they?"

"Never mind the bunkhouse, what are you getting at? What about your aunt in Antlers?"

"I didn't even know there was such a place as Antlers, Oklahoma, until I checked the map yesterday. I . . ."

Charlie's mind was spinning, freewheeling through a dozen notions of plots. It showed on his face, and Calvin leaned toward him.

"Look, dammit. I don't know what the shrinks told you and I don't care. I know you better than they do anyway. And I'm worried about you, like it or not. Now, I'm on my own time and driving you up here was no big deal. I wanted to check you out, see how you handled yourself out in the world . . ."

"And?"

"So far so good. And that would have been enough for me yesterday. But this deal you're getting into up here . . ."

"What about it?"

"You know what I'm saying. It's right back in the frying pan. I'm not sure you're ready. Are you?"

"There's one way to find out."

"Right, and a hell of a way. Look, I'm not going to beg you to let

44

me help you with this. I'm available and I didn't have any vacation plans anyway. If you don't want me here, just say so."

"Did Branville send you to spy on me?"

"If you can't tell the difference between a spy and a friend, just get the hell out of my car and good luck to you."

Charlie got out of the car and reached into the backseat for his bag. Calvin slammed his Mercury into reverse before Charlie spoke, the passenger door still open.

"What's in it for you?" Charlie asked.

"Not a goddamned thing, and shut the door before I decide to charge your paranoid ass cab fare."

"I don't even know what the job pays yet," Charlie said. "If you stay, we'll split it, whatever it is."

"Make up your mind. I don't mean to spend my vacation sitting here arguing with you."

Charlie looked at the man behind the wheel, tried to look inside him past the angry face, tried to get a feel for him. He knew Calvin, he told himself. He never lied to me before. Charlie made up his mind what he would do and decided to sort out how he felt about it later. There would be time. Once he had decided, he felt relieved. He would not mind having Calvin around.

"Park it," Charlie said. "Let's not keep the guy waiting."

CHAPTER SIX ■

THERE WAS A RECEPTIONIST IN THE OUTER OFFICE who asked if they would mind waiting a minute or two, Mister Childress was on the phone. Charlie and Calvin declined coffee and sat on a sofa near the window until the lawyer was ready for them. Charlie was impressed with the office. It was expensively paneled and tastefully appointed. There were photographs on the wall: Childress bare-chested with windblown hair on the deck of a boat, squinting into a bright sun, with lettering on the gunwale in the background that said something about a dive shop in Cozumel; a couple of shots of Childress and the rest of a golf foursome at some kind of tournament; and a lot of pictures of boats.

Things went well enough when they met with Mister Childress. It was not a problem to include Calvin in their plans, the lawyer assured them, then put in a call to Poppa McKendrick at the ranch to let him know there would be one more for supper.

"The money will be the same," Charlie assured Childress. "Whatever it is."

"It didn't slip my notice that you didn't bring up the matter of a fee the first time we met. The going rate for an investigator is two hundred dollars a day and expenses. Is that satisfactory?"

"Yes."

"For both of you?"

"That's right. We'll work out the split."

"Two for the price of one. I can't quibble. You're the geneticist Poppa's brought in for the horses. Your friend?"

"My graduate assistant. Working on his thesis."

"Why not?"

There was some more chatting after that, background stuff on the family tree, a chart Childress had drawn with all of Mom and Poppa McKendrick's children and grandchildren so Charlie could get the names straight. Childress asked if Charlie needed an advance to cover expenses. Charlie had twenty-five dollars left and some change, so he let the lawyer give him two hundred up front. There was a contract for them to sign and some details about reporting. Childress had a pager and he gave Charlie the number so he could get him any time. And then they were off to see the ranch.

North out of Paris on the road that would take you to Hugo, Oklahoma, if you stayed on it and crossed the big iron bridge over the Red River, they slipped in and out of the little traffic there was, Childress driving his Lincoln faster than Charlie liked and talking all the way. There was Camp Maxey on the left, he said, pointing at a squad of barracks and Quonset huts the other side of the railroad that paralleled the highway. Big deal during the war. National Guard camp now. Forty-ninth Armored Division. Childress had been in the Forty-ninth back in sixty-two when they were called up during the Berlin crisis and had spent nine months in Fort Polk, Louisiana. Great fun, the lawyer laughed, then added that his time was worth too much now to be away from his practice that long ever again.

Within sight of the Red River bridge at a place the sign said was Arthur City, Childress turned right onto a country road and said it would not be long now. But it was a long time before they saw the ranch, roaring too fast along the little road past a lake they could not see for the trees, an old lake the lawyer told them about, nothing like the new one the Corps of Engineers put in over on the other side of the highway, Pat Mayse Reservoir. He was an affable and knowledgeable guide, the thin well-tended lawyer, finding more to say about the country they passed through than Charlie could imagine to ask. He seemed to know every place along the way, all the endless farms and pastures, the nice and shabby houses, the families and what had become of their kids and who the places had once belonged to. Charlie did not listen to most of it, waiting to see what lay ahead at the one place that concerned him, the McKendrick place. He thought that Childress seemed different today than yesterday at the Institute, and hoped it was because the lawyer felt good about what they were doing.

Finally they were there. From the top of a hill Charlie saw the road run down a long slope and disappear around a curve to the right. There were trees along both sides of the road, pin oak and live oak and a smattering of pine. Heavy brush, and trees Charlie did not know the names of. It did not look like the land was being put to much use, he thought.

"There it is," Childress announced, aiming his skinny right arm like a deer rifle in front of Charlie.

Charlie followed the line of the lawyer's arm and did not see anything except more trees. A long way off to the right, maybe a mile away, he saw what looked like a small hillock rising out of the woods.

"What?" Charlie asked.

"The Shaman Tree. See it?"

"Oh," Charlie said, looking again at the hillock and seeing this time that it was a tree instead. "Is it on a hill or something, or is it just that much taller than the rest of them?"

"Just a damned big tree."

"How big?" Charlie wondered, shading his eyes from the sun as he looked.

"Hundred feet tall."

"An oak you said."

"Yessir, a live oak."

"Didn't know they grew that big," Charlie said.

"That's the thing. They don't."

Childress laughed and Charlie looked at him. From the backseat Calvin laughed too, but his heart was not in it.

They took the curve to the right about twice as fast as would have been safe and the Lincoln fishtailed from ditch to ditch as Childress fought it back under control, talking all the while.

Once clear of the curve and satisfied they would not crash, Charlie looked up and saw that the land was being put to very good use indeed. At least on the right-hand side of the road. The woods on the left went on as far as he cared to look, but on the right side a whitewashed board fence that appeared suddenly ran in a wiggly line that traced the terraced land and the meandering road as far as he could see, until it disappeared over the next hill. They were coming up on a break in the white fence, an open gap where the lawyer turned in. More white fence on either side of them from the road back west for almost a mile to an oversized gate like you would expect to see in a movie. Beyond the gate a big house stood waiting, white with a blue shingle roof, two stories tall with big white pillars and a porch that went all the way around. There were barns to the left and corrals made of the new rustproof pipe. As the Lincoln skidded to a stop in the circular drive in front of the house, Charlie saw between the barns and the house and farther back a pair of sheds and a gravel lot with tractors and a couple of pickup trucks.

"Here we are," Childress announced.

"Thank you, Jesus," Calvin muttered from the back.

"You okay?" Charlie asked.

"Yeah, but when we leave, I'll do the driving."

"I'm with you."

Childress opened the trunk of his Lincoln with a button in the glovebox before he shut off the big car and rambled off like Ichabod Crane toward the steps that led up to the porch. Charlie and Calvin clambered out of the car, glad to have survived the trip, and were taking their things out of the trunk when they heard voices.

"Molly!" Childress yelled.

He was answered by a long shrill whoop and dialect out of *Gone With the Wind*. "Lawzy, Missah Chiduss! Come in dis house!" Something like that. Charlie and Calvin exchanged looks.

They went up the steps the way Childress had gone to the porch that was chest high to Charlie when he stopped in the yard to take a look at the house.

An old woman, still talking like Butterfly McQueen, motioned for them to put down their bags just inside the door. Childress showed them both into an honest-to-God parlor and before they could make themselves comfortable the old woman was back with lemonade for them. She announced that "Missuh MaKenderk" was expecting them and had told her to tell them when they came he would be with them "fo long." Then she left.

"Who is that?" Charlie asked.

"Molly. She's been with them for years. Sweetest old thing in the world. And a hell of a cook."

"Do . . . uh . . ." Calvin began, cautiously. "Do many of the black people around here talk like that?"

"What? Oh, I see what you mean. No, I don't suppose they do, anymore," Childress answered, as if he might have thought it a shame.

They heard a truck pull up out front and two doors close, then footsteps up the steps and across the porch. The three of them stood to meet the McKendricks, Mom and Poppa, returning home.

"Poppa, Mom, this is Doctor Gants and his assistant, Mister . . ."

"Rakestraw," Calvin said, stepping forward to shake hands with the McKendricks. "Calvin Rakestraw."

Mom recoiled from him at first, then tried to make it less obvious by stepping across the hall outside the parlor to lay her broad-brimmed straw hat on a table.

"How do you do," she said, from her safe distance.

"Rakestraw. Glad to meet you." Poppa shook his hand. "I'm Bob McKendrick. How was the trip?"

"Fine," Calvin answered, not wanting to talk about the way the lawyer drove.

"And you're Doctor Gants. Glad to meet you. You come highly recommended."

Poppa McKendrick took Charlie's hand and Charlie smiled. That doctor business would take some getting used to.

"Please," he said. "Just call me Charlie."

"Charlie it is, then. We've got a room for you upstairs. Mister Rakestraw, I'm afraid, you're in the bunkhouse. We didn't know you were coming, and we have all the children staying with us, so we're a little short on room. I hope you don't mind."

"No, sir." Calvin smiled at Charlie. "The bunkhouse is fine. The closer to the horses the better."

"Good. Good." McKendrick looked around at their bags. There was only Charlie's canvas overnighter and a plastic softsider Calvin had brought with him. "This isn't all of it, is it? You have some more stuff in the car?"

"No," Charlie said. "This is it. We travel light."

He was wearing his jogging suit again and his business suit was in the bag with his shoes. He and Calvin could run into town later and pick up whatever else they needed.

"I'll say you do. Well, if you need anything, we can probably find it around the place somewhere."

"No problem," Charlie assured him.

Mom excused herself as if the August heat was too much for her. Which it may have been, except that the big house was cooled by unseen air conditioners Charlie could hear rumbling in the background. He could see past Poppa that the truck they had driven up in had the windows rolled up. It was air-conditioned, too. Whatever the source of her distress, Momma McKendrick flittered up the stairs and was gone. Mister McKendrick gave Molly her instructions for supper and Charlie looked him over.

There was something open and straightforward about the man. He was in his sixties easily, but lean and fit looking, with rough hands and a sunburned face. As he talked to his cook, McKendrick took off his straw cowboy hat and ran a handkerchief across his brow. Charlie saw that the old man had the giveaway tan of a man of the land, red from the chin up to the line of the hatband, white above that. He did not look or

50

act like a rich man, and he had a peaceful air about him. He was not trying to impress anybody.

When Molly was gone to see about supper, McKendrick offered to show them around. Childress stayed inside with the lemonade and Calvin excused himself at the one-story white frame bunkhouse. Mister McKendrick showed Calvin which of the dozen bunks were taken and let him pick the one he wanted. He said that he had only two ranchhands on the place now. In the old days they needed a lot more men to work the ranch, but machines did most of it now. There was a room at the back with a door into the big room with the dozen bunks, and Charlie had noticed there was another door that opened onto the yard. That was the foreman's quarters, McKendrick told them. Calvin picked a bed and started unpacking, saying he would like a nap to calm his nerves after the drive out from town. McKendrick told him to make himself at home and left with Charlie.

They took the truck and McKendrick switched off the air-conditioning and they rolled down the windows. The air was for Momma, Charlie thought. The old man liked the feel and smell of the place.

It took an hour or so for McKendrick to take Charlie around. They drove through the hay meadow where four men were baling hay and loading the bales onto a flatbed truck. Charlie had done that one summer. He remembered it was the one last thing that convinced him to move to the city and get a job somewhere away from the land.

McKendrick pointed out the men to Charlie as they passed between the baler and the truck, not stopping to interrupt the work by introducing him to them.

"Angel loading. That's my grandson Wes driving," he said, pointing at the two men working the truck and pronouncing Angel like the English word angel. "That's Red Jackson, my foreman," he said, meaning the big man driving the tractor that towed the baling machine behind it. "On the sled there, that's Juan."

"You haven't gone to the round bales?" Charlie asked.

This was the way he had worked hay twenty years ago. He thought the whole world had gone to the big truck-sized round bales by now. One machine made the bales, one man on a tractor with the right attachment moved the bales. One or two men could do the whole thing.

The way McKendrick was doing it, you needed one man to drive the tractor pulling the baler, one to ride the sled behind the baler and stack bales, then put them off the sled so two or three men with a truck could come along behind and load them. And stacking a load was a trick in itself if you did not want it coming loose and falling off at the first ditch or terrace you came to.

"Not yet," McKendrick answered, turning to look him over. "A man ought to, I guess, if he's got enough hay to come out on the cost of the equipment. Don't take as many hands. But with lining 'em up outdoors the way they do, a feller'd loose a right smart to weather. Keep more hay this way and it's a heap handier feeding the horses. They're stabled, most of 'em, when we feed, and it'd be more trouble than it'd be worth getting the hay to 'em off one of those big bales. We just put up what hay we need, don't worry about selling it. If I knew what I was doing, I'd probably sell any extra to one of these guys around here that hauls hay for a living. But I don't count money as hard as I used to."

Charlie had no way of knowing it, but that was a long speech for McKendrick to make, and he did not say anything more until they drove into the woods on the east side of the house. From where they got out of the truck Charlie had a clear view of the Shaman Tree. It was bigger than anything he had ever seen in that part of the country. But McKendrick did not say anything about it, so he did not either.

There was a lane that ran ahead of the truck up a gentle hill away from the house. It looked like a right-of-way of some kind, but Charlie did not see any reason for it, no pipeline or cable. Power lines ran in to the house from the road along the driveway, he remembered.

McKendrick walked ahead of Charlie up the slope and stopped when he got to the top of the hill. Charlie knew what it was before he came alongside the old man. He knew when he saw the wrought iron that rose out of the ground taller than Poppa McKendrick, when the old man took off his hat and stood silent and still.

Worked into the black iron crosspieces that made the top of the gate was the name *Terry*. It was a family cemetery.

Charlie joined McKendrick and saw the fresh grave, the rich dark earth upturned like a furrow for planting. There was no stone yet, nothing with her name. There she was, he thought. Amber McKendrick.

Poppa McKendrick had a way of talking that Charlie knew too well, the same way his own father had, a roundabout way of getting at what he meant if it was anything that mattered to him. Before he worked his way in to his dead daughter, Poppa circled with the history of the land.

It all started with the Indians, of course. Mom's people, the Terrys were some of the first whites in these parts. They knew it for some of the richest land in the Red River Valley, and they set themselves on having it. They did not run the Indians off like you see in the movies. They offered to buy them off the land. The Indians, Caddoes as best he could remember, did not know about owning land. The land was just there, always had been, always would be. They'd have taken trade goods and moved on, humored the white men, if it had not been for the medicine man, the shaman. He allowed as this was sacred ground, where their people were buried, and he would see it sold over his dead body. And that is what happened. The old man died, one way or another, and the Terrys got the land. It was handed down among the Terrys, father to son, for over a hundred years. Mom's daddy lost it in the thirties. Lot of land lost in the Depression.

"My first wife and I had the next place down the road," McKendrick said, and that was the first Charlie knew of another Mrs. McKendrick. "She passed away and I married Mom a couple of years after. Mom and I bought this place back and fixed up the house and everything. It meant a lot to Mom to get back her home place."

He was half an hour telling it that far, and still had not said anything about the tree or Amber. Charlie knew it was best to let him set his own pace.

"It's the lawyer's idea to bring you here," McKendrick said, turning for the first time from the graveyard to look at Charlie. "He's worried there's some kind of conspiracy afoot. I don't hold with that, and I told him so. But he feels like Amber wanted you up here and . . . well, that's reason enough, I guess."

"What about all the accidents?" Charlie asked. "Amber said . . ."

"I know what she said. She told me the same thing, before she ever went to Childress or to Dallas to see you. She was strongheaded. Got it from Mom, I guess. Couldn't understand why something couldn't be the way she wanted it to be, like wanting it bad was reason enough.

53

Stubborn. I've been at this all my life, Charlie, around horses and cows and machinery. Seen a lot of accidents. Enough to know sometimes they come in cycles. Kids nowadays, everything is happening for the first time. We had good luck for a long time and Amber figured it was always like that. But I'll tell you, the things we've had happen around here that got her het up, I've seen a lot worse."

"What kind of things?"

"Horse killed one of my hands. It's the kind of thing that happens. If a man ain't paying attention, messing around with a highbred horse. They're nervous, high-strung, you know. Spook over nothing sometimes."

"I know."

"Wes, my grandson. You saw him driving the hay truck. He fell out of the hay loft and stove himself up pretty good."

"How did that happen?"

"Board came loose."

"Somebody could have made that happen."

"Sure could. I'd expect you to think that way."

"What else?"

The hottest part of the day was over, and the sun was on its way down to their left, the west. Charlie noticed for the first time that he could see water between the trees. The lake where Amber had drowned.

"This and that. Nothing world shaking. Couple of my hands left, though. Superstitious, I guess."

"Superstitious?"

"That's how I wound up with just Angel and Juan. They don't speak enough English to know better, I guess."

"What do you mean, superstitious?"

"I figured lawyer Childress would have told you all that."

"He said something about a tree."

"And our family curse, too, I expect."

"Something."

"It's the old Indian getting even, you see. As the story goes, the old medicine man was buried on the place. Over there between the house and where the lake is now."

"Where the tree is."

"Right where it stands. That's why it's so big, because the medicine

54

man put a spell on it. Or it grew up out of his heart instead of out of an acorn, I can't remember how it goes. Anyway, he put a curse on the place and any white man who owns it."

"Did Amber believe that?"

"No. She believed in herself."

"Then why did she come to me? Why did she think I could help?"

"Why not you? You're a private eye, ain't you? Or are you some kind of ghost hunter?"

"She looked me up because . . . I'd had some experience with a similar case."

"A family curse?"

"Kind of."

"Oh. Then maybe she thought you could show this business up for a fake, get to the bottom of things."

"What did she think was behind all of it, the accidents and talk about the curse?"

"She never said. Probably somebody trying to scare us off the place. Greed is evil enough for all the meanness I've ever seen."

"Is anybody interested in buying your ranch?"

"I imagine. Somebody usually is. But it ain't for sale. The kids can sell it after Mom and I are gone if they want to. Probably will. It doesn't mean much to them, I don't think."

"That's a shame."

"Yeah."

The old man turned back to his graveyard and did not have anything else to say. Charlie stood to one side and looked around him at the woods and what he could see of the lake. Looking back over the pickup, he could see the house, and sounds of Molly rattling around in the kitchen reached him on a southern breeze up the hill. He heard the noise of a car on the drive coming up from the road toward the house, too, but a stand of trees screened his view of the front of the house and he could not see who it was. The hands knocking off for supper, he guessed. Early, he thought. He looked back at the old man as the sound reached him of car doors slamming, and a trunk lid.

Poppa cleared his throat and daubed his brow with his handkerchief again. Then he put his hat back on and he was ready to go.

"You have any children, Charlie?"

"A little girl. Elizabeth."

"That's good. Any plans for a son someday?"

"I'm divorced."

"Sorry to hear it. I didn't mean to pry."

"No, it's all right. I would like to marry again, raise some kids."

"Your little girl lives with her momma, I reckon."

"Yeah. They moved to Houston this summer."

"That's the way of it, I guess. Kids go with their momma usually."

"I'm afraid so."

"Except Jeff there. He stayed on when his momma moved away."

"His parents divorced?"

"No. His daddy died in the war. Vietnam."

The old man pronounced it the way Lyndon Johnson did, to rhyme with "ham."

"Did you go over there, Charlie?"

"No, sir."

"Good for you."

Charlie was relieved that Poppa did not hold it against him that he had not been in the war.

"We put a stone up for him, there with the rest of us," McKendrick said, swinging his arm back toward the top of the hill behind him to show he meant the family plot. "And buried the box they sent us. Hope it was him. Damned shame. Send your son off and they send you back . . ."

He did not finish and Charlie hoped he would not cry. He was entitled, but Charlie knew the old man would think less of himself for it. But he did not cry. He only wiped his handkerchief across his forehead again and put his hat back on.

"You ready to go to the house, Charlie?"

"If you are."

They turned and walked the rest of the way down the hill to McKendrick's truck.

Charlie's hand was on the door of the truck when something caught his eye, movement in a screen of trees on the other side of the clearing, behind McKendrick, in the direction of the house and the lake.

And then he saw her. Dressed in black, a somber hat low across her face, she picked her way soundlessly through the last of the trees and stepped into the clearing. Charlie saw McKendrick look at him, the puzzled look on the old man's face before he turned to see what Charlie was gaping at. And then all Charlie could see was the girl, coming toward him soundlessly, with long supple strides, her long blond hair feathered across one shoulder as if there were a breeze.

It was the dead girl, Amber McKendrick.

CHAPTER SEVEN ▪

CHARLIE WAS CARRIED AWAY SCREAMING AND FIGHTing back to the Institute where Sam Cartwright and her head-shrinker boyfriend shook their heads and clucked their tongues and agreed that there was nothing else to be done for him except possibly a lobotomy. He recoiled from the door handle of McKendrick's pickup truck and skittered backward like a hermit crab halfway up the trail toward the McKendrick cemetery before his backward impetus overtook his scrambling feet and he sprawled spread-eagled like a captive about to be tortured by Indians and lay there, unable to move. He screamed and hid his eyes behind his hands and screamed again, his heart pounding, as every touch and taste and smell of his times with the other ghost, the ghost of the dead captain, came back to him. It was all happening again, and he had sworn he would rather die than live through that again. He pushed himself away from the pickup truck and hurled himself headlong down the hill beyond the enormous live oak tree and into the waters of the lake beyond. Amber McKendrick had led him to this place and now he would follow her to the deep black water and the sleep of dreamless death . . .

All of that happened in Charlie's mind, in a gust of time collapsed upon itself, an eternity of his inner life that passed for the others in the time of a heartbeat. For the others on the outside, there was no sign that Charlie Gants had been elbowed over his private precipice and might have disappeared if he had not seen the yellow taxicab pass beyond the screen of trees on its way from the circular drive in front of the big house back toward the road, its tires crunching the driveway gravel as it went. It was such a prosaic and not-belonging thing, which he was almost sure was real because of the gravel-crunching, that it meant to Charlie that he was not seeing a ghost this time. It was all that saved him.

Charlie held on to the door of the pickup and felt as if the world had suddenly gone vertical like the deck of a ship hit by a tidal wave, fighting to hold himself erect and to hide from the others how he felt inside. Like the duck, he told himself, knowing it was a good sign that he could think this way: calm on the surface, paddling like hell below the waterline.

The girl froze on the clearing's edge and looked from McKendrick to Charlie and back. McKendrick stood nearer her than Charlie, on the driver's side of the truck, looking at Charlie. He stood looking at Charlie and not at the girl for what seemed to Charlie a long time, long enough that Charlie wondered . . . But then the old man did turn to the girl and she smiled and ran to him the last few feet and they hugged each other and cried and Charlie almost cried himself, he was so unbelievably happily relieved that McKendrick saw her too.

Charlie tried not to intrude on McKendrick and the girl by watching too directly or listening too closely, and only heard her say she was sorry she had come home too late for the funeral, something about making connections, then something more that he could not make out. McKendrick's answers were like only sounds, no words in particular, he spoke in such a low and gently rumbling voice that the words tumbled indistinctly over each other and did not matter, because the sound of his voice by itself meant it was all right, he was glad to see her, he was glad she was home, and all the rest she had hoped to hear. When that was done, McKendrick introduced the girl to Charlie.

"Doctor Gants," Poppa said, gesturing back and forth from Charlie to the girl, "this is my daughter Jade, come home from the other side of the world. Baby, this is Doctor Gants. I've asked him to visit with us here on the place for a while."

"How do you do?" she said.

"You're Amber's sister," Charlie answered, as if a question had been asked.

"Yes."

"Her twin sister."

"Yes, that's right. Did you know Amber?"

"You look very much like her," Charlie explained, trying to listen hard enough to Jade's voice to see if there was some distinction he could be sure of.

"That's often the case with twins, isn't it?" the girl answered, her voice purportedly amused, deniably arch. "What kind of doctor are you?"

"He's a geneticist, baby," McKendrick informed her, as if he were afraid that Charlie would botch it or might have forgotten. "I asked him here some time ago to do some work with the breeding stock. It would have been a boogerbear to reschedule . . ."

"I see," the girl said. "No, you're right. It's important to get on with things. How's Mom holding up?"

"You know your mother, baby."

The girl nodded and then she and her father hugged again, leaving Charlie to wonder what it meant that she knew her mother, what that said about the way Mom was holding up. He did not ask and only waited until Poppa and Jade were ready to go, and they got into the pickup. Charlie opened the passenger door for the girl and then climbed into the back of the truck, insisting it was no trouble, and they drove back to the house for supper.

CHAPTER EIGHT

AFTER HE HAD FRESHENED UP IN A BATHROOM OFF THE hallway next to his assigned room, Charlie followed the gentle hubbub of voices and the scraping of chairs on a hardwood floor back down the stairs and found himself in an enormous dining room. The room ran lengthwise from the front to the back of the old house, and extended beyond the original back wall to make one end of a screened porch that overlooked the bunkhouse and the barn beyond that. There was one table, a polished monster of dark wood set simply with a bounty of steaming roasts and simple pottery dishes alive with corn, beans, potatoes, and fresh bread.

Charlie thought that the table was about the length of a Gulf fishing boat, and wide enough that two people sitting opposite each other would have to stretch to join hands across it. He could not see any seams in it, no sign of leaves that could be added when company came and then taken away when Mom and Pop dined alone, and he wondered if they used this table when it was just the two of them, if they sat at either end of the thing and had the old cook shuttle between them to pass the salt.

There were a dozen places set, six to a side, and one at each end, to make fourteen. Charlie wondered for a moment about name cards, but of course these people were all family and knew their places. All except Charlie and the lawyer, who took Charlie by the arm and steered him to his place.

Pop was already seated at the head of the table. Or the foot, Charlie thought, depending on your point of view. At any rate, Pop was to Charlie's left, facing down the long table toward the rear of the house. The lawyer pulled out the end chair on the near side for himself, to sit at Pop's right hand, and pointed to show Charlie that the next chair was his. Charlie nodded and put his hand on the chair but did not sit down. He looked to his right and saw that the next two places were taken by a couple who looked as if they might be either side of forty; they were seated, talking to each other. She was wholesome as opposed to striking and wore her hair pulled back. He was dark and balding, with sharp features and exaggerated eyes behind spectacles. Beyond them a sullen young man slouched brooding into his plate, tapping a fork arhythmically. The ghost or twin or whatever she was who had so recently shocked Charlie by appearing in the woods leaned an angular hip upon the corner of the table at the far right end, chatting with Mom, who stood at right angles to her, arms folded across her bosom.

Directly across the table from Charlie's assigned place stood a high chair with straps dangling and baubles attached. The child for whom it waited dangled dully from the jabbing hands of a woman Charlie took

60

to be its mother. She and the man with her, who looked old enough to be her father and granddad to the kid, had been edged backward a step by the woman who pressed in on Pop, bobbing the baby toward the old man repeatedly in a way that made Charlie think of a priest sprinkling holy water. Pop was smiling patiently, his eyes wincing, as the kid lolled his head and drooled.

Looking along the other side of the table to his right from the thing with the kid, Charlie saw two young men talking behind two empty chairs. At the end of the far side, nearest Mom, another chair stood empty, waiting.

Charlie thought the empty chair must be for Calvin and wondered where he was.

"Do you know where Calvin is?" Charlie asked the lawyer.

"Who?"

"Calvin. My . . . assistant."

The lawyer pointed toward the rear of the house and returned his attention to making a fuss over the dangling kid.

The dining room was big enough that Charlie did not bother anyone as he made his way along the table to his right and out through the door, again to his right, that opened onto the screened porch.

There was another table set up there, perpendicular to the one inside and centered along the porch. It was hardly half as big as the one inside, but the food was the same and smelled delicious. Calvin and the two ranchhands Charlie had seen working in the hay meadow earlier had dispensed with socializing and were eating heartily.

"What's going on here?" Charlie demanded.

"Supper, what do you think?" Calvin answered.

The other two did not look up.

"What are you doing out here? Why don't you come inside and eat with us?"

"Because this is where my food is, Charlie. The cook said eat here and that's what I'm doing. Have you had any of this yet? This is the real stuff, man. All these vegetables are fresh. I had forgotten how real food tastes."

"This isn't going to get it," Charlie said. "Come on, you're going to eat inside with the rest of us . . ."

61

"In case you haven't noticed," Calvin answered. "That is not us in there. That is y'all. Us is out here."

"This is bullshit."

"When in Rome, man . . ."

"Bullshit, Calvin."

"What is your problem, Charlie? I thought you grew up in this part of the country. What did you do, forget to set your watch back ten years when you crossed the county line? Did you expect these people to have a room for me in the big house? You think they'd let two meskins and a nigger eat at their table?"

"You don't have to do this. You don't have to put up with . . ."

"If it doesn't bother me, why are you so upset?" Calvin reluctantly rested his fork on his plate and turned in his chair to face Charlie. "This is nothing, man. Nothing I can't deal with. You've made your point, it wasn't your idea. You don't go along with it. You're morally outraged. Now shut the fuck up and go eat your supper before it gets cold."

Charlie went back inside and settled into his chair and looked up to see Mom smiling at him acidly.

"We waited for you," she said, in a tone of voice meant to let him know he had been rude without being rude in turn. He was company, after all, and she forgave him his bad manners. "Son," she said then, nodding regally at the middle-aged man who sat at Pop's left hand, beside the baby who had by now been restrained in the high chair.

At this imperial signal, the man bowed his head. Everyone else at the table bowed, including Charlie, and the man said grace. Or at least he took a stab at it, starting with "God be great, God be good . . ." then catching himself before rattling off the rest of the childhood rhyme that sounds adorable when offered by a toddler, daft by a grown man and oldest son. After an awkward throat-clearing harrumph he finished off with something about blessing this food to the nourishment of our bodies and amened as if he really meant it.

"Thank you for saying the blessing," Mom intoned when the man had finished and everyone had murmured amen.

That is right, Charlie reminded himself. Up here you don't say grace, you say the blessing.

Pop took it upon himself to make the introductions, pausing when

62

required to do so to turn a hand in the clockwise passing of the dishes so that all the plates could be served.

Charlie smiled and nodded at each of the faces and paid no attention to the names. He was not good with names and knew he would not remember them, not this many. He only tried to understand the relationships, who each of them was.

The poor man who had been called upon to say the blessing was Pop's oldest son by his first marriage. Not that Pop or anyone else at the table would have been so indelicate as to put it that way. But Charlie quickly noted that some of these people Pop introduced as "my oldest boy" and so forth, while some he said were "our daughter" or whatever. It was a useful code, easily understood without hurting anyone's feelings who did not choose to be overly delicate about it. Apparently no one did.

The baby did belong to the oldest son and the woman who looked much too young to be his wife but was anyway. The wife, upon being introduced to Charlie, halted the getting acquainted process long enough to make another fuss over her baby and to make sure Charlie understood that her little boy was the apple of Pop's eyes. It put Charlie in mind of the Tennessee Williams play *Cat on a Hot Tin Roof*, the daughter-in-law who campaigned so desperately with her children to make her husband Big Daddy's favorite. The notion of Pop McKendrick as Big Daddy so occupied Charlie's attention for a moment that he did not keep up with the introductions for a while, but he did pay more attention after that.

Going down the far side of the table first: There was Pop's third child and second son, a slender man with an air of delicacy; next came "our" grandson, the young man who lived on the ranch. No mention of his parents. Next came the empty chair, and Pop paused long enough for everyone to fidget uncomfortably before moving on without explaining it. By now Charlie realized the empty chair, with a place set before it, was for the dead girl, Amber.

On his side of the table, starting with Amber's twin, Jade, Pop worked back toward Charlie. The sullen young moper who had stopped tapping his fork on the table to jab disconsolately at his food was Pop's second grandson, a student at Southern Methodist University and a proud member of one of the fraternities there. Next was the boy's father, the dark and quiet man with the glasses, a son-in-law, and then Pop's second child, a daughter, the mother of the frat rat. She was the wholesome-looking one, and Charlie imagined he saw something more in her face than a friendly welcome. Like the lingering smell of cordite after a gunfight, there was an air of something bitter and unresolved about her . . .

That only left Charlie and the lawyer, whom everyone knew.

By the time all the family had been introduced and Pop had explained that Charlie was a geneticist, with the polite if uninterested questions that engendered, it was time for dessert.

The cook, who had been absent during the meal except to pop her head in from the kitchen to make sure there was plenty of everything, cleared the table, stacking dirty dishes onto a wheeled cart. She or the cart creaked as they trundled away and there was clattering offstage as the dishes were transferred to a sink to be washed later. Charlie looked beyond the polite conversation of the woman to his right to see a look of puzzled interest on Mom's face as she studied him.

With a muffled bang the kitchen door closed behind the cook as she returned, her cart now laden with slabs of homemade apple pie in dishes, a gallon of ice cream, and a parlor scoop centered among them.

They eat well, Charlie thought, and wondered if this was standard fare or special for family gatherings. He could not imagine Pop eating this way all the time, not as lank and lean as he looked.

When dessert was finished Pop stood and all the men, as if by a prior agreement, followed him into the den. Not the living room, with its sofas and chairs with curliqued legs standing on imitation lions' paws, but through that formalish and tastelessly cool and stylish room and across the hall through an open sliding door into a more human and comfortable room with a worn and lived-on couch and a brace of recliners and a plebeian television for watching Dallas Cowboy games and having a drink, maybe even for eating dinner for two on TV trays. Pop produced a bottle of decent bourbon from a cabinet and someone else a Tupperware bowl full of ice cubes and a two-liter plastic bottle of Seven-Up from a little refrigerator that was big enough for Mom and Pop's needs and saved either of them a trip across the house to the kitchen when there were only the two of them. Charlie was happy to be led to so practical and comfortable a room in the big house he had begun

64

to think of as a stage set where he imagined Mom directed them all in badly written plays and the daughter-in-law with her poor baby would insist on bringing Tennessee Williams into it.

Only the men went into this mannishly practical room, and Charlie heard the women talking and more clattering of dishes after the door of the dining room had closed behind them. The daughter-in-law was at it again with the baby and the kid started to cry. Charlie heard the crying move from the dining room into the hall and then up the stairs. Good, put the poor thing to bed, Charlie thought. You've worn him out jostling him around and using him. Let the kid get some sleep.

Somebody wanted Coke with his bourbon instead of Seven-Up and Charlie noticed this time that it was the oldest son, the poor man who had stumbled through the blessing, who had produced the ice and everything else from the refrigerator and who now interrupted himself in the middle of taking glasses out of the same cabinet where Pop had found the bourbon to go back into the fridge and find a bottle of Coke. It was a lesson in group dynamics, Charlie realized, in family ritual, just as dinner had been. He was drawn to this oldest son, because he had fumbled the praying and was making himself so desperately useful now as if to make up for it. No one offered to help him get the mixers or the glasses or the ice, as if they understood without anything being said that doing all that was somehow a way for him to recover. Or, Charlie thought, a way to show he knows things, knows his way around Pop's privacy at least, knows where things are, that he can be useful. The others even seemed content to wait for the oldest son to find the Coke so that he could pour the drinks. All except the frat rat, who swaggered up to the cabinet where the whiskey and ice were laid out and poured himself a drink.

"Here's my idea of a mixed drink," he announced. "A generous helping of firewater and add ice."

He plopped a couple of ice cubes into what would have been a triple if he had been paying for it and threw down a slug. He made a face when it hit him. He coughed and play-acted hitting himself in the chest with a fist.

"Attaboy, Pop. It pays to buy the best," he laughed, slapping Pop on a shoulder before strutting away to plop himself into one of the recliners.

The men, Pop included, ignored him and waited for the oldest son to start pouring their drinks.

Charlie asked for a bourbon and Seven-Up and made a note of the ratio: about two to one whiskey. He let the others take their drinks and move away, then settled beside the oldest son as he made his own drink. Charlie was drawn to the man out of a sense of kindred ineptitude, but soon regretted it when the man, assuming Charlie, whom he took at face value as a geneticist, would be interested in his real estate business. The man was a developer, and had plans for the ranch someday. Charlie did not like the plans and soon resolved that he did not like the man very much either. Fumblers can be endearing when they resort to sensitivity, but not when they press on to bombast and foul their nests with the spoor of desperation. The man had gotten only as far as the industrial park he envisioned beyond the barns where the horses were now, which he thought would complement the resort development designed to capture the water sports potential of the lake itself, when Charlie excused himself and went outside.

The sun was gone but from its place beyond the lake it still made the western sky pink and purple and left a quivering trail of light on the water. Charlie skirted the big tree and came to the water's edge without knowing that he was looking out over the place where Amber McKendrick had drowned.

When he began to notice it, the sound had already been there for some time. There was never silence in nature, he knew. Especially in the dark. Along the edge of the water birds and bugs and fish and frogs kept the night alive with ripples and splashes and bumps and croaks. It took him a while to realize that this sound was different from the random and rhythmical "bumps in the night" that are always there. It was too . . . purposeful. A ripple on the water caught his eye, then another. He thought it odd at first, then understood that it had direction to it. He looked out along its line toward the middle of the lake and saw nothing except night settling in. Back from the spot where the ripple had been, his eyes followed the line to the shore and up into the tall grass to the silent figure of a man sitting stoop shouldered and silent beside a tree.

Charlie started, unable to contain a partially swallowed gasp that echoed across the still lake. The figure on the bank turned its head as if to look at him.

"Jesus," Charlie barked, stomping a tight circle in the beaten trail to get his pounding heart under control. I must be in better shape than I thought, he told himself. Twice in one day these guys pull this crap and I'm not dead yet. "You might let a guy know you're around, for Christ's sake. You scared the hell out of me."

The man might have grunted, but Charlie could not be sure.

"Who are you?" he asked. The shadowy figure did not answer. "Calvin, is that you?"

Still no answer. Charlie, wishing he had brought a flashlight, moved toward the man. From two feet away he could not make out anything about the face in the shadows. It occurred to him that whoever this was might be up to no good, and that he would not get any closer until he had a better idea what was going on.

The man sighed, a loud and patient sound of resignation, and began a twirling of his hands that made the splashing sound come alive again. When the cork and bait popped free of the water and wriggled up the bank toward the figure, Charlie realized the man had been fishing.

When the line was snug around his cane pole, the fisherman laid the pole down and lit his pipe. In the matchlight, Charlie saw an old dark face, its eyes squinted in wrinkled folds against the glare of the match, with a nose like a hawk's beak.

"Not biting anyway," the old man said, as if, like Mom at the dinner table, he had forgiven Charlie for his bad manners.

"Oh. Well, I'm glad I didn't scare them away when I had my heart attack. You could have said something, let me know you were here."

"You didn't see me?"

"No."

"I wasn't hiding."

"You might as well have been."

"I wasn't, though."

"Okay, I believe you." Charlie started to sit down beside the old man just as the old man stood up to go. Charlie was surprised at how tall he was, but his shoulders still were humped as if he were sitting on the bank.

67

"I'm Charlie Gants. I'm a friend of Pop McKendrick's. Actually, I work for him. I'm here to help with the breeding . . ."

"Breeding?"

"Yeah, the horses. Breeding the horses."

"You breed horses?"

"That's right."

The old man laughed.

"You know what I mean, I help Mister McKendrick breed studs to mares to improve his lines."

"You a vet?"

"No, a geneticist."

"Unnh." It was a grunt full of meaning, that told Charlie the old man did not know what that was and was not interested in learning.

"Who are you?" Charlie asked.

"What difference does it make?"

"None. Is it a secret or something?"

"No."

"Do you work for Mister McKendrick?"

"I'm too old to work."

"Oh."

The old man was ready to go, his pipe clenched between his teeth and his pole in hand. Charlie wanted him to stay awhile longer without knowing why. He was trying to think of something more to say, of a way of making the old man stay and talk, when he heard the scream.

It cracked the still night sky like lightning and Charlie turned toward the house, its source, and then the dying echoes of the first scream were followed by another and then caught up in a keening wail like he had never heard before, that stabbed across the lake and careened back upon itself until it seemed the world itself was wailing.

Like a banshee, Charlie muttered. It was like a banshee, a dying endless scream reverberating to fill up the whole world with anguish.

Charlie dashed up the trail toward the house, stopping beside the big tree to look back at the old man. He was gone, and Charlie ran toward the house. He knew what it meant when a banshee wailed.

It meant death.

CHAPTER NINE ▰══════════════════

THE LATE AUGUST SUN STARED DOWN AT THE HUDDLED crowd like the unblinking and merciless eye of God. There was no shade or shadow on the hilltop except beneath the green awning where the family sat on metal folding chairs arranged upon a sheet of carpet made to look like grass.

Brother Whitehead was a meaty, well-fed man with a pasty white face that showed red circles on his cheeks from the awful heat. Sweat glistened on his lips and ran in streams down his neck, ruining the starched and strangling certainty of his white shirt beneath the black suit that must have felt like punishment. He was a Baptist preacher.

Charlie and Calvin stood off a way, leaving the canopied darkness to the family. Beside them stood the sheriff and a pair of his deputies, half a dozen of the McKendricks' neighbors and the county commissioner. Flowers of all kinds stood in bunches and clung like ivy upon wire frames jammed into the hard dry ground, so many that they spilled over from the freshly dug grave and straggled among the tombstones of other McKendricks.

Charlie loosened his collar and the tie he had taken from his bag along with his old suit. He was sweating heavily, and envied Calvin, who was wearing just his nicest sport shirt and slacks. Charlie looked from one to the other of the people in attendance and wondered about each of them, about their secret thoughts. Sometimes I wish I were psychic, he thought. Something drew him away from the hilltop and the ceremony, and he looked over his shoulder toward the trees and the lake beyond. He thought he saw something there, in the shadows.

The trick was to look between the trees, not at them. But it was not easy, standing in the white heat of the hilltop that bleached all the world to a grayish brown, to see into the dark shadows beneath the trees. He thought he saw a movement, small and furtive. There was no wind, and

69

the trees, even in their smallest branches, were still. Charlie remembered the old Indian and reminded himself again to ask about him when the time was right.

Brother Whitehead was reading from the Bible now: ". . . Suffer the little children to come unto me, and forbid them not: for of such is the kingdom of God . . ." He paused with a tremor in his voice and fetched the handkerchief from his breast pocket to dry his tears. Charlie thought the preacher's tears were only sweat that stung his eyes, and doubted that the preacher had ever known the dead one. ". . . Verily, I say unto you, whosoever shall not receive the kingdom of God as a little child, he shall not enter therein."

The baby's mother screamed again at that, the way she had two nights before, the banshee's wail that had brought Charlie running back from the lake and the old Indian. She threw herself out of her chair upon the casket where it lay poised on straps above the yawning grave. It was a pitifully small thing, the casket, Charlie thought, not much bigger than a doctor's bag. The baby's father, Poppa's oldest son, sat unmoving in his chair, a big and flaccid heap. He was drunk, Charlie knew, and hardly saw his wife. Jade and the other daughter, the smoldering wholesome one, went to the baby's mother and drew her back within the dark shadows of the family. She screamed again and Charlie thought the doctor from town would have to be called for her.

". . . And he took them up in his arms, put his hands upon them, and blessed them," the preacher intoned, his East Texas country dialect barely undercutting the pompous tone he had learned at seminary. "We take comfort today, my friends, in the certain knowledge that today, as it was then, Jesus Christ our Lord and Saviour stands with open arms to welcome the children unto Him. Yes, little Ben rests in the bosom of the Lord this morning, my friends. We weep not for him, for he has gone home, he has gone before us and we take comfort in the certain knowledge that we will all see him again."

Then the preacher led them all in what was supposed to be a recitation by the group of the Twenty-third Psalm. It was half-hearted and spotty, because most of them were lost in themselves or did not know all the words. But finally it was over and the preacher stepped from the sunlight into the canopied shade to speak to each of the family members in turn, the baby's mother and father first. Whatever he

70

offered them, Charlie noticed, they paid him no mind. At last they were free to leave the place and go back down the hill to the big house. The baby's mother could not bring herself to leave, to abandon her child to be lowered into the dark hole, and she had to be borne away by her kinswomen. Her husband stumbled into the light and Poppa led him by the arm away.

The polite coterie of friends among whom Charlie and Calvin stood shuffled and the lawmen put their straw hats back on. They did not intrude upon the family to express themselves and Charlie knew their presence was the message and their shared sense of having failed somehow to save the baby spoke without words in their tight-lipped downcast faces and the humble set of their shoulders.

Only Mom paid the wilted preacher any mind. Poppa having taken his first son in hand, she availed herself of Brother Whitehead's arm and let him escort her down the hill to the house.

"Your words were such a comfort to us all," Charlie heard her say as she and the preacher passed by without looking at him.

When the family was gone into the house, the two ranchhands, who had waited patiently off to themselves, took up the job of burying the child. Charlie turned and followed behind the lawmen as they made their way back toward their waiting squad cars. Calvin, with an instinctive reluctance about approaching them, stayed behind.

Charlie overtook the sheriff as he reached his car. The two deputies had already climbed into theirs and the one driving raced the engine of the big Ford to get the air-conditioning going.

"Sheriff, have you got a minute?" Charlie asked.

"I guess."

The sheriff turned with his hand on his open car door and took Charlie in. He was a few years older than Charlie, square-built with a paunch but brawny arms that stretched the short sleeves of his shirt as he peeled off the jacket of his western-cut dark blue suit. He tossed the jacket into the back seat of his car and jangled his keys in his hand. Charlie noted the blue-steel Government Model .45 in a worn and well-made holster high on the man's right hip, cocked and locked, the tattoo on his left forearm, "U.S.N.," and the name of the ship he had served on.

"My name is Charlie Gants . . ."

"Some kind of a doctor, right?"

"Uh, that's right. I'm a geneticist. Poppa brought me in to help with the horse breeding."

"Don't say."

Charlie was not sure he bought that.

"Yeah. I was wondering what the tests showed. The autopsy."

"Little out of your line, isn't it?"

"I guess."

The sheriff swung into his car and shut the door. He cranked the engine and Charlie saw him adjust the air conditioner. When the sheriff rolled his window down, Charlie stepped closer.

"I'm not trying to be nosy," Charlie explained. "If it's a secret or something . . ."

"Nothing secret about it," the sheriff offered, pulling a pack of Red Man chewing tobacco down off the sun visor over his head. "Just kinda private."

"I understand."

"You're some kind of a medical man, aren't you? Geneticist, that's some kind of a vet or something, ain't it?"

"Not really. More . . . theoretical."

"Uh-huh. I understand it was you that did CPR on the baby. Where'd you learn that?"

"Just picked it up. It comes in handy sometimes, working with range animals there's not always a hospital handy."

"Uh-huh."

"That's the thing, see. I . . . gave it my best shot, but it wasn't good enough. I was just wondering . . ."

"Ever heard of something called 'SIDS'?"

" 'SIDS'? Yeah, 'Sudden Infant Death Syndrome.' Crib death. But I don't know what causes it."

"Neither do the doctors as far as I can tell. But that'll be the official cause of death. From what they tell me, there probably wasn't much you could have done."

"I appreciate that."

"Uh-huh."

The sheriff studied Charlie through the window and did not offer him a seat in the cooling car.

"I don't suppose all the results are in, though," Charlie offered.

"No, it'll take a week or two to get everything back. You asking for a reason?"

"No, just . . . you know."

"Where are you from, Doctor . . . ?"

"Gants. G-A-N-T-S. I'm from A and M."

"I see."

"Mr. Childress will vouch for me."

"The lawyer."

"Yeah."

"Hmm."

The sheriff was looking him over, and Charlie thought about telling him everything. Let Childress handle that, he decided. He knows the setup around here better than I do. The badge does not automatically make this one a good guy.

His two deputies pulled alongside, Charlie between the two squad cars, and the passenger officer rolled his window down with a look that asked the sheriff if they would be needed. The sheriff waved and told them to get back to work.

"Run by that place and see if anything's stirring," he told them. "Give me a holler."

"Right."

With that the deputies were off, out the long drive toward the road, where they turned right, not the way back to the highway or town.

"Where are they going?" Charlie asked.

"Where I sent them," the sheriff answered. "You ask a lot of questions, Doc."

"Sorry."

The sheriff revved his engine and tested the air blowing through the vents with his hand.

"Look, I don't want to butt in, it's just that I've taken a liking to Mister McKendrick and I'm concerned about what's going on, the accidents, his daughter's death, this thing. If there's anything I can do . . ."

"I appreciate that, Doc. I'll keep that in mind."

"Okay." Charlie stepped back as the sheriff put his car in gear.

"Sheriff!" It was Poppa McKendrick calling from the front porch. "Come in and have something to eat with us. There's plenty."

"Thanks, Mister McKendrick, but I guess I'd better get back on the road. If there's anything I can do . . ."

"We appreciate it, Sheriff. You be careful now, hear?"

The old man waved from the porch and the sheriff waved back.

"We'll be seeing you," the sheriff called to the old man. To Charlie he said, "And I'll be seeing you, too, I guess."

"I guess."

Charlie watched the sheriff's car turn left at the gate onto the road and disappear over the hill going back toward the road to the highway.

"How did that go?" Calvin asked, joining Charlie now that the lawmen were gone.

"Not great. About like a scene from *In the Heat of the Night*, if you know what I mean."

"Charlie, y'all come in out of the sun and get something to eat," Mister McKendrick called.

"Yessir, thank you," Charlie answered.

"Lord, lord," Calvin muttered.

"What?" Charlie asked.

"If you're Mister Tibbs, where the hell does that leave me?"

CHAPTER TEN

THE BIG HOUSE WAS FULL OF FOOD AND AS THE AFTER-noon wore on the driveway was busy with friends and neighbors bringing more. Some of them stayed and some only brought their offerings and left.

There was an unspoken etiquette to it. Mom McKendrick was in seclusion in her bedroom upstairs, attended by her daughters. The oldest and closest women friends made their way up the stairs to pay their respects to her and stayed as long as their closeness made them welcome. The baby's mother slept sedated in the upstairs room she shared with her husband and saw no one. Molly sat with her in case she awoke and needed anything. Poppa and the baby's father were in the den with the sliding doors closed. A few of the men who called, most of them Poppa's age, went in there to pay their respects. The parlor, with its plastic-covered "good" furniture and formal air, was for the rest of them, the lesser lights who came and went and some of whom stayed long enough to eat something.

The big kitchen was for the food and with Molly upstairs everyone helped himself. Flowers were everywhere and there was a book on a stand inside the front door which the funeral home had provided, where all who came in signed their names, each for his own reasons.

There might have been a dispensation made for Calvin due to the occasion, since Poppa had seemed to have meant that he and Charlie should come inside and eat something, but this alone of all the arrangements seemed unclear. It was not something these people had practiced, having a black man share this ritual with them. There was a loose and at first unseemly air around the kitchen table, with here and there three or four men gathered at one corner of the big table or around a particularly tempting plate of food; women likewise knotted themselves as friendships dictated or right allowed. It was a noisy and even sometimes raucous business, with jokes passed and memories reenacted. It was like every funeral Charlie remembered from his own youth, on a grander scale. Like his own father's, except that in his mother's little frame house there was too little room for so much demarcation, and the guests had spilled out onto the porch and into the yard, sneaking shots of whiskey against the chill of the winter day. He preferred winter for funerals.

Charlie and Calvin found plates and helped themselves to some of the food. Calvin gave no indication of noticing the ripple of uncertainty he carried with him, the almost subtle change of pitch in the murmuring of conversation that went before him, the looks and cocked brows that trailed in his wake. The men looked up at them and made no sign at all, the women smiled too much. When their plates were full, Charlie moved through the door out onto the porch and Calvin followed, leaving the mourners to put their patterns back together.

They sat at the table on the porch where the hands ate their meals and Calvin especially enjoyed the home cooking. Charlie had no appetite except for the aromas of it and the memories it conjured.

"I've had enough of this 'Green Acres' bullshit. Me and Jeff are gonna go out and scare up some action!"

It was the kid Charlie remembered from his first dinner at the ranch, the one who drummed on the table with his fork and played with his food. His mother was the wholesome one who had sat next to Charlie, Poppa's daughter with the dark and silent husband, the one with glasses. The kid was at SMU, a fraternity guy. He was talking to his uncle Chris in the back yard.

"Lower your voice, Chip," Chris chided him. "Show a little respect."

"Screw it. I don't even know why I'm here at all. You don't know what I'm missing out on or you'd call me a fool for hanging around. Rush, man. All the chapters are doing it, parties, the women, jerking off the fish, you have no idea. No fucking clue."

"It'll all be there when you get back. It's a funeral, Chip."

"This whole scene is a funeral. It's bullshit."

"The baby died, for heaven's sake. Doesn't that mean anything to you?"

"Damned straight. It means one less slice in the pie."

"What?"

"What, my ass. The estate, the big payoff. Tell me you wouldn't have minded the kid getting the lion's share. Why do you think his mommy is so damned torn up about it? She was shoving that little fucker down Poppa's throat, angling for the payoff just like everybody else in this family, including you."

"You need your butt kicked, you pigheaded little . . ."

"Take your best shot, faggot."

"Chip!"

The frat rat's father rounded the corner of the house as the two squared off.

"Take a hike, Dad. We got business."

"No you don't. Knock it off."

"Butt out, Dad."

"I said knock it off. We don't need a spectacle."

"Right, Dad, don't want to lose any points with the old-timers."

76

"Shut up."

"You shut up! Leave me the hell alone."

The father spun the boy around and tried to put an arm on his shoulder but the kid shook him off. Chip turned his back to the house and stalked away. His father followed after him, with an apologetic look back at Chris. The father and son talked quietly and then the father handed his son what looked like car keys and the boy stomped off. The father turned to Chris, who stood planted in the yard as if still ready for a fight.

"Sorry about that, Chris. You know how he is."

"Yes, I'm afraid I do," Chris snorted and walked away in the opposite direction his nephew had gone.

Chip's father stood looking around the corner of the house until Charlie and Calvin heard a car engine roar to life and the sound of wheels racing away. Then he shook his head and mounted the back porch steps. He stopped when he stepped inside the screened porch and saw Charlie and Calvin sitting there.

"Hello," he said.

"Hi," Charlie answered.

"I guess you heard all that."

Charlie nodded.

"He's a hot-headed kid. Talks without thinking sometimes."

The kid's an asshole, Charlie thought, but then you know that.

"Kids," Charlie offered. "What are you gonna do, huh?"

"Yeah," the man nodded and joined them at the table. "Kids."

He took off his glasses and wiped his face with a handkerchief. Then he wiped the glasses and offered Charlie his hand.

"Simon Goldman," he introduced himself. "We were introduced the other night at dinner, but I don't imagine you remembered all our names."

"Charlie Gants. No, I'm afraid I haven't sorted them all out yet."

"Well, we're quite a horde. And you are?" Goldman offered his hand to Calvin.

"Calvin. How do you do?"

"Calvin, I hope they've made you comfortable."

"Can't complain."

"Can't you? Well, I hope . . . you're comfortable."

"I am. Thanks."

Goldman put his glasses back on and put his hands together on the table in front of him.

"I hope you won't get the wrong idea about Chip, my son . . ." he began.

"Don't worry about it. It's none of our business one way or the other," Charlie said, and meant it. He was in no mood for the long and unfelt apology he saw in the father's face. "The heat alone is enough to make a person crazy. And I'm sure your son misses school."

"You give him too much credit, I'm afraid. He misses the autumn rites of his fraternity. I don't imagine he's bothered to find a classroom yet. But then he's only a junior."

Goldman laughed a little and Charlie and Calvin laughed with him, to put him at ease and make him understand they were not interested in hearing very much more on the subject.

"I envy him," Charlie admitted.

"So do I," Goldman agreed. "You can't help thinking if you'd had the same opportunities . . . but, you can't tell kids anything."

"Not much."

"I take it you two plan to stay on?"

"Yeah, Mister McKendrick wants to get on with things," Charlie said, thinking that he had not been told as much by the old man.

"That's good," Goldman said. "Get on with things."

"Yeah."

An awkward silence settled in as the three men rummaged through their thoughts, and then Goldman brightened.

"We all will be staying a while too, I think. Through the Labor Day weekend, anyway. Maybe I can help you sort out the cast of characters."

"Or give us a program." Charlie smiled.

"It's simple if you don't get bogged down in who is his, hers, and theirs. They don't make any distinctions anyway. Bill Junior is the oldest, his wife is Tess. You know them, of course."

The baby's parents. Yes, Charlie thought, I know them.

"My wife, Ruth, is next. Then there was Jeff's dad, he died in the war."

"Poppa told me about him."

"Jeff's mother went away after that. I'm not clear what became of

78

her. Jeff has lived here with Mom and Poppa ever since. You know Jade."

Amber's twin. Yes, Charlie remembered the shock of her arrival.

"That just leaves my son Chip and his uncle Chris."

"Chris isn't married, right?"

"Hardly. No wives or kids to clutter the picture. And that's all of us."

"I think I've got it. I may have to jot down a couple of notes."

"Yes. Well, I think I'll look in on Poppa and Bill Junior in the den. Can I get either of you anything?"

"No thanks."

"Well, make yourselves at home."

"We will."

Goldman opened the kitchen door upon the sounds and smells of the food and mourners and then he was gone. The door closed behind him and Charlie and Calvin were left alone in the warm shade of the porch.

"Nice guy," Calvin offered.

"Yeah."

"The kid's an asshole."

"Yep," Charlie agreed. "Makes you wonder who he takes after."

"Every other spoiled little shithead in the world. They didn't beat him enough when he was little."

"You're probably right." Charlie laughed. "Well, what do you think about all this so far?"

"I'm not sure. I might have been better off minding my own business."

"Probably. But, hey, don't feel like you're locked into anything. Any time you get enough, just say the word."

"Right."

"I mean it, damn it. You aren't obligated on this thing. And I sure as hell don't want to feel responsible if anything happens to you."

"Sweet-talk me some more, Charlie. Goddam."

"As long as we understand each other."

"Right."

Calvin went back inside for dessert and Charlie sat alone on the porch. He was wondering how it must be for Simon Goldman, a Jew among the McKendricks.

CHAPTER ELEVEN ▪══════════

THE SUN LOLLED LOW OVER THE LAKE AND ETCHED long shadows like fingers toward the house. The last of the well-wishers had gone and Molly had left Tess with Ruth to come down and put things away in the kitchen. Calvin had gone off with Red Jackson, the foreman, and the two hands to see what he could see and Charlie found himself in the parlor wondering if he would be welcome inside the den when he heard the commotion.

First there was screaming, a man's voice, and the crash and thud of things falling. Behind the doors inside the den there was a struggle of some kind.

Charlie stepped through the doors to find Bill Junior held by Poppa and Simon Goldman. Chris stood to one side, a drink in his hand. Bill Junior was crying and very drunk.

Charlie looked at Goldman.

"Is there anything I can do?" Charlie asked.

"Come on in," Poppa assured him. "Make yourself a drink if you like."

Charlie helped himself to what he found set out, not wanting to rummage through things to see if there was any scotch. When he had his Ancient Age and Seven-Up mixed and iced to suit him, he took in the scene.

Bill Junior was a sodden lump on the sofa between the two recliners now and no longer needed to be held back from doing any damage. He was sobbing brokenly and hopelessly into the hand-knitted afghan that covered the sofa.

Goldman and Poppa made themselves drinks while Chris watched from as much distance as the room permitted.

"He's taking it awful hard," Poppa said to Charlie.

80

"Of course," Charlie said. He tried not to imagine himself in Bill Junior's place if anything should happen to his daughter Elizabeth.

"Little Ben was his whole world," Goldman offered, thinking to add, "practically," to avoid excluding Bill Junior's wife, Tess.

"Hardest thing in the world," Poppa said. "Losing a child, outliving one of your kids, it's the hardest thing in the world."

They knew he spoke from experience and were silent in the memory of Amber and the son who died in the war.

"The doctor should have given him something," Chris said.

"Couldn't have," Poppa answered. "On top of all that liquor, it'd kill him."

"Just the same . . ." Chris shrugged and left his thought unfinished.

"Charlie, I don't know what to say to you. You've caught us at a terrible time," Poppa said, shaking his head.

"No, I . . ." Charlie began.

"Then he can leave, can't he?" chirped Chris. "You can leave if you like, Doctor Gants."

"Or stay, if he's of a mind to," Poppa countered.

"But surely you feel you're intruding. Don't you, Doctor? Don't you feel . . . intrusive?"

"Yes, I do," Charlie admitted.

"I mean, you're here about horses, aren't you. Bloody horses! As if they mattered . . ."

"They do matter," Poppa cut in. "To me."

"Yes, Dad, I understand that. You've always thought more of them than . . ."

"All right," Goldman interjected. "All right now, let's don't lose sight of things now, let's don't argue at a time like this."

"Don't mix in, Goldman," Poppa warned. "Let him have his say."

Simon Goldman blanched a little at Poppa's use of his last name as if there were special significance in it. He set his unfinished drink on an end table and excused himself, closing the door softly behind him as he left.

"Go ahead, Son. You were saying?" Poppa invited Chris, settling in behind his drink.

"If we're going to have a family feud, mightn't we wait until we're alone, Dad?" Chris asked, eyeing Charlie.

"Yeah, I need to be going . . ." Charlie began, about to finish his drink and leave.

"No, stick around, Charlie," Poppa insisted. "The subject was horses, I believe. That's what you're here for, isn't it?"

"Yeah, but . . ."

"Take your time with your drink. You're not intruding on this. Go ahead, Son, get it off your chest."

"I was just saying that you've always thought more of your horses than your sons. That's all."

"Sons? Did you say sons?" The old man raised his eyebrows in exaggeration.

"Your children, then. Is that better?"

"More accurate, anyway. I guess 'children' covers all the possibilities."

"I wonder, Dad," Chris began, then paused to collect himself. "I wonder if this once we could have our fight without any of your jibes about gender? Could we just set that issue aside for now and fight about what's important?"

"Kinda man to man, you mean."

"Forget it!" Chris spat and stalked toward the door.

"Wait, wait!" Poppa called out to stop him. "Hell's bells, I'm . . . I'm sorry, Chris. God as my witness, I truly am. Don't run off, boy. Stand your ground and let's fight it out."

"There's no point . . ."

"The hell there ain't. There's no point in much else. I . . ." Poppa bowed his head and then looked up at his son again. "Stand your ground, boy."

"Does he have to be here for this?" Chris insisted, jabbing a finger in Charlie's direction.

"I don't have to be here," Charlie offered.

"Both of you just hold what you've got and let's get on with it. I don't expect you to put much stock in this, Chris, but Charlie's here for a reason and all this is rolled up in things. . . . He needs to know how we feel."

"Of course. I expect the horses need . . . okay, enough of that.

I'm not like you, Dad. Of course, I expect that's the understatement of the century, but I mean, I'm not the strong silent type, the . . . that's not what I mean either." Chris drank and paced a tight circle to pick his words. "I'll never have children."

Poppa bit his tongue and buried his nose in his drink to keep from saying anything. His eyes met Charlie's and Charlie tried hard not to intrude.

"No snappy comeback, Dad? You are making an effort, aren't you?"

Chris looked from Poppa to Charlie and back to his father.

"A geneticist. My, my, a man who's devoted his life to the notion of a master race. God, my dad would kill for me to have turned out like you."

The words "master race" struck Charlie like an out-of-tune piano key, and with a single brush stroke darkened his picture of the old man who had insisted he stay. He thought of Simon Goldman again.

"I'll admit that," Poppa conceded. "But you didn't. Go ahead."

"So the fundamental difference between us . . . a fundamental difference . . . is that I have no illusions about the future. I have no hopes, no plans for what comes after. No interest in bloodlines or dynasty. History ends with me, for someone like me. You, on the other hand, are not the end result of anything. You are a link between the past and the rest of it, the generations you hope will come. You, Father, are a custodian, a steward. You preserve whatever it is you think is valuable, whatever you imagine is worth preserving about our . . . what? Our family? Our lineage? It's so pretentious, really."

Emboldened by his father's forbearance, Chris finished his drink and made himself another, and Charlie thought he was surprised that the old man did not take advantage of the pause to attack while he had the chance. But Poppa said nothing, only waited patiently while his son prepared to go on.

"Life matters to me, my life. There is nothing beyond myself that I feel sure of. I don't see myself as a link in any chain. Can you understand that? Can you understand how unconnected, how superfluous I feel to your obsession with arrangements you hope will pay off after you're dead?"

"I hadn't thought about it like that," Poppa admitted.

"I know." Chris softened a little. "It's never been that I don't care about you, about the things that are important to you. I didn't one day decide to be gay, you know. I didn't 'turn queer' to spite you."

The old man started to say something but thought better of it, or could not figure out how to go about it, and kept his peace.

"I know I've disappointed you . . ." Chris's voice broke and his eyes swelled with tears. "Shit, I don't want to cry, I don't want to go to pieces, I want . . ."

"Take it easy, Son," Poppa almost whispered. "Take your time."

Charlie set down his empty glass and turned toward the old man. "I really have to be going," he insisted.

"Don't run off," Poppa said, and it occurred to Charlie that somehow this business with his son was easier for the old man with Charlie there.

But there was a limit and he was intruding.

"I'll see you in the morning, Mister McKendrick."

"Call me Poppa."

"Poppa," Charlie obliged, thinking about what Chris had said about "master race."

"Wait a minute, Charlie," the old man said as Charlie opened the sliding doors. "I'll need some help getting Bill Junior there up to bed."

"He'll be all right where he is," Charlie answered. "The doctor's already been here and given Tess a sedative. She won't miss him tonight."

"Guess you're right. Good night, Charlie."

"Good night," Charlie answered; he met a look from Chris and added, "Good night, Chris."

"Good night," Chris answered.

Charlie pulled the doors closed behind him and stood in the entry hall of the big silent house. He decided to walk down to the lake and leave the old man and his son to work things out between them.

Chapter Twelve

OUT THE BACK DOOR OF THE HOUSE AND ALONG THE
trail, Charlie made his way in the gathering twilight in hopes that he
would see the old Indian again. While he had not found the right time
to ask about him around the family, Charlie had a hunch that the old
man would be of some use, might know something. He had not shown
up at the funeral and had not, as far as Charlie knew, been one of the
gaggle of solicitous mourners who had come to the house afterward.
Maybe he was not a friend of the family. Whatever, he was a source. If
not a friend, maybe he would be even better placed to shed some light
on things.

This time of year it did not get "good dark" until after eight
o'clock. It was nearly that when Charlie stopped on his way to the lake
to examine the big tree.

The Shaman Tree. He wondered about the stories without particularly coming down on any side about them. He knew of no reason why
such a tree would grow so big because an Indian had been buried among
its roots. What was it, the Indian's heart instead of an acorn? Whatever.
He could not think of any reason, for that matter, why this particular
tree should grow so much bigger than all the rest, bigger than such a tree
was supposed to ever be. He was in no mood to dismiss the magic
angle, not in the darkling hour that lay about the lake. Not with the
memory of his own impossible story about the murdered police captain
fresh in his mind. No, he was poorly equipped to play the skeptic.

As he walked a circle around the tree, he noticed for the first time
something jutting out from its trunk a little higher than his own head. In
the gloom of evening it might have been anything, but he finally made
it out: the head of a double-bit axe. Someone years ago had taken a
pretty good shot at chopping the tree down and had left the axe-head

buried irretrievably in its bark as proof of the effort. Charlie stretched up and touched the rusted blade, but could not budge it.

Charlie pushed on past the tree toward the lake and wondered how Calvin was getting along with his bunkhouse pals. Knowing Calvin, he was sure they were getting on. Calvin had a way about him.

When he reached the shore of the lake, Charlie looked carefully to his left from the trail that ended in the water, hoping the old Indian would be there again, fishing. But he saw nothing. No form among the shadows beneath the trees, no line or ripples upon the dark water. Only the moon a shimmering bridge across the water to the unseen other side of the lake.

To his right, he saw nothing. He noticed the water level was low, to be expected this time of year. There was a strip of smooth unworried mud ten feet wide that ran from the edge of the underbrush to the water's edge. At a loss, he pushed off to his left to see if the old Indian might have found a more promising place farther away from the trail and the occasional interruptions of blundering city boys.

Charlie had gone less than fifty yards when he heard something. He stopped to listen and there was a troubling of the water back behind him, in the direction of the trail. It was dark now, and looking back the way he had come he could not make out anything except the edge of the underbrush that screened the trail from him. He started to call out to see if anyone was there, but thought better of it and instead began as silently as he could to work his way back.

Now and then as he worked along the edge of the lake back toward the trail a stealthy noise brought him up short. Once a splash he did not hear again that he decided had been a fish feeding on the surface, or maybe an alligator gar rolling the way they do in the evening when bugs are on the water. Another time, a gasp like someone gulping air. Tingles ran down his spine and he took himself to task. "Don't start imagining things," he told himself. "You know how it is in the woods at night. Thousands of things alive out here, and every leaf that bends sounds like a . . ." He did not finish his admonishment because the sound of a sigh, a definitely feminine sigh, washed over him borne on an evening breeze. He pushed on.

At the trail, he stepped gratefully from the mud at the water's edge upon the smooth and beaten ground as if he had survived something. He scraped the mud from his shoes as he told himself he and Calvin would need to go to town again and buy themselves some boots and jeans, ranch clothes that were meant for . . .

He shot up straight at the sound of her, the o-o-o-o-o-h he knew without question was a sound made by a woman, a sound made for a reason, laden with the necessity of effort or air. Another sound, the leaden shimmering of a broken wave, froze him to the spot and turned him toward the dark water. That was when he saw her.

She was a long way out, just this side of the starkly moonlit fingertips that marked the tree-lined channel, when he saw her. Moonlight shimmered on her long blond hair as she came in toward the shore where Charlie waited, scissoring her long legs and stirring little eddies in her wake. Closer she came, coming toward him as if drawn to him, the blithering of the water before her where her arms worked with purposeful strokes. There was no sound upon the lake that Charlie heard, no chirp or croak nor the sigh of any wind as he stood transfixed and watched in hopeless wonder as she drew steadily nearer.

Gliding the last few yards on her kick alone, she judged where the shallows began and in a graceful turn spread her arms wide and righted herself, her legs curling down beneath her until her foot sank into the mossy mud. She sloshed ashore with her arms spread wide for balance, her hips rolling with the lithe and sinewy, arrogant grace on an athlete. She shivered and paused, the water at her knees, to push back her hair with both hands. She wrapped her arms together over her flanks so that her breasts lay upon her wrists as she shivered and took her next step.

Charlie stood speechless upon the trail at the water's edge and watched her as she made her way to him.

When she reached the lazily lapping water's edge and found him waiting there in the benighted brazenness of disbelief, she opened her arms, exposing her breasts and glistening belly to him and the moonlight, descended in graceful supplication to her widespread knees at the water's edge and reached out to him.

"Are you . . . who are you?" he asked.

She did not answer. Her hands at his hips drew him toward her and the primal lake mud, into the gentle rhythm at the water's edge, drew him down to her and opened him and drew him out. She took him in her mouth and he felt his cock come to life in its warmth. After so much, after so long . . .

She devoured him and bore him down into the warm mud and he held her, drove her down beneath him and they fucked until his need gave way to terror, as it dawned on him that she would draw him into her and annihilate him, that she would make off with him to the dark deep water and bear him down with her and then at last he came and in his need and horror spent himself in her without caring if he died.

And then she was gone and he might have died in earnest for all he cared until he came to himself and the water was still and dark and there was no trace of her. He picked himself up and made his way back to the big house.

CHAPTER THIRTEEN

CHARLIE LET HIMSELF INTO THE HOUSE BY WAY OF THE back porch and stopped to take off his muddy shoes before stepping into the kitchen. He was surprised at the quietness inside, and looked at his watch. It was later than he had thought; he had lost some time at the lake. He shivered at the thought of it, of the woman arising from the dark water. Jade. It was Jade of course, he told himself. Don't start . . . Amber is dead, and that is that. He wondered if Jade was about, but from the empty silence of the house he did not think anyone was stirring. A lamp had been left on in the kitchen but as he made his way into the dining room he found himself in darkness.

A single light from the landing above lit the stairs and cast dim shadows across the parlor below. Charlie stepped gingerly between the sofas and chairs to the foot of the stairs and started up, then halted. He turned and stepped across to the sliding doors of the den with the idea of looking in on Bill Junior.

The doors slid open with a low rumble of rollers in the track and a plaintive soft screech of wood on wood. Charlie looked in and saw in the dark room the prone figure of the poor man on the couch, the afghan over him. Charlie went to the couch and pulled a curtain to one side so moonlight came in by the window above the couch and fell upon the sleeping man.

Bill Junior slept soundly, his breathing deep and regular, with the open-mouthed wet rumbling of breath that came with whiskey and defeat. Charlie snugged the afghan under the poor man's chin and retraced his steps to the sliding doors and pulled them closed as quietly as he could manage. He would spend the night with Bill Junior in case he awakened and needed someone. In case Charlie's dark and troubling sense of evil lurking in the house should prove more than paranoia. Charlie picked his way in the moonlight from the window to one of the recliners. He settled into the big chair and worked the lever on the side beneath the armrest to lower the chair a couple of notches. He folded his arms upon his chest and waited for sleep to come, his thoughts on the lake and the woman.

She was Jade. He assured himself of that and focused himself on puzzling out her motives. Why on earth had she been in that place at that hour, as if she were tempting fate or proving something by re-creating Amber's fatal swim? No one in the family had spoken much of Jade, and he remembered her homecoming. She had been too late for her sister's funeral. Where had she been? Had her dark swim been a tribute of some kind, or a dare? Had she been mourning her dead twin or exulting? Her passion had had an edge of madness to it.

Charlie pushed himself out of the chair and, watching Bill Junior for any sign that he was disturbing the man, went to Poppa's desk. There was blank notebook paper in the shallow middle drawer, and Charlie took one sheet. He folded it twice so it would fit in his shirt pocket. He borrowed a sharp yellow pencil from a coffee mug full of pens and pencils and, stepping back into the moonlight from the window, jotted down a few notes. A list of names, beside each either a check or an *x*, with lines connecting the names of the family members who had been together here and there in the time between when the baby's mother had put him down and the discovery of the little body. When he had accounted for everyone, he returned to the recliner.

He lay back to think, and his eyes grew heavy and his head nodded. It had been Jade, he promised himself. Otherwise . . .

A glimmer at the window startled him, a flutter on a moonbeam, and he was stunned to see the figure of a woman swimming down the shaft of ghostly light through the window into the room. She emerged naked and beautiful from the moonbeam stream and showered the dark room with droplets of light, like sparks shimmering up from a campfire or fireflies. She trailed moonbeam shards like water drops as she came toward him, and her wonderful breasts and belly were aglow with twinkling beads of light as he sat spellbound. There was a soft and plaintive rumbling like far-off thunder and Charlie thought he heard the floor squeak ever so softly at her feet.

She came to him and mounted him, her moonglow thighs astride his lap as he sat in the big chair too stunned to move or speak. Her luminous face drew near to his, her dark and sparkling eyes transfixed him as her lips opened.

He wondered dumbly if he was dreaming but did not stir, even when he chilled at her icy breath playing on his cheeks. Even when he saw her draw back her hand and he noticed idly that it was the taloned paw of a beast. Even when she swung the rough and heavy paw down with all her might and he felt the blow explode at his temple, he did not stir himself to awaken. He pushed out sluggishly, impotently, to free himself of her, but felt nothing where her shimmering flesh should be. Darkness came over him and he could not see her anymore. He forced his eyes open, but still could not see. He felt himself rock forward in the chair, heard the sound of the recliner banging upright and felt his feet beneath him on the floor as he shoved himself toward her blindly to drive her away. He pitched forward, arms outstretched futilely searching for her, and fell with a heavy thud upon the floor. And then he did not dream anymore.

CHAPTER FOURTEEN

CHARLIE AWOKE HALF A DOZEN TIMES, or tried to. The light through the window behind the couch had turned to sunlight, soft and sunrise amber at first, then warmer and more insistent as early morning dew and mist burned away and the August day began in earnest. Charlie lay upon the floor, his left eye blinking at the sun's insistent intrusion. He turned his face away from the light, but that brought the left side of his head down on the floor and the bolt of pain in his left temple jolted him awake. He rolled over and sat up, his hand to his head, and noticed the afghan crumpled on the floor by the empty couch. Bill Junior was up and about, he supposed.

His head felt odd, the left temple mushy and damp to his touch, and Charlie drew his hand away and saw blood on his palm. He struggled to his feet and held himself erect while a wave of dizzy nausea passed. He looked around the room and when he felt steady enough moved toward the closed sliding doors. His foot hit something on the floor and he caught himself to keep from falling. He held his head carefully with his left hand as he looked down and saw a stick of firewood at his stockinged foot. There had been an armload of firewood in a brass basket near the hearth, and now the stumpy logs, each about two feet long and about as thick as his arm, lay scattered about the floor. The basket itself sat on its side, almost empty.

Charlie found a damp and crumpled towel beside the ice bucket where they had mixed their drinks the night before and he folded the towel and pressed it to his head to stop the bleeding and soften the throbbing pain. Then he stepped over the spilled firewood logs and opened the sliding doors.

From outside he heard sounds of life, a truck drove by and the voices of the hands rang out. Inside the house the sluggish silence of sleep insisted, and Charlie thought he was alone until he heard from the kitchen the scrapes and rattles of plates and pans, the reassuring sounds of Molly making breakfast. He steadied himself against the frame of the den doors for a moment and checked the towel to see how badly he was bleeding. It did not look as bad as he had thought, there was not as much blood as he expected from the way his head felt.

The kitchen door banged open as Molly bustled through with her cart to set the table. Charlie pressed his towel to his head again and pushed himself away from the door, making it rattle in its track. Molly heard the noise, and left her setting of the table to come into the parlor to see who was up.

"Oh, it's you," she said, coming into the room to find Charlie. "Lawd, what's the matter?"

"Bumped my head," Charlie answered.

"Here, let me get you something," Molly offered. "You need to put some ice on that."

Charlie looked up for the first time to tell Molly he would appreciate that and to ask if she could bring him some coffee too, but he did not say anything. He only stood open-mouthed as he looked above the woman and to the right of her, at the thing dangling in the early morning shadow of the stairway landing.

Molly turned back with her hand on the door to the dining room, as if to make sure Charlie was all right, or maybe to see if he was bleeding on the floor and making a mess. But when she saw him looking so odd, his face upturned and fish-belly white, she did not push through the door. She followed Charlie's gaze up into the grayness beneath the stairs and saw something. She could not make it out from where she was, so she moved toward Charlie, across the parlor toward the stairs, until she could see clearly. And then she screamed and fainted dead away.

Charlie paid poor Molly no mind. He was taken with the sight of Bill Junior hanging by his neck from a banister rail, his feet dangling waist high above the floor.

Charlie could see from where he stood that the man was dead, had been dead for some time. Bill Junior's blackened tongue lolled thick and turgid from his swollen and discolored lips. His eyes bugged out and his face was purplish and swollen. Charlie knew he was dead, but he set about cutting him down anyway, because he wanted to spare the family the sight of him. He stepped over the fainted cook on his way into the dining room where he grabbed a chair and found a butcher knife in its place in a drawer of the sideboard beside the table.

"Molly?" a woman's voice called from one of the rooms upstairs; Charlie couldn't be sure which woman it was. "What's going on down there?"

Charlie hurried to get it done before anyone came down. They had been through enough without something like this, he thought, as he placed the chair beneath the dangling corpse and climbed up. His head hurt from the effort, and with the dizzy pain of it and the feel and smell of the befouled dead man as he steadied the body and reached up with the knife, it was all Charlie could do to keep from retching.

He sawed through the rope, noting as he did that it was a hemp lariat like you would expect to find on a ranch. He saw that the loop end was snugged around the dead man's neck, cutting into the flesh so deeply that he could just make out one end of the leather guide that held the loop open so the rope would pass through cleanly when a loop was twirled and thrown. He did not take time to notice much more because he heard shuffling footsteps above him as here and there the house awakened in dread and a sense of alarm.

"Molly?" the woman's voice insisted from above, as Charlie heard the opening of a door and then more voices.

With a sudden thud the body slumped to the floor as the knife worked through the rope and Charlie was not able to hold the weight of it and let it down more gently as he had hoped. He stepped down quickly from the chair and dashed into the den as he heard someone coming down the stairs. He quickly snatched up the afghan and returned, laying it over the dead man as Poppa made his way down the stairs, followed closely by some of the others.

"Charlie, what in the world?" Poppa asked, looking from Charlie to Molly, who was coming around and mumbling to herself where she lay on the floor. Then to the afghan shroud and its crumpled horror.

"You better have the women wait upstairs, Mister McKendrick," Charlie offered.

The old man fixed Charlie with a hard and wondering look, and Charlie realized he was still holding the butcher knife. He laid the knife on the chair beside the body and showed Poppa his empty palms.

McKendrick stopped two-thirds of the way down the stairs and turned to see who was behind him. The Goldmans, Simon and Ruth, were at the top of the stairs, and Charlie saw Jade behind them, looking down at him.

"Simon, come here," McKendrick said, his voice with a tinge of wonder but meaning business nonetheless. "You girls go back to your rooms for now. Let's see what's going on down here."

Ruth and Simon exchanged glances before she turned back and Charlie heard her moving away down the hall calling her son's name.

Simon came down the stairs behind McKendrick and Charlie saw that Jade ignored her father and followed Simon.

"What is it?" McKendrick demanded.

"Bill Junior," Charlie warned. "I found him when I came out."

McKendrick looked up at the severed rope and down at the mess on the floor beneath it.

"He's dead?" the old man asked, knowing the answer.

"Yes, sir. I cut him down before . . ."

Charlie did not bother to finish, full of the knowledge that he had failed the old man.

McKendrick knelt in his bathrobe beside the body and tugged the afghan back to see for himself.

"You might not . . ." Charlie began, but he knew the old man would have to see for himself.

Charlie stepped away to give McKendrick room and Simon Goldman stood on the last step of the stairs, his hand upon the banister, and looked curiously at Charlie. Jade pressed by him and brushed past Charlie. Their eyes met briefly but her look told Charlie nothing about what she felt or the night before.

Goldman left the stairs to go to Molly. He helped her up and led her to one of the parlor chairs.

"Good god almighty," McKendrick murmured, looking down at his ruined son.

From above came a terrible scream and a thunder of footsteps and Charlie looked up to see Momma McKendrick careening down the stairs.

"DearJesusalmighty . . . oh, JesusLordandsaviour . . . omercifulsaviour . . . godalmighty . . ." she chanted, her hysterical incantation strung together as if she was speaking in an unknown tongue. "Poppa, Poppa, Jesus, Jesus . . ."

And then as she swirled around the banister at the bottom of the stairs and came upon her husband bending over the corpse and she saw the dead man's face she lost the gift of language altogether and screamed.

Charlie looked up from the spectacle of the old woman to see Tess, the dead man's wife, standing at the top of the stairs. She had buried her baby the day before and now stood in the misty cloud of the sedatives

94

they had given her, staring down at them with a muddled and curious look.

"Bill?" she called out. "Bill Junior?"

Ruth and her son Chip appeared behind the woman and Ruth took her in hand. Chip craned his neck to look down over the banister with a look like he was annoyed at being awakened.

Poppa took his wife in hand and tried to lift her off the dead man where she had thrown herself, full of weeping and incoherence.

"Ruth," McKendrick called up the stairs. "Ruth, get her back to bed."

The old man struggled with his wife to keep her off the body. She screamed and beat her breasts with her fists and screamed again. He looked at Charlie and then at Simon Goldman, who stood comforting Molly.

"Goldman!" McKendrick shouted. "Never mind that nigger woman. Come here and help me with Momma."

Goldman did as he was told and he and McKendrick were able to drag the old woman away toward the dining room.

Charlie went to a phone to call the sheriff.

CHAPTER FIFTEEN ▬▬▬▬▬▬▬▬▬▬▬▬▬

CHARLIE SAT IN A CHAIR ON THE SCREENED PORCH AND Calvin did what he could with the wound on his head.

"You could use some stitches, Charlie."

"A couple of butterfly patches ought to do," Charlie protested. He wanted no part of a hospital and did not mind that the doctor was too busy with the others to see to him. Calvin had found a first aid kit somewhere and was doing all that needed to be done about Charlie's head.

"They'll stop the bleeding and hold your hide together, but you'll have a scar."

"It doesn't matter."

"I guess not. I think I've got it cleaned out, doesn't look like I'm leaving any tree bark in there."

"I'd appreciate it."

"Hold still."

"Yes, Doctor."

Calvin closed the laceration with two butterflies and then applied a small gauze patch which he taped neatly in place.

"That sheriff got around to you yet?" Calvin asked.

"Not yet."

"Good. What are you going to say when he does?"

"I'll just tell him what happened. What do you mean?"

"I'm talking about this undercover business. You going to level with him or do you aim to still be Doctor Gants?"

"I guess I'll just play it by ear."

"Well, Charlie, I guess that ain't good enough. Make up your mind one way or the other so we can keep our stories straight. One of the last things in the world I want to do is to get on the wrong side of some redneck lawman for attempted bullshitting."

"Yeah."

"And, I'll tell you, the way old Red Jackson has been pumping me about you, I wouldn't be surprised if the jig wasn't up anyway, if you'll pardon the expression."

"What do you mean?"

"That either Red Jackson is a damned curious man or else the high sheriff has put him up to doing some prying."

"Do you think he suspects something?"

"Do you think I convinced him I was your graduate assistant? How the hell do you spell 'geneticist,' anyway?"

"You want out?"

"That's up to you, Mister Tibbs."

"Tibbs?"

The sound of the voice in the doorway behind him startled Charlie. It was the sheriff.

"Morning, Sheriff," Calvin smiled.

Charlie turned to face the sheriff as Calvin made himself busy putting the first aid kit back in order.

96

"Tibbs?"

"It's a little private joke," Charlie said, with a small smile.

"Uh-huh."

"How's everybody doing in there?" Charlie asked.

"Like you'd expect. How's your head?" The sheriff eyed Charlie's bandage carefully and then looked Calvin up and down.

"Not too bad," Charlie said.

"Not something you'd likely die from, I guess."

"No."

"Then you might've waited till the doctor could take a look at it."

"He had his hands full. Calvin took care of it."

"I see that. Only I might've wanted the doctor's opinion."

"I see."

"You some kind of doctor, too?" the sheriff asked Calvin, and Charlie expected him to add "boy," but he did not.

"No, sir. I was a medic in the service," Calvin answered.

"Which service was that?"

"Ours," Calvin said, smiling good-naturedly. When he saw the lawman was not amused, he hurried to add, "Army, First Cav."

"Vietnam?" the sheriff asked.

"Yes, sir."

"Me, too," said the sheriff. "One hitch on river boats."

The two men nodded at each other as something mutual seemed to arise between them.

"You?" the sheriff asked, pointing his question at Charlie.

"Uh, no," Charlie admitted. "I wasn't in the service."

"Uh-huh." The sheriff looked back over his shoulder toward the interior of the house; he pushed his hat back on his head and settled heavily into a chair near Charlie. "Mister Tibbs, huh?"

"It's just a little joke," Charlie laughed uneasily.

"Uh-huh. And that'd make me Gillespie, I guess."

"Who?" Charlie asked, genuinely puzzled.

"Chief Gillespie. Rod Steiger. I saw that goddammed movie too, Doctor Gants."

"Oh."

"Or whatever you are."

"What . . ."

"Don't waste my time," the sheriff interrupted. "Old man McKendrick vouches for you. Lawyer Childress vouches for you. I don't have time to play games with you right now, and I'll know all I need to about you before it's over, so let's don't play any games."

Charlie and Calvin exchanged looks but neither said anything.

"Just tell me what happened," the sheriff ordered, settling in his chair to listen carefully.

Charlie told him everything, starting with his waking up on the den floor. He did not say anything about the business at the lake with Jade (Amber?) or anything about his dream of the succubus swimming in moonbeams.

"How did you come by that lick on your head?" the sheriff asked when Charlie had finished.

"I can't say for sure. Either I got up during the night for some reason and fell, or . . ."

"You think you fell and hit your head on the firewood?"

"Could be. It was spilled out on the floor . . ."

"You been drinking?"

"A little. We had a couple of drinks after the funeral."

"Drunk or not?"

"Not."

"Or what?"

"I beg your pardon?" Charlie asked.

"You said either you got up and fell or . . . or what?"

"Or somebody hit me with a piece of firewood and dumped the rest to make it look like I fell."

"Uh-huh."

"I guess you're doing a crime-scene search?"

"Meaning what?" the sheriff demanded.

"Meaning I wonder if you found the piece I got hit with."

The sheriff eyed him levelly, then turned toward Calvin.

"Would you excuse us for a little bit?" the sheriff asked.

"No problem," Calvin assured him, taking the first aid kit with him as he cocked an eyebrow at Charlie as if to say he should not underestimate the sheriff and pushed the screen door open.

Charlie watched him as he traipsed across the yard toward the bunkhouse. He understood that the sheriff wanted to question them separately.

98

"You are doing a crime scene?" Charlie asked.

"On a suicide?" the sheriff asked, with something in his eyes.

"On an exceptional death," Charlie began. "You can't assume . . ."

"Who the hell are you?" the sheriff demanded suddenly.

"I'm a . . ."

"Horse doctor, right. And I'm a . . ." the sheriff caught himself and did not lose his temper. He took off his hat and leaned toward Charlie. "We're doing the scene, Mister Tibbs, or whoever you are. We're not as ignorant as you might think."

"Then you've checked the rope," Charlie said.

"Yeah, we're taking a look at it. And that brings up a question I'd like to ask you. The way I get it, you cut the man down right quick."

"Yeah."

"But you didn't bother the rope. You didn't loosen it around his neck."

"No, I didn't."

"You didn't make any effort at all to see if he might still be alive, try to use your CPR on him."

"There was no point."

"Meaning?"

"Meaning he was dead. He'd been dead for some time."

"How would you know that? How could you tell so sure from a quick look?"

"It was obvious."

"Uh-huh. Then why the hurry to cut him down?"

"I didn't want the family to see him like that."

"Sensitive of you. Only you kinda played hell with the crime scene, didn't you?"

"Not really. Physiologically . . ."

"Just a minute . . ."

"Really, the post-mortem lividity . . ."

"Never mind that for right now," the sheriff insisted. "Tell me what you were doing there in the first place."

"What?"

"You decided to sleep in a chair in the den when you had a room of your own upstairs. Why?"

"To . . . to keep an eye on Bill Junior," Charlie said, knowing as he said it where it would lead. He had thought it all himself.

"Why?"

"He got drunk as hell after the funeral."

"That's understandable," the sheriff said.

"Of course. But I . . . I wanted to keep an eye on him, make sure . . ."

"Make sure of what?"

"That nothing happened. That he didn't do anything foolish."

"Well, you did a hell of a job, didn't you?"

"Didn't I."

"It was a nice thought," the sheriff offered. "Shame you ain't a light sleeper."

That was the thing, one of the things, that had been bothering Charlie. He *was* a light sleeper.

"But let's get back to the rope for a second," Charlie said. "Did you notice the marks between the body and the anchor point?"

"What marks?"

"That's the point, there weren't any. But how about on the other part of the rope, the part between the banister post on the landing where the rope passed through and the stairway railing where it was tied off?"

"What about it?"

"Look, it was like this . . ." Charlie gestured with his hands, describing the suspended body here, the rope running up from the dead man's throat to one of the banister posts on the landing above where it was not tied, but just run through, and from there across to the banister post halfway up the stairs where it was tied. He ran his finger through the air to indicate how the rope ran from its tied-off anchor point on the stairway up and across to the landing, around the post there and then straight down to the dead man. "See what I mean?"

"Yeah, I know how the rope was rigged. We took photos before we took it down. What's your point?"

"And it was a new rope, right?"

"Uh-huh."

"New hemp. With bristles that stand out, right?"

"Uh-huh."

"Only, the bristles between the anchor point and the wrap-around on the landing didn't stand out like the rest. They all were mashed down, all of them bent over toward the wrap-around, toward the weight of the body. Like a scrape or a kind of a burn. See what I mean?"

"You mean that part of the rope was pulled across the landing banister with some weight on the other end."

"Exactly!"

"Meaning Bill Junior didn't hang himself, not unless he . . ." The sheriff stared Charlie down with a look that made Charlie wonder if the lawman had figured this out on his own already. "Meaning somebody put that loop around Bill Junior's neck and then ran the rope around the landing post and hoisted the poor sonofabitch up like a side of beef."

"Yeah, and too far up."

"What do you mean too far?"

"I'll grant you there's damned few murders by hanging, but suicides usually don't hang so high, unless they step off a chair or something."

"And how would a horse doctor know that?"

"Well, I . . ."

"You're fixin' to lie," the sheriff cut in on Charlie. "I can see it in your face."

Hell of a trick, Charlie thought. Trouble is, he's right. I'm not much good at this, I guess. Charlie was on the sheriff's side. He wanted to level with him, but he did not know if the man could be trusted. If he's legit, Charlie noted, I owe him a drink when this is all over.

"Sheriff, I . . ."

"Don't waste my time, man. If you ain't gonna shoot straight with me, just don't by god bother."

Charlie met the big man's stare, but did not say anything.

"This is my county," the sheriff went on. "My turf, and all this is my business. It's my goddammed job! Do you understand me?"

Charlie did understand, better than the sheriff could have imagined.

"I may look like some kind of bumpkin to you, but I know what I'm doing and I take my job mighty serious, whether you believe it or not. Now, I ain't gonna ask you twice. Why are you here?"

Charlie did not look away, but he did not answer, either.

"Because I asked him to come here," Poppa McKendrick said from the doorway behind them.

"Mister McKendrick," the sheriff said, rising to his feet.

"You asked me about Charlie already," McKendrick said, an edge to his voice. "I told you he was all right. Charlie's not the problem here. I expect you to take my word on that."

"Yes, sir. I understand that. But . . ."

"But what?" the old man insisted in a level tone.

The sheriff looked at Charlie like he thought Charlie knew how he felt better than the old man could, like he wondered what it was between Charlie and the old man that made things the way they were.

"But nothing. I'd better get back inside and see how they're coming along."

"I think that's a good idea," McKendrick said, nodding.

"We'll be out of your way as soon as we can."

"Take your time, Sheriff. It's important work."

"Yes, sir."

The sheriff went back inside and McKendrick took his seat.

"How much of that did you hear?" Charlie asked.

"Some."

They sat without speaking for a moment.

"The sheriff's a good man," Charlie said.

"Probably."

Charlie waited for the old man to ask the question and did not mind that he took his time about it. It was a bad business. While he waited, Charlie tugged the folded sheet of paper out of his shirt pocket. Again he used the borrowed yellow pencil to make a list of names, beside each his own system of symbols and connecting lines, trying to coax a pattern out of all of it. He had done all he knew to do with that when Poppa turned to look at him. Finally, it came.

"Did my boy kill himself, Charlie?"

"No, sir," Charlie answered, looking the old man in the eye. "It was murder."

CHAPTER SIXTEEN

THAT NIGHT CHARLIE HEARD THE WOLVES FOR THE first time.

He had intended to make his way back to the lake for reasons he had not made himself think through. Part of it was the woman and another part was the old Indian. What they had to do with each other, he was not sure. What any of it meant, he . . . it was murky.

Charlie Gants was a man of many parts as he turned his back on the lighted but somnolent eyes of the big house and all the misery that cried itself to sleep beneath the old gabled roof. Tess, Bill Junior's widow and the late Little Ben's mother, was gone now, taken away to parts unknown by the doctor in an ambulance and a narcotic fog that Charlie suspected would never lift.

The rest of them, he imagined, had stalked circles around their beds like wary dogs and lain down with slitted yellow eyes to await the morning.

So there was this part of him that longed for more of the woman. The woman of the lake, the emerging nymph who seduced him in the primal mud and awoke in him fires of passion that scoffed at death and madness. This part of him needed her again, needed more of her and did not mind if the woman he took her for walked about the big old house in the dreary daylight without a sign that anything had passed between them in the secrecy of the night.

That part of him was mad, he knew, or so nearly mad that on a given day it was a matter of mood and energy, not to mention a certain clinical facility he had picked up at the Granville Institute. He did not deny that part of himself, not now, not as he stood at a place in the trail that led from the house down to the lake past the big tree. It was a special and appropriate part that endorsed him to the night and the old place with its mysteries.

And then he heard the wolves for the first time.

Plaintive and timeless, one and then another called across the night sky, answered and emboldened. Like the ghosts of ancients, the old devils talked their talk like the drumbeats or smoke signals of ancient unseen Indians.

Charlie jumped and almost screamed at the touch upon his elbow and flew back with a thump against the hard-barked trunk of the big tree. It was the old man from before, the one Charlie had come upon fishing the night the baby died.

The old man stood calm and still beside him as Charlie caught his breath and tried to find the strength to speak.

103

There was this part of Charlie too that had hoped to find the old man, that, as much as the other wanted the woman to fuck him wanted the old man to find him, for reasons he could not fathom. And now here the old man was, and Charlie was at a loss for what to say.

"Wolves?" he asked finally, for want of anything else.

"Hmm," the old man answered.

Charlie stood beside the old man beside the big tree and wondered . . .

"Hunting, I think," the old man said. "There's a chill coming, maybe."

"A chill?"

"Hmm. They don't stir much in the hot time."

"Oh."

The old man started off toward the lake and Charlie followed.

"Going fishing?" Charlie asked.

"Not tonight."

"You didn't happen to be out here last night, did you?"

"Can't remember last night," the old man offered, over his shoulder.

"You'd remember. There was a woman swimming, out in the lake."

The old man pulled up short. He turned to face Charlie, his face in shadows but his eyes alive with the light from the moon or somewhere.

"Last night?" the old man asked.

"Yeah, did you see her?"

The wolves howled again, sounding nearer.

"Did you?" the old man said.

"Yeah."

"Then what difference does it make?" the old man asked, turning away toward the lake.

"What are they hunting?" Charlie asked, hurrying along the trail until he caught up with the old man.

"Food."

"I know, but what?" Charlie insisted.

The old man did not answer and Charlie did not ask again. He fell into step with the old man as they followed the trail toward the lake and Charlie's thoughts turned again to the woman. He wondered if she would be there again tonight, if it would matter that the old man was

104

there, if she would show herself to the two of them, or . . . He made himself stop thinking about her.

When they reached the end of the trail where it led off into the smooth mud and the water beyond, the old man stood silent and still, his head cocked to one side. Charlie heard the wolves talking again, different now.

"They have something," the old man said.

"What?"

"Who knows?"

"You can tell by the sound of them?"

"Can't you?"

"No."

"Oh, that's right," the old man said. "I forgot."

"Who are you?" Charlie asked, remembering finally something of what it was he had hoped would come of finding the old man again.

"What difference does it make?" the old man asked.

"I am Charlie Gants," Charlie said.

"Funny name," said the old man. "It doesn't tell you anything."

"What do you mean?"

"Like who was your father, your mother's people, what medicine you have. It's a funny name, isn't it?"

"I don't think so."

"Maybe it's just me," the old man shrugged.

"You're an Indian, aren't you?"

"Indian?" the old man asked.

"Yes."

"I don't think so. I don't know what it means."

"I thought maybe . . . there are a lot of Indians in this part of the country. Across the river, a lot of Choctaws, Cherokees farther north . . ."

"Caddo," the old man said.

"Caddo?"

"Sure. You haven't heard of us?"

"Yeah, I . . . I'm sure I have."

"You don't know much."

The old man seemed disappointed in him, and Charlie was at a loss to recoup himself. He was puzzling this and listening for the wolves

105

again when he heard a noise behind him, from the direction of the house. He turned and caught sight of moonlight on long blond hair.

"Here she comes," he said, turning to tell the old man that the woman was coming. But the old man was gone.

CHAPTER SEVENTEEN

CHARLIE STEPPED OFF THE TRAIL INTO THE SHADOWS of the undergrowth, not really hiding, he told himself, as he wondered where the old Indian had gone and at the same time what the woman coming down the trail toward him had in mind.

He stood rock still as she walked to the trail's end and stood quietly looking out at the lake, almost within his arm's reach. She was dressed in something white and soft, a dress that moved softly with the light breeze and he wondered if she would take it off and step into the water. He wondered for a moment, and then he felt like a spy and stepped out of the shadows and spoke her name softly.

"Jade," he said.

"What?" she shrieked, and jumped the way Charlie had when the old Indian had touched his elbow up the trail by the tree.

"It's okay," Charlie reassured her. "It's just me."

"Who?" she demanded, half-turned as if she might dash up the trail to the house and awaken everyone.

"Me, Charlie. Take it easy, it's just me."

"My god, you scared me half to death," she said, not as if she trusted him or thought that it being only him meant she was safe. "What are you doing out here hiding in the bushes?"

"I wasn't hiding, I was just . . ."

"The hell you weren't. What are you up to?"

"I really wasn't hiding. I was just trying to see where the old man went."

"What old man?"

106

"The Indian. I don't know his name, the old guy that fishes here. You tell me."

"I don't know what you're talking about."

"The old guy . . . Never mind. Relax, relax."

"Yeah," the girl said. "You, too."

Charlie realized he was tensed like a drawn bow, full of expectation. He made himself take a deep breath and put his hands in his pockets. He stepped back from the girl, circling a little so that he put his back to the lake and did not block her way back to the house if that was where she wanted to go.

"Sorry, guess I'm a little tense myself," Charlie said, laughing softly.

"Yeah."

"I . . . I hope I'm not intruding," he said.

"Of course you are. I'd hoped to be alone down here."

"Oh."

"You don't mind, do you?" she asked pointedly, giving him to understand she wanted the lake to herself.

"No, of course not," Charlie lied, puzzled.

He skirted around her, walking like a crab, so he wouldn't intrude on her or alarm her, and then backed away up the trail toward the house, smiling doltishly back at her.

"You're sure you wouldn't like me to stay?" he asked.

"Perfectly sure," she answered.

"I see," he said.

Charlie turned away from her and started back up the trail, and then the silliness of it stopped him and he went back.

"Look," he said. "There's no sense in you're being this way, after last night, I . . ."

"What?" she asked, and he could see her big eyes in the moonlight off the lake, full of disbelief and indictment. "What about last night?"

"You know as bloody well as I do, and knock off this stupid act . . ." he began.

"Get away from me!" she hissed, and he knew she would scream next, loud enough to awaken the house.

"All right," he said, holding up his hands and stepping back from her. "All right, have it your way. Last night never happened. Is that better?"

"I don't know what the hell you're talking about!" Jade insisted. "You just stay the hell away from me, you hear me?"

"All right, all right. Take it easy. My mistake. Take it easy." Charlie worked to make his voice sound reasonable and not threatening at all, while his mind whirred like a haywire clock; she means it, he thought. Then who was that last night? Oh, god, what's going on here? "I don't want to upset you, ma'am. If you want to be alone, that's fine. I'll go back to the house."

"Like hell. You think I'm going to stay down here with you on the loose somewhere? Like hell, mister. I don't know what's going on around here, but the damnedest things have been happening since you showed up, and now this talk about last night . . ."

"Have it your way," Charlie assured her. "You go back to the house and I'll wait here until you're safe inside, how about that?"

"You keep your butt out here where I can see you, you hear me?" she said.

"I promise."

"We'll see what my daddy has to say about all this."

"Right," Charlie said. He was in no mood to argue.

"Stay where I can see you," the girl said once more as she walked away.

"You bet," Charlie promised.

He stood in the middle of the trail at its lakeside end and watched the girl's blond hair disappear up the trail toward the house. He could see her as far as the big tree, and then he lost sight of her around the curve as she went the rest of the way home. He did not move even after she disappeared beyond the tree, giving her plenty of time to make it to the house before he left his place. When finally he figured she was there, he shook his head and started back, turning once more to wonder where the old man had gone.

"Silver-tongued devil you," a voice sang out from the darkness.

"Jesus Christ, Calvin!" Charlie swore, too wrung out to jump this time.

"I have to hand it to you, Charlie, you really know how to talk to the women."

"Shut up."

"And, uh . . . I give up, what did happen last night?"

"Nothing."

"Yeah, that's what she said."

"What the hell are you doing out here, Calvin?"

"Keeping an eye on you, man. And don't try to tell me you don't need it."

"I won't. You been out there long?"

"About as long as I care to be. You okay?"

"Tops. You saw the girl, right?"

"Naturally."

"And the old man?"

"Who?"

"Never mind."

"Right. Now what?"

"I don't know, Calvin. What do you think?"

"I think I'll be glad when you white people all go to bed."

CHAPTER EIGHTEEN ▪

SINCE THE WHOLE FAMILY WAS AT THE RANCH AL-
ready and there was no reason to think Bill Junior's wife Tess would be
in any better shape any time soon, there was no reason to put off the
funeral. By the time the autopsy was done and the body released to a
funeral home in town, the arrangements had been made. The family
buried Bill Junior two days after he died. Brother Whitehead did the
honors again.

Charlie and Calvin would have skipped the funeral altogether
except that their absence would have raised too many questions and they
felt obliged to be there out of respect for McKendrick. As soon as it was
over and the family withdrew to the house to repeat their rituals of food
and condolences, the two outsiders excused themselves.

Poppa had put one of his pickup trucks at their disposal and Charlie made his way from the little cemetery toward the truck with Calvin in his wake. Charlie stopped long enough to ask the sheriff if there was anything new, but the big man answered brusquely that it would be a while before the autopsy results were in. He did not volunteer anything more, and also did not ask Charlie any of the questions that showed in his eyes. Charlie did not press the matter. He and Calvin got in the truck and drove away toward town.

They needed some things, the right kind of clothes for the ranch and some boots. Calvin's loafers and Charlie's running shoes were not fit for the rough country, and the only clothes Charlie had brought with him were a sweat suit and the one dress suit. It had come in handy for the two funerals, but Charlie hoped he would have no more need of it. If anyone at the ranch wondered why a horse doctor and his assistant had not come better prepared to spend time on the range, none of them asked any questions. They had plenty of other things on their minds.

Poppa had told Charlie where to go and to get whatever they needed and put it on McKendrick's bill at the store. But Charlie insisted he would pay.

Charlie took a deep breath as he wheeled the pickup onto the highway off the smaller road and swung left toward town. He looked back over his shoulder toward the hills that rose between him and the McKendrick ranch, half expecting to see a dark cloud settled in over the hilltops and stretching out toward the ranch. There was no cloud, of course, but Charlie felt as if the sky had brightened as they took to the highway and left the McKendricks behind them.

Calvin seemed to brighten, too, and Charlie decided to tell him about Jade, that he had made love to her at the lake shore the night of Bill Junior's murder.

When Charlie had finished his story, Calvin did not say anything, just shook his head and looked out his window at the passing country-side.

"What?" Charlie insisted when Calvin showed no sign of giving his opinion.

"You," Calvin answered finally. "What is it with you and women, man?"

"Same as anybody else, I guess. So what do you make of it? Why

110

do you think Jade acted the way she did at the lake the second time? She acted like nothing had ever happened between us."

"Who knows?"

"Thanks a lot. You're a great help."

"Charlie, the girl is . . . she's not on the same page, know what I mean?"

"What?"

"Not on the same page in the hymnal, a little out of step with the rest of the congregation."

"Crazy?"

"Whatever."

"You really think so?"

"Charlie, I don't know much, but I know crazy when I see it."

"Yeah, I guess so. I didn't . . ."

"Of course you didn't. You were too tied up in your own head deal."

"Meaning?"

"The first time you saw the girl you freaked. Isn't that what you said? You thought it was the ghost of the other one, Amber. You got all wrapped up in that deal, feeling bad that maybe you could have done something and Amber wouldn't have died . . ."

"Aren't you going a little fast there, Calvin?"

"Am I?"

Charlie thought it over. He remembered seeing Jade for the first time, beside the cemetery, the way he had felt.

"No."

"Thank you. That's your problem with the girl, you let yourself get all mixed up between her and her sister. Whose dying, for the record, was not your fault."

"It wasn't, huh?" Charlie asked.

"Not unless you sneaked out of the Institute and killed the bitch yourself."

"You don't understand . . ."

"Hell I don't, mister po-lice. You're sliding right back into the kind of thinking that got you in the Institute in the first place. Everything's your fault, you're the one, you're supposed to be some kind of . . ."

"I get the point, Doctor Rakestraw."

"I hope you do."

"So what you're saying is Jade is so schizo she jumps my bones one night and doesn't even remember the next?"

"Either that or she was shamming when she acted like it never happened. Or else it wasn't her you laid by the lake."

"Then who . . ."

"The ghost of Amber, naturally. That's what's rambling around in your head, isn't it, Charlie? Tell the truth."

"Well . . ."

"Bullshit. Don't you start that ghost bullshit again, man, or I'll drop a dime on your ass so quick . . ."

"Okay, okay," Charlie said. No ghosts. So Calvin was right, Jade was crazy, or else . . . Or else she wanted Charlie to wonder about it, to wonder if it had been Jade or Amber that night by the lake. Why? Unless Jade knew about Charlie. But how? Could she have found out from Amber somehow?

Charlie had not gotten anywhere puzzling it out by the time they got to town. He went to Lawyer Childress's office first, where he signed a receipt for another advance against his pay and Childress's secretary gave it to him in cash.

"Come in, come in this house," the friendly man welcomed them as they entered. He met them halfway between the door and the tables where jeans and shirts were stacked in neat piles. "What can we do for you today?"

"We need some jeans and boots, I guess," Charlie offered. "Nothing fancy."

"You bet." The man put his hand on Charlie's shoulder and led him toward the boots. "Do you know what size you need?"

It was not as easy as it should have been. The friendly man insisted on showing them boots made of what he called exotic skins, ostriches, lizards and different kinds of snakes. There was one pair he said was made from elephant hide. Last forever, he said.

Charlie opined that he did not need a pair of boots that would outlast him and asked if they weren't still making some boots out of leather. They finally found boots in their sizes that had not contributed to the extinction of any species and cost less than a hundred dollars apiece. Since he expected to do more walking then riding, he chose

112

boots with straight low heels and rounded toes. Calvin was taken with a particularly garish yellow pair with dogger heels and pointed toes, with brownish warts the size of dimes. The friendly salesman assured Calvin the bigger the warts the better the boots, and he insisted they were "genuine" ostrich. Charlie had no idea if there were such a thing as fake ostrich boots, and less interest. He assured Calvin that boots like he had chosen for himself would be more practical and at last the matter was settled. The jeans were less of a problem and they bought two pair apiece.

They needed shirts and Charlie passed up the fancier styles the man showed them first and they wound up with what they needed. Charlie did not think they needed belts, even when the man offered to throw in a couple of oversized buckles at half price. Charlie chose a cap to protect his head from the sun, a plain number that adjusted to any size. Calvin stood his ground this time and insisted on a cowboy hat. They found a straw one and that was that.

"Okay," the friendly man said, piling their choices on the counter beside the cash register. "Two pair of ropers at fifty-nine ninety-five."

The man rang up the boots on the register and Charlie caught the edge of contempt in his voice. Ropers, not real cowboy boots.

Four pair of jeans, the shirts, Charlie's cap and Calvin's rakish cowboy hat. The total came to a little less than three hundred dollars, with tax. Charlie handed over three one-hundred-dollar bills and got back less in change than lunch at the truck stop across the road would cost. It left Charlie with a hundred dollars.

They changed into their new clothes in the dressing room and Calvin was much taken with his new image. Charlie had other things on his mind, and on their way back to the ranch Calvin chided him.

"Enjoy the moment, Charlie," Calvin said.

"You've got to be kidding."

"The hell I am. I'm not insensitive to the fact that we're in the middle of a terrible deal here. I'll buy your version of Bill Junior's hanging. If you say it was murder, that's what it was. Maybe Amber didn't drown without some help. Even the little baby, that could be skulduggery too. Hey, it's as bad as it gets, somebody's killing off these nice people for some reason. Okay. You're gonna have to do something about that, because that's your job. No argument. But we're not going to crack this case between here and the ranch, are we?"

"I don't imagine," Charlie admitted.

"Then seize the moment. Kick back, revel in the new threads. Enjoy the frigging moment, man."

"You sound like my old partner," Charlie said, remembering the hundred times he had heard the same lecture from Wes Braverman.

"A wise man," Calvin said. "He'll live long and prosper, no doubt."

"I don't think so," Charlie said. He did not remind Calvin, in case he had forgotten the story in Charlie's file, that Wes had been dead for a while already, that he had watched a crazy woman slice Wes to shreds with a straight razor. Calvin did not press him about it, so maybe he had remembered.

"Charlie, you hungry?" Calvin asked.

"Not particularly."

"I am."

"There'll be enough food for an army back at the ranch."

"I'd just as soon not go through that again," Calvin said. "They're all great cooks, but I don't mind if I don't have to face all that business in the house again this soon."

"Yeah, I guess you're right."

They found a little place alongside the loop before they got back onto the highway that looked all right. It was midafternoon, but there were half a dozen cars and pickups parked in front and the sign in the window said BEST BURGERS HOMEMADE.

After they ordered Calvin excused himself and went outside to a pay phone that stood between the café and a paint store next door. He told Charlie he needed to call Dallas and "check on things." Charlie got the idea it was a woman he was checking on and smiled.

From the booth Calvin looked back and waved at Charlie, who was seated at a table near the café's big window. Charlie waved back smiling and Calvin doffed his new hat with a grin. Charlie laughed.

Calvin fed coins into the phone and tugged a little spiral notebook out of the pocket of his new jeans. He thumbed through it to the last page and looked for the number. There were seven or eight names scrawled on the page, each with a phone number. The Branville

Institute topped the list, with the main number. Above that he had penciled in a second number, Doctor Branville's private line. Calvin listened to the ringing on the line and thumbed back to the middle of the notebook, to the pages where he had made his notes. Finally, after half a dozen rings, a man's voice answered.

The two hamburgers and Calvin's large order of fries had already been delivered by the waitress who called Charlie "hon" and Charlie was eating by the time Calvin rejoined him.

"That took long enough," Charlie said.

"Serious business," Calvin smiled, pronouncing it "bid-ness." "Plenty serious."

"I 'magine. Guess she's just waiting by the phone in case you call."

"Who? That was no lady, Charlie, that was my uncle. Serious family bid-ness."

"You needed your notebook to talk to your uncle?"

"Absolutely. You have to keep your paperwork straight."

"Paperwork?" Charlie laughed.

"It so happens my uncle's business is in the area of . . . investments, let's say. You have to keep track of your investments."

"Commodities, you mean."

"Kinda. Short-term stuff."

"Would there be any sports connection by any chance?"

"You could say that."

"You mean he's a bookie."

"Gosh, Charlie, I'd never thought of it in just those terms."

They both laughed and Calvin ate heartily. When he had cleaned his plate and Charlie had done his best with his, they climbed back into McKendrick's pickup. Calvin insisted that they run by the lawyer's office again so he could pick up his car and drive it back to the ranch, where he could keep an eye on it. Charlie still had a lot on his mind, but on their way to get his car Calvin found a radio station that came in clear and sang all the way there, teaching himself the sad country and western songs they played in this neck of the woods.

"Damn, Calvin, listening to that crap on the radio is bad enough. Do you have to sing along?"

Calvin stopped singing about love gone wrong and thumped his new hat back on his head with a thumb.

"Shucks, pardner," he smiled. "I'm just trying to get in the mood of the thing."

"I wish you wouldn't. Can't you find some decent soul music on that thing?"

"This is soul music, man. Ain't you never heard of Charlie Pride? Country Charlie Pride?"

"I give up. You're having too damned much fun."

"You ought to try it, Charlie. It couldn't hurt."

"Yeah, yeah."

CHAPTER NINETEEN

CHARLIE CAUGHT SIGHT OF POPPA MCKENDRICK AS HE wheeled the pickup into the wide drive in front of the house, with Calvin following in his Mercury. The old man had changed from his funeral clothes back into work clothes and was walking from the house toward the stables. Charlie braked the truck to a halt and slid out.

"I'll see you later," he said to Calvin. "Take care of this stuff for me, will you?"

Calvin patted the brown paper bags with their extra new clothes and their old things in them and winked at Charlie, who walked away shaking his head as he heard Calvin and the Mercury's radio singing something that sounded like "All my ex's live in Texas."

Charlie overtook McKendrick between the house and the stables. The old man heard him coming and turned. He looked Charlie over and smiled.

"That's a little more like it," he said. "Now you look like you belong on a ranch, anyway."

"Yeah, feels better, too," Charlie said.

"I hope you put it on my tab like I said," the old man said.

"No, I appreciate it, but it wasn't necessary."

"I don't guess it makes much difference," McKendrick admitted. "My tab or if Lawyer Childress pays you out of Amber's estate."

"I hadn't thought it through that far," Charlie said. "I've got enough to cover it without it costing . . ."

"Hell, Charlie, I don't give a tinker's dam one way or the other. It doesn't matter, that's all I meant."

"Yessir, but I don't feel like I've earned any money from you or Amber either. I . . ."

"You're doing your best. You can't be everywhere."

"No, but I was where I needed to be the other night, for all the good it did Bill Junior."

"Ain't your fault somebody cold-cocked you in your sleep."

Charlie let it go, not feeling up to explaining to McKendrick that it was his fault, everything that had gone wrong since he came to the ranch was his fault, as far as he was concerned.

"Good thing you're here," McKendrick said. "You being a horse breedin' doctor."

"Oh?"

"Yeah. We're fixing to do a little breeding. You might learn something."

Charlie smiled and fell in alongside McKendrick.

"I don't know how this looks to you, Charlie. Right after the funeral, here I am fooling with the stock."

"I don't . . ." Charlie began.

"Seems right, though." Having cut Charlie off, McKendrick took as much time as he needed to choose his words and then went on. "You heard that between me and Chris the other day, what he had to say about me being a link, some kind of a custodian."

"I remember."

Charlie heard what sounded like a scream from the stables on the other side of the barn, a long and terrible screech full of need or horror. He looked that way and then at McKendrick, who took no notice of the sound. Charlie followed the older man's example and wondered at what he had heard.

"He is right. I've always figured there was more to things than just a man's life, disconnected, kind of."

McKendrick stopped long enough for Charlie to realize that he expected an answer.

"I see what you mean," he said.

"It's a wonder if you do," the old man smiled at him. "No better than I am at explaining it. The way I look at, it don't add up to much if you just take a man's life unconnected that way, no more than anything else, a tree or a dog or anything. You're born, you live, you die. The end. See what I mean?"

"I guess that's where religion comes in," Charlie offered.

"I guess, if you're turned that way. That's how Momma . . . Anyway, the way I see it, it makes more sense if a man ain't just . . . if he's connected, see? If he's part of what's gone before and then he's kind of connected at the other end, too, passing it along to the next one. That way, there's a pattern to the thing, it makes some kind of sense."

"Yes, it does," Charlie agreed, and he meant it. He felt that way about his own father, dead now, and his little girl.

"So that's what Chris was talking about. Funny thing is, he's understood how I see things better than the rest of them. And he's . . ."

"Gay?" Charlie put in, trying to help.

"A dead end," McKendrick said. "He's a stump on the tree instead of a limb."

"I see."

"So does he. That's our trouble."

Another scream, and still no reaction from McKendrick. Charlie tried not to give himself away.

"But as long as there are the others to pass . . ."

"Don't work that way," the old man cut in. Charlie noticed the conviction in McKendrick's words, more feeling than he was used to from the old man. "It don't just pass from one to the next. Everything in nature, Charlie, it's either growing or it's dying. It's either getting stronger, better, or it's withering away. Nothing just passes along unchanged. That's the way of things."

"I hadn't thought about it that way," Charlie said, and thought again of his feelings as he had listened to Chris and the old man in the den the other evening, when the words "master race" had struck him so. There was a side of this that was dark and troubling, and Charlie was having trouble squaring that with what he had seen so far of the old man.

"Most don't," McKendrick said. "A man has just so many kids, mainly sons, the way things are, to improve the line in his next generation. One like Chris, a dead-end stump, he cuts down your chances of breeding the line up the way it needs to be. Bill Junior wasn't much better."

"I beg your pardon?" Charlie asked, puzzled and a little shocked.

"You heard him, the first night you were here. I heard him too, for the thousandth time, his plans for the ranch."

"Yeah, he wanted to subdivide. He thought it had potential as a resort of some kind."

The old man shook his head.

"A resort," the old man snorted. "It's about like if you wanted your boy to be an airplane pilot and all he wanted to do was fly kites, I swear."

"Kids," Charlie said with a smile.

But McKendrick was not smiling.

"There's blood in this ground, Charlie. Ours and others. The land is everything, been that way since Bible days. Jacob and Esau, all the way back. My people and Momma's, they've died over this land, and killed for it, too. A resort!"

McKendrick said no more and Charlie was lost in thought as they rounded the corner of the barn and came upon the stables where Charlie saw Red Jackson, the foreman, and the two hands. They had a mare and a stud in hand, in separate pens. It was the stud, a handsome big bay, his nostrils flaring, who was doing the screaming. He reared and pawed the air, full of lust and the scent of the mare who answered with nervous tosses of her head and a mincing prance at the end of a lead rope held by one of the hands.

Charlie drew close to McKendrick and whispered, "Guess I'm supposed to know all about this."

"Yeah."

"You want to give me a tip or two?"

"Just lean on the fence . . ." The old man turned toward him for emphasis. "On the outside of the fence . . . and try to look like you've seen it before."

"I can do that."

"Good."

It was a hell of a thing to watch, and Charlie could see there was no place inside the pen for anybody but experts. They led the mare around her pen and backed her up to let the stud sniff and snort over her, to revel in her timely scent. He did not need much encouragement, Charlie thought, by the look of him. When it was time, the stud was brought in with the mare and all hell broke loose. He bit the mare's neck and she whirled like a dervish, kicking out at the stud viciously. The three men handling the horses strained at the lines and cursed and cajoled them, sweet-talked them both, and made lewd remarks. McKendrick himself stood aside, ready to step in if there was any need for it. It was not easy for Charlie to look bored when the animals finally progressed to the next step. He shook his head in wonder at the power of the two of them and that was when he saw Jade watching from the shadows of the barn.

She was intent upon the horses and paid Charlie no mind. He saw the way she stood, the heavy way she leaned upon a post at the side of the barn door, and thought her eyes glistened in the shadows. She was still wearing the black suit she wore to the funerals, and made a strange and compelling figure, her high heels buried in the straw on the barn floor, her legs parted, one hand to her lips. She said nothing and did not move. Charlie was drawn from her to the action in the pen by the shouts of the men and he saw they had their hands full with the stallion. He had failed an attempt to mount the mare and charged her in frustrated rage. One of the hands lost his footing and went down, scrambling to his feet to retrieve the swirling rope as men and beasts thundered around the pen screaming.

When the stallion was finally under a semblance of control and again stalked the mare hungrily, when she had ceased to fight him and stood wide-legged in the center of the pen, her head thrown back in the direction of the snorting stud, Red Jackson called out to Charlie.

"Doc, I don't suppose you'd like to step in here and show us how y'all do it at A and M," he said.

McKendrick turned to look at Charlie but did not offer to interfere.

"Artificial insemination usually," Charlie answered. "We've found it's easier on the hired help."

120

McKendrick tipped his hat down to hide his face for a moment and Charlie smiled broadly at the foreman. Screw you, he thought, glad they were not likely to ask him to say any more about the insemination process than that. He had just told them all he knew.

"I see," Red Jackson answered, daring to turn away from the stallion long enough to throw Charlie an angry look without putting any words with it. "Thoughtful of you."

Charlie nodded at the hot and angry man and said no more. He was happy to quit while he was ahead.

Before long it was done, and Charlie thought that the act itself was over quickly. Hardly worth all the turmoil, he thought. He was not surprised when he looked toward the barn again and Jade was gone.

Chapter Twenty ▪

"YOU HANDLED THAT ALL RIGHT," McKendrick assured Charlie as he handed him a drink. The two of them had retreated to the cool privacy of the den after McKendrick had seen to it that the mare and stallion were put away in good order and neither was the worse for their coupling. "Old Red didn't know much to say about that artificial insemination business."

"I'm damned glad. I wouldn't have had any answers."

"Don't worry about him. He's a good man, and I don't think he'll push it any further with you."

Charlie took a thirsty drink and enjoyed the effect of the whiskey as he looked over the books on McKendrick's shelf. He pulled one down and thumbed through it.

"Just the same, Mister McKendrick, I'd like to borrow this for a while. It couldn't hurt if I knew something about horses."

"All right. But take this one here."

McKendrick handed him another book and showed him a chart in the back of it.

"Yeah, this is good," Charlie said.

"See here, this is the start of it all," McKendrick said, pointing to the top of a chart that ran the length of the page. He read off the names. "The Darley Arabian, the Byerly Turk. The Godolphin Arabian. They were the daddies of all the Thoroughbreds, or great-great-granddaddies, however you want to say it."

"Shows how much I know," Charlie said, looking over McKendrick's shoulder. "I had no idea Thoroughbreds came from Arabians."

"Neither do any of my kids, Charlie. That's all the interest any of 'em have ever showed in it. Except for my oldest, that is."

"The son you lost in the war."

"Yeah. He took after me where horses were concerned, anyway. Not about the war, though. It never made sense to me to go that far off to fight over somebody else's land. Just a waste. Jeff's a pretty good'un, I guess."

"He's your grandson, the boy who lives here with you."

"Yeah. His daddy didn't come back from the war, his momma went off. We've raised him here. He knows a horse from a donkey, I guess."

"That's good. Somebody to carry on with . . . your work, the breeding, and everything."

"I reckon."

There was a note of reservation in the old man's tone, but Charlie did not pursue it. He did wonder what there was about the boy Jeff . . .

"My other grandson, Chip . . ." McKendrick did not bother to finish.

"The frat rat," Charlie nodded. "If Chris is a dead end, what does that make Chip?"

"A step backward, I'd say," answered McKendrick. "A giant step. Ruth and that husband of hers, I don't know. . . . They spoiled the boy, that's plain."

"You don't think much of Goldman, do you?" Charlie asked.

"Not much."

"Because he's a Jew?"

"Jews are all right," McKendrick said. "So are Tennessee Walkers, or Appaloosas. Just not my breed, that's all."

"I see."

"Do you?"

122

Charlie thought he did, but the stench and gloom of anti-Semitism did not square with what he thought he knew of the old man. He wanted to think it through before he went any further.

"I'm trying," he said finally.

"Fair enough."

Charlie finished his drink and left the house. It was an hour or so before sundown and he did not want to be in the house with the others. With his horse book under his arm, he went looking for Calvin. The bunkhouse was empty. There would be no supper that night, everyone being left on his own to eat when the mood took him, all the funeral food arrayed on the kitchen table and the sideboard, most of it brought today for the family to have after Bill Junior's funeral, some of it still left from the baby's mourning.

There was no sign of the foreman or the hands either, and Charlie made a circuit of the house and outbuildings looking for them. All the trucks were in place in front of the house so he knew that wherever they were they were afoot. Or horseback. He thought of Calvin on a horse and it made him laugh and worry at the same time.

The sound of a voice led him to the men, a voice with menace in it, an earnest malevolence that set Charlie's juices running. He had heard that kind of a voice plenty of times, and he knew it meant business. He hurried toward the sound of it and came upon the four of them, Calvin and the three hired men. It meant business, all right.

The foreman and the two Mexicans were in a semicircle in front of Calvin, who had backed up to the far wall of the barn for protection. It was Jackson doing the talking. Calvin was stony-faced and silent, his eyes moving from one of the men to the other and back again. There was a knife in his hand.

The two Mexicans were armed too, after a fashion. They stood eyeing Calvin, one with a hay hook in his hand, an evil-looking tool with a round handle that ran across your palm so that the hook itself ran out from the handle between your fingers, curled up and in and came to a point. The point of this one was shiny, as if it had just been sharpened. The other Mexican was holding a long-handled shovel, the blade shoulder high. They could be trouble if it came to that, Charlie figured, but he did not think their hearts were in it. Red Jackson was the real problem.

123

The foreman turned toward Charlie as he came into view and Charlie saw that he had a knife too, bigger than Calvin's.

"Evenin', Doc," Jackson said, bearing down on the "Doc." "Damned nice of you to join us."

"I'd have been here sooner if you boys had just invited me."

"Never too late for a little party, Doc."

"I wouldn't want to interrupt," Charlie said, smiling. He saw the look on Calvin's face out of the corner of his eye. He was not sure what Calvin expected of him, but it was probably something a little more direct. "Why don't you go ahead with what you're doing. I'll wait."

"How about that, Mister Calvin?" Jackson taunted the cornered man. "He don't seem too eager to help you out, does he?"

"No need," Charlie said, keeping his voice light and even. "He's already got you yellow sonsabitches outnumbered."

"Big talk," Jackson snarled, getting as mad as Charlie had hoped he would.

"How long has he had the three of you treed? What's your plan, Red, you waiting for reinforcements?"

Red said something to the hired hands in Spanish and they exchanged worried looks between them, the one with the shovel shifting nervously and ducking his head to swallow.

"I ain't waitin' for a goddam thing," Red said, his voice low and thick with malice as he turned toward Charlie, leaving the Mexicans to keep Calvin where he was.

"Good," Charlie said, moving to his left a couple of steps to turn Red a little, so Charlie could see Calvin and Red had his back to the other three men. "There is one thing, though."

"Yeah?"

"If you want your ass kicked, throw down the knife and let's start."

"If I don't?"

"I'll kill you."

"No shit?" Red smiled broadly, but not convincingly.

"No shit. I'm scared of knives."

"You oughta be."

"It's getting dark. What do you want, big man, a whipping or a killing?"

"I'm gonna stomp a mudhole in your ass," Red promised. He

124

turned and called the Mexican with the shovel by name, and tossed the knife to the ground at his feet. The Mexican picked it up, looking from Red to Charlie. "Is that better?"

"That's fine, Red. You're not as dumb as you look."

The big man's face was a deeper red than his hair, and his breath was strained and ragged, rage building in him. Charlie liked that.

"Of course," Charlie added. "Nobody's as dumb as you look."

With a muttered curse the big man came at him. He was more than a head taller than Charlie, with broad shoulders and long rangy arms. He charged across the few feet that separated them with his jaw set and fire in his eyes, reminding Charlie of the stallion going after the mare that afternoon. He came fast, but he was clumsy and came too hard, his weight all forward and his arms out wide.

Charlie stood relaxed and upright until the big man was on him, his big hands clinched into fists that looked as big as boxing gloves, until Red reached for him with one hand pawing, as if to measure the distance, and the other swinging in a wide arc at Charlie's head. And then Charlie ducked, dropping into a crouch that brought his head beneath the whistling right hand of the big man. He leaned forward from the waist and the big man charged into him, his momentum carrying him too fast to catch himself. Charlie drove out of the crouch like a guard hitting a blitzing linebacker, and he heard Red grunt with the force of the impact in his chest, heard the wind go out of the big man. Charlie dug forward and upward, lifting the cowboy off his feet, then grabbed his legs and pulled up hard. Red's feet came off the ground and Charlie straightened his back to get as much height as he could, holding Red's knees up, then turned the big man and drove him beneath his shoulder hard into the ground. They hit with a jarring thud, Red's back landing flat, Charlie's shoulder driving down again into his chest. Charlie rolled off before the stunned cowboy could get a grip on him and sprang quickly to his feet.

A quick look at Red was all Charlie needed to see that he had knocked the wind out of him and hurt him. He took a couple of seconds to make sure the Mexicans were staying out of it. They were, the two of them and Calvin had not moved.

Red groaned and swore and rolled to one side, both his hands on his chest, fighting for air. Charlie measured two quick strides and kicked

125

the big man, driving the toe of his boot hard into his lower back alongside his spine. Red screamed and arched like a bow, one hand flying to the place just above his belt where Charlie had hurt him for the second time.

Charlie watched Red scramble up to one knee, sputtering and clawing. When he had gotten that far, Charlie went at him again. He stepped in close to the man's back and looped his right arm out and around his neck, pulling back hard on it with his left hand to work his forearm underneath Red's downturned chin. When he had the hold he wanted, Charlie stretched himself out and laid his weight on it, pulling Red over as far as he would go onto his back. Charlie did not have to strain, his weight and the other man's position did all the work for him. Red struggled briefly, to no effect. In a few seconds his hands fell away and he went limp. Charlie held the pressure for another second and then let go. He got to his feet as Red slumped over on his back on the ground, out cold.

"Well?" Charlie demanded of the two Mexicans.

They exchanged a few words and then went away, walking backward at first to keep an eye on Charlie, toward the bunkhouse.

Calvin came forward smiling, folding his knife and returning it to his pocket.

"You saved that man's life, Charlie. If you hadn't come along, I was fixing to kill him."

"Yeah, that's the way I had it figured."

"You didn't kill him, did you?" Calvin asked, stooping to make sure Red had a pulse.

"Probably not," Charlie answered. He thought he could see the man's chest rising and falling. "What did you say to get them so mad at you? You weren't singing again, were you?"

"That's just it, I wouldn't sing. Red was pumping me about you. He didn't like my answers worth a damn, either."

"He didn't buy my cover, did he?"

"Not hardly."

"What did you tell him?"

"Everything I could remember from high school biology about plebiscites and protozoas and shit like that, footwork and bullshit, trying to sound like a graduate assistant. What else?"

126

"How is he?" Charlie asked.

"The usual for being choked out. He pissed in his pants, but he's breathing. He'll be back among us in a minute."

Red had begun to stir and Charlie had stopped worrying that he might have overdone it when McKendrick and the two Mexicans showed up.

"Hear y'all had a little trouble," McKendrick said.

"Not particularly," Calvin offered, smiling. Charlie thought for a moment Calvin might put one foot on Red's back like a big game hunter with a dead lion, but he did not. "Nothing we couldn't handle."

"I see. The boys here came and told me."

Charlie noticed the Mexicans had stopped by the bunkhouse long enough to pack. Each of them had what looked like a duffle bag over his shoulder.

"Looks like they're going somewhere."

"Yep. Red, too, if he's able."

As if he had heard his name, Red coughed and flailed about, trying to sit up.

"I wouldn't want them to lose their jobs on our account," Charlie said.

"Speak for yourself," Calvin told him.

"Man works for me, he does what I tell him," McKendrick said. "And don't get into this kind of foolishness."

Red finally got himself into a sitting position. He sat bleary-eyed on the ground and rubbed his throat with one hand, his back with the other.

"Mister McKendrick," the foreman said, then coughed.

"Red, get your stuff and get off my place. I'll settle up with you when you're ready to go."

"Look here," the big man protested. "You know I wouldn't . . . this man here's not . . ."

"I expect you thought you were looking after my interests, Red. But you know better than to pull this kind of business. Now, go on."

Red had nothing more to say. He struggled to his feet and walked off toward the bunkhouse to pack, with a look back toward Charlie that had in it a little wonder and plenty of spite.

They all headed back to the house, McKendrick and Charlie and

Calvin, with the two Mexicans trailing behind. McKendrick climbed into his pickup and opened the glove compartment to get a checkbook. He took out another book, a small hardbound journal, and did some figuring in the margin. Nothing was said as he did his sums and wrote out three checks. He handed one check to each of the Mexicans and stood with the third in his hand as he watched Red make his way toward them from the bunkhouse. The white man had more gear than the other two, one big suitcase and a cardboard box tied up with twine.

A pickup with a horse trailer in tow pulled in beside them as they stood waiting and Charlie watched Jeff and Chip climb out.

"Poppa," Jeff said as he sauntered over. "What're y'all doing?"

"Settling up," the old man said, looking his grandsons over closely. "Where've you two been?"

"Delivering."

Both the boys were grinning and loose-jointed, their eyes damp and reddish. Charlie was trying to decide whether they had been drinking or smoking dope or maybe both.

"Oh?"

"Yep," Jeff answered with a smug grin. He and Chip looked at each other and giggled, for no reason Charlie could see.

"This ain't all my stuff, Mister . . ."

"Let us know where you'll be, Red," McKendrick cut him off. "I'll have the rest sent."

"Mister McKendrick . . ."

"This is what you have coming," the old man said, handing over the third check.

Red took it without looking at it and stuffed it into his shirt pocket. He did not try to say anything else.

"Take the red truck. Keep it till you get something else. Let me know and I'll send for it."

"I'll just drop it off," Red offered.

"I don't want you back on the place, Red."

"Yes, sir," the ex-foreman said, with a look at Charlie. "Let's go," he said to the Mexicans, and they threw their gear in the bed of the red truck and climbed into the cab.

"What's going on here?" Jeff demanded.

"I'm firing 'em."

128

"What the hell for?"

"There ain't no call for this, Mister McKendrick," Red said through the driver's window of the pickup as he cranked the engine. "I was just looking after you."

"What did he do?" Jeff insisted.

"Go on," McKendrick told Red.

"I'm going, but I'll tell you one goddammed thing. If that son-ofabitch there is any kind of a horse doctor, I'm a . . . ."

"Go on, Red, you've done lost that fight."

With an angry clamp-jawed nod, Red left, driving McKendrick's pickup slowly out the drive and down the long gravel lane toward the road. Charlie saw the big man's head turning from side to side and imagined that he was taking a last look at the McKendrick place.

"Delivering, huh?" McKendrick turned to Jeff. "Guess I know what you were delivering."

"I guess you do," Jeff said, looking proud of himself. "That bay colt."

"To Bud Witcher, I guess."

"Uh-huh."

"For him to take to the races."

"Oklahoma City, this weekend."

"Thought I made it clear I don't want my stock raced."

"He ain't your stock, Poppa. He's mine." Jeff made sure his pal Chip was suitably impressed with his defiant tone of voice. "You said so yourself."

"Poor judgment on my part, I guess," McKendrick said softly.

"So what's the deal with Red and the hands?" Jeff demanded.

"I told you, I fired 'em."

"What the hell for?"

"They forgot who runs this place."

Jeff stood looking at his grandfather with his brows furrowed for a moment, then snorted a cocky laugh as if he had decided there was no meaning in the old man's remark for him after all. He turned away and waved for Chip to follow him into the house.

"C'mon, Chip, let's go in the house and see if there's any food left."

"Yeah," Chip answered, falling in alongside his cousin. "I've got the munchies big time."

Charlie watched the two boys walk away, kindred spirits, and wondered how much they had in common, the city kid and his country cousin.

"Kids," Charlie offered, with a shrug.

The old man did not answer. He handed Charlie the horse book he had forgotten in his scrap with Red.

"You dropped this," McKendrick said.

"Yeah, thanks."

CHAPTER TWENTY-ONE

CHARLIE MOVED INTO THE BUNKHOUSE WITH CALVIN that night, without much fuss being made about it by anyone. Mom had taken to her bed to grieve her double loss and the Goldmans were keeping to themselves. Jeff and Chip had left again after eating, and Chris and Poppa McKendrick were in the den, talking softly. Charlie took his bag and left without intruding on them.

Calvin turned in early and Charlie lay in one of the bunks reading his horse book by the light of a small lamp until he lost track of time. It was late and the moon was up when he heard something.

The night was full of sounds, alive with furtive scurryings as life went on among the wild things and the livestock. A breeze stirred enough to make noise in the tree limbs and underbrush that hovered at the fringes of the huddle of buildings at the center of the big ranch. Crickets and unknown forms chimed in to make a kind of jumbled song and Charlie was thinking that the old folks had told him when he was a kid that the crickets meant a change in the weather, a cold snap coming.

He had laid the book aside and snapped off the lamp when he heard it. It was an odd thing that he could not put his finger on at first, lying

130

in the new darkness of the big room among the empty bunks and Calvin's deep and steady breathing. And then he realized, understood that what had caught his attention was a sudden hush, a break in the murmur and chirp of the night. It meant someone was about, the song-makers hushing as someone passed. Charlie turned toward the window and looked out, toward the house. Nothing.

Trying to make no sound himself, he eased out of his bunk and slipped into his jeans, tugged on his boots. He stopped then to listen again, and thought he could tell by the way the night noises came and went that someone was out there, moving stealthily somewhere between him and the house itself. He tiptoed to the bunkhouse door and held the screen door spring with one hand to dampen its groaning as he eased the door open and stepped outside. The moon was almost full and cast the yard in a silver luminescence like a stage set at the curtain, waiting for a play about ghosts. He moved to his left into shadows at the corner of the bunkhouse and tried to see into the scattered shards of darkness here and there around the back of the ranch house.

A furtive movement caught his eye, a sliver of silver twinkling in the shadows at the far corner of the house. He fixed his eyes on it and discerned that it was moving away, toward the trail that led past the big tree down toward the lake. He waited while the thing that moved stopped and changed and then moved on again, and then he followed it, keeping in the shadows and breathing with his mouth open so he would not make a sound. He could see the phantom ahead on the path to the tree when he reached the edge of the yard at the path's beginning, and he turned to survey the yard and buildings behind him before he went on, assuring himself that there was nothing there behind him, that he was not leaving anything or anyone stirring near the house.

Shimmering like a mirage, the silver thing went on ahead in fits and starts, more or less along the path, stopping now and then to change its shape and then moving on. Charlie stayed well back and took pains to lift his feet and set them down straight and soft, keeping his weight on his planted foot until he was sure of the next step before moving on. It was slow work, and the phantom gained on him as it approached the looming big dark tree. And then it stopped.

Charlie stopped, too. He watched from dark bush branches alongside the path as the thing moved without going on, lingering about the brooding tree. And then it was gone. Charlie blinked and looked again but the silvery form had vanished. Behind the tree, Charlie told himself. Whomever it is just went around behind the tree. He waited to see if the thing would reappear but it did not. After a time, he crept forward. As stealthily as he knew how, he worked himself forward along the edge of the path toward the tree, stopping now and then to look and listen. When he was close enough to reach out and touch the cool and rocky bark, he stopped. He looked up and saw the bit of the axe jutting out of the tree's hide in the moonlight. He moved in a crouched shuffle, circling around the tree until he reached a place where he could see beyond it down the path toward the lake, but the phantom was not there. He squatted in shadows to wait.

The touch upon his arm froze his blood and stopped his heart, but he did not cry out or jump, only stiffened in his crouch and held himself in check. No sound came with the feel of it on him, and he turned to see the phantom.

She hovered at his shoulder, the silver of the moonlight tipped and daubed upon her features like an artist's trick. Her touch was light on his arm and she seemed to quiver on the night breeze like a spider's web, and he saw that it was her robe or gown that he had followed, moonlight on her robe had been his phantom. It lay upon her shoulders like a band of light and luminous, diaphanous, clutched her breasts and thighs like a shroud upon a death mask. Her long blond hair spilled down in shadows, framing her face with here and there a touch of moonlight gemlike in its soft mass.

No words came and her touch was not insistent. He could not make out her face, only panes and angles of moonlight and darkness together, impressionistic. He rose to his feet and she turned away, going toward the lake. He followed and she turned without stopping as if to be sure he was coming.

Beside the dark water where the moonlight lay like a bridge and the breeze stirred the surface of the water languorously, she touched him again. Her hands reached out to him and took his face between them, turned him toward her and moved in solemn and sensuous circles around him, leading him in a slow and silent dance at the water's edge.

He did not lift his hands to touch hers or to protect himself against her, awash with dread in the darkling notion that she was not real.

"Jade?" he murmured.

No answer came except the glint of teeth between her blood-dark lips to show she smiled at that.

"Jade," he insisted, as she closed her slow-turning circle in on him and drew him toward her. "Ja . . ."

"Whooo-e-e-e-e!"

The yell like a battle cry rattled and banged down the hill past Charlie and the phantom, tumbling out over the lake toward the unseen trees and darkness on the other side.

"What the . . ."

Charlie looked up from the ghost in his arms toward the raucous sound and saw the big tree on the hill back-lighted, its heavy, upflung limbs like arms on fire. From beyond it came the heavy, clumsy sound of booted feet, slamming doors and drunken giggling. A young girl squealed unseen.

"Skinny dip! Skinny dip!" a voice chanted drunkenly, and Charlie knew that was Jeff.

"Last one in's a virgin!" Chip.

Drunk and loud, full of booze and the night and hot red blood, they came stamping and galloping, crashing down the path past the tree toward the lake where Charlie stood, and he turned and saw that his ghost was gone. He stepped deep into the shadows of the underbrush beside the path and watched the kids charge down to the water. He watched unseen as Chip won the dash to the lake and then could not stop himself and charged headlong out into the lake waist deep and stumbled and pitched into the water with a flailing splash and disappeared. Jeff and the two girls drew up at the end of the trail and rimmed the lake with peals of drunk laughing. Before the turgid water closed and smoothed the signs of his entry, Chip burst out of its grasp and held a whiskey bottle aloft like a trophy overhead.

"Didn't spill a drop!" he cried.

"Hang on, Chip, she'll save you," Jeff called out. He grabbed one of the girls, who, unsuspecting, had stooped to peel off her jeans, and heaved her into the lake where the water drowned her squeal.

Chip charged the hapless girl as she struggled up and they churned

133

the water to froth with their wrestling before he finally let her go to throw her jeans and boots out onto the shore.

Charlie turned away and looked for the silver phantom, catching sight of her as she moved through the underbrush back toward the top of the hill, toward the big tree. With a long look over his shoulder at the naked couples, all of them in the water now, he started off in pursuit of her.

He wished Calvin were here as he moved away from the lake, torn between a certain inkling that he should stay, that the kids, careless and stupid with lust and whiskey, were in danger as they frolicked heedlessly in the same dark water where Amber McKendrick had died. If Calvin were here, he could stay and watch them, while Charlie chased his ghost. Alone, he had to choose, and he paused to look back once more.

Jeff and one of the girls stood in water not quite waist deep, and Charlie watched the young boy's strong hands maul her breasts. She stood with her back to the boy, arched against him, her own hands curled back upon his muscled shoulders as he explored her, one hand working down over her belly to the lapping ripples of the water's surface where it played between her thighs. Beyond them Chris and the other girl gamboled like dolphins.

Turning back toward the tree, Charlie saw the silver ghost disappear, moving away from the tree and the path back to the house, moving deeper into the woods and he knew that she was moving toward the cemetery he could not see. The mystery of her, the sight of her going and the thought of losing her drew him up the hill away from the lake. Once begun, he hurried up through the brush, not worried about the kids hearing him. They were oblivious.

Without catching sight of his ghost again, Charlie hurried through the dark brush toward the cemetery, as best he could judge his directions in the moonlight and gloom. It was the only place he knew, the only thing he had seen, off in this direction. He did not know where else she could be going.

A stumble and a soft curse brought him out of the brush into a clearing that, when he took his bearings, he took to be a trail, narrower and not as well worn as the one that led to the lake, than ran from the big tree through a swale between that hill and the one where the cemetery stood waiting. He caught his breath and moved off a fast pace

134

to his left, across the little vale of a creek that fed into the lake and up the slope on the other side. Soon the little path he was following joined a broader one and Charlie looked to his right along that and saw the ranch house looming in the distance. This was the way McKendrick had brought him the first day, to show him the family burying ground. The day he had seen Jade for the first time. He knew the cemetery was just a few yards down the wide path, again to his left, and he hurried that way.

She was there, poised like a tombstone angel at the head of Amber's grave. Without a sign that she knew he was there, she trembled in the breeze across the hilltop, her gossamer shroud of a robe billowing gently. Charlie closed on her and reached out for her, but she turned and took his hand in hers and was off again, leading him through the family plot out to the edge of the little hill and down the other side into the darkness of the woods beyond.

Unnaturally light and swift, she threaded her way down still another path, little used and overgrown, and Charlie labored after her, drawn by his hand in hers.

Around a bend the path slithered through a huddled stand of scrubby oaks and broke through them into a clearing within a ragged circle of what looked like cedar trees. It was a smallish place, like a hole in the earth, with a broad roof of starry sky that narrowed like a funnel to the clearing floor. She let go of his hand and went ahead, disappearing into a thing that squatted upon the clearing floor, a dark and stolid thing that might have swallowed her up.

Charlie stood at the clearing's edge to catch his breath and blink his eyes until he could see clearly. He made half a turn to run away, out through the stand of oaks where he imagined the way he had come already had closed behind him, but he caught himself and stood his ground. His breathing quieted and the thing that had swallowed the ghost took shape.

It was tall, sharp-shouldered and broad, dark and old. There was lace about it, like a collar. Not lace, of course, but . . . flowers. Charlie moved nearer the waiting thing and saw that there were flowers all around it except for a space the width of its gaping dark mouth where the ghost had gone. He touched them, and drew back a bitten finger.

135

Roses. White and dark, on thorny stems and bushes black in the moonlight.

He took it finally for a tomb of some kind, a mausoleum, cool and smooth to the touch, with walls he was surprised to find were made of dark and ancient stone. He traced them from the nearest corner across the face of the thing until his hand slipped off its hard veneer into openness that was its mouth. He stepped inside.

Moonlight fell in muted shafts through windows he had not seen, one above him, over the door, another from his left. He saw that the windows were not clear, but murky with some design he could not make out. There were pews, rough-hewn and patient, on either side of him, describing a narrow aisle that he followed toward the waiting ghost. She sat as if suspended in the haunted stillness and the aisle led him to her. He reached out for her, afraid she would vanish, and she did not. He moved near her, into her arms, and found that she sat upon an altar of some kind, made like the pews. She drew him near and kissed him, her lips warm and pulsing upon his.

"Jade," he whispered.

She drew back and from behind her produced a circle of darkness that she laid beside her on the altar. His eyes were drawn to it and wondered what evil lay there, and only knew she rose from the altar when he felt her body against his, and heard the whisper of her robe. He turned to see her white shoulders emerge and followed the slowly slithering robe as it dreamily descended of its own infinitesimal weight and her breasts and belly, her flanks and then her hips, her thighs, the silvery dark and potent mound, revealed themselves as if created for him as he watched, born whole among the shimmering folds of the dying silk that fell into the darkness at his feet. The musky scent of her rose from the darkness amid the ageless and musty stones and rough-hewn timber of the place, the thing that had swallowed them both.

Her hands reached up to him and he stood without defense as they played down his cheeks and throat, as they tugged at his shirt with languid, spellbinding need until he was naked to the waist. He took her in his arms but she turned and he saw her raise the dark circle from the altar and in the silvery moonlit darkness of the place he saw a smile

136

glimmer on her lips. He took her wrists in his hands and looked at the thing she held. It was a wreath, a braided loop of flowers. In the muskiness of her he caught the sweeter scent of the roses and he let her set them lightly on his head. He crushed her to him and found her lips with his and then she pressed the circlet down upon his brow and half a dozen hiding thorns bore down into his flesh. He straightened with the pain and grabbed the crown of thorns off his head.

"Jesus Christ," he muttered.

A deep and evil lusty laugh rolled up her throat and over him at this, the only sound she had made, and she drew him to her hungrily. He closed with her, full of passion and anger, driving her beneath him upon the altar, forcing himself between her thighs as the rose wounds throbbed and a trickle of blood traced down his forehead and across his eye. With one hand he pinned her down as he reared up and with his other hand fumbled with his belt to free himself. The blood burned in his eye and he wiped it away with his hand. She took that hand in hers and drew it to her lips. She kissed his hand and sucked the fingers clean, then licked his bloody palm like a cat.

A shadow flitted past the window and Charlie saw it in the corner of his eye. He looked down at the woman for a stony instant, then broke away from her and charged up the aisle and out the door.

Charlie raced around the corner of the chapel to his right, toward the window where he had seen the shadow pass and thought he saw something, a form or shadow scampering away toward the surrounding trees. He chased whatever it was into the trees and lost his way, with no more hint of it to guide him. He waited for a moment, listening, and heard nothing, his rampage through the woods having silenced the night as far as he could hear, only the breeze in the trees oblivious of him. He retraced his steps to the clearing and was not surprised when he went inside the chapel to find his ghost had vanished.

His stomach churned with the banked and troubling fires she had lit in him and a foreboding sense of being lured away. The lake was not far straight through the woods but he knew best the way along the paths and started back, hoping as he ran and stumbled along that he would be in time.

He was on the path between the spirit tree and the lake when he heard the long and lingering scream.

CHAPTER TWENTY-TWO ▰▰▰▰

IT WAS NOT DEATH THIS TIME THAT THE WOMAN'S
scream announced, except the longed-for murder of desire. It had been
Chip's girl who screamed, as he brought her off beside the lake in the
mud in a bleary drunken act. Jeff and the other girl lay tangled on the
ground not far away, her head between his legs.

Charlie came down the path so urgently and noisily that they would
have heard him if they had not been so intensely drunk and preoccupied.
When he saw how it was, Charlie pulled up short and moved off the trail
into the brush to keep an eye on them.

He settled down in a place where he could sit and see them while
being hidden himself, knowing they were not likely to find him anyway.
It was late when he took up his post, the moon had traveled far, and he
wondered how long they would stay.

The two boys bragged back and forth about the girls, and Charlie
heard Jeff tell Chip he wanted to swap, that his had passed out in the
middle of something important. Chip agreed and allowed he would
wake her up. If either of the girls protested, it did not amount to much
and soon it began again.

Charlie sat in the brush and kept himself awake with thoughts of his
ghost and the pain of the wounds the thorns had made. He thought about
ghosts and sacrilege, naked writhings on a chapel altar in midnight
woods. He wondered . . . It had been Jade, he told himself. You
know what a ghost is, he promised himself. And flesh and blood. Don't
let it get out of hand, Charlie boy. You're okay, you're doing all right.

And then he wondered why. He puzzled about Jade, the day and
night difference she had shown him, and asked himself . . . No, none
of that crap. It all happened. All of it. And it was Jade. Amber was
dead.

Before long Charlie had the night to himself, as far as he knew. The

138

boys and girls all passed out beside the lake and there were no sounds from the direction of the house. He sat and thought and the sound of the night arose around him after a while as if he were not there.

The moon set and Charlie warned himself to keep his guard up in the inky stone-dead hour before sunrise, the loneliest and sleepiest time. He shifted now and then and wished he had cigarettes, but did not leave his post and found himself hoping that something would happen, that whoever was behind all this, whoever it was, whatever it was, would show up and take a crack at one of the drunken McKendrick heirs. He did not feel too chipper, but he would prefer a showdown in the dark to another day and night of trying to figure things out.

Nothing happened except that the night surrendered to the struggling sun and gray dawn came, and then the prettiness of the colors the early sun made in the sky and on the lake. With daylight, Charlie figured his job was done. People would be stirring soon, and there had not been any mischief yet in daylight. Besides, the craziness and wonder of the night had some time ago ebbed and now his aching bones and empty stomach elbowed their way into his thinking. Daylight eased his puzzled sense of doubt and his haunted uncertainties gave way to a less threatened bemusement that he told himself would be best cured by a good breakfast and a cup of coffee.

The kids asleep beside the lake stirred now and then in the cool and dewy briskness of the morning, but had drunk too much to awaken unaided. As the sun edged over the horizon, Charlie took to chunking clods at them until finally one of the girls sat up and shivered. They had to go, she announced. They'd be in a world of trouble if they didn't get back before someone woke up. Charlie could not make out who it was they would be in trouble with, and he did not care, as long as they got up and got on their way so he could go on his. The boys awakened enough to slip back into their clothes against the chill, then each of them told the other to take the girls home. The girl doing the wailing woke the other one and they dressed. It was not until the girls threatened to walk to the house and wake up Mister McKendrick that the boys finally came to and lurched to their feet. It was a noisy and hung-over crew that stumbled back up the hill to the pickup, only to find it would not start because they had left the headlights on all night. Charlie had not bothered to turn them off because he had not wanted the kids to try driving anyway. The last Charlie saw of them the two couples, snarling back and forth like yard dogs, disappeared up the path toward the house with the intention of borrowing one of the other trucks.

When he was sure they had gone and filled with the satisfaction of having seen them safely through the night, Charlie rose creakily and started up the path the way they had gone.

He had hoped to smell breakfast cooking, but from the look of the house as he topped the hill he supposed everyone was still asleep. The hands were gone, so there was no one except maybe Molly the cook to be up this early. None of the rest of them had anything to do of any importance. Disappointed, Charlie dismissed a notion to slip into the house on the off chance there was a pot of coffee left living. Breakfast would have to wait, he decided, but it would not be long. His second choice would be a little sleep, and he had the bunk in mind as he drew nearer the house and met Mrs. McKendrick coming out.

"Good morning," he said, his voice soft to let her know he was there without startling her.

"What? Oh, good morning, young man."

She stood awkwardly, one foot on the last step down from the back porch, the other on the ground, and Charlie thought she looked as if he had caught her at something. He did not know what and was not much interested.

"You're up mighty early," she said.

"You too, Mrs. McKendrick. Is there anything I can help you with?"

"No . . . I . . ." she paused, looking behind into the house as if she was afraid someone might be listening. "Well, if you wouldn't mind?"

"Of course not," Charlie lied.

"If you're sure it's no bother, I could use a little assistance."

That's what your goddammed grandsons are for, Charlie thought, trying not to let it show on his face.

"Glad to help."

"You're so kind. If you could come with me, please?"

Charlie fell in behind her and she led him without much more conversation except that they agreed it was a beautiful morning and sunrise was the nicest time of day and some other crap Charlie paid little

140

mind to. By the time the dottering old woman reached the burying ground, Charlie was so hungry he could have eaten her hat, a broad-brimmed straw bonnet with a long string tied in a bow at her chin and a band of bogus daisies tucked around the crown.

When they were there at last, she leaned against one of the old stones and looked down at the two new graves, Bill Junior beside the baby.

"They're better off, you know," she said.

Charlie had heard this before, said of his own father and every relative he had ever known who died, men, women, and children of all ages. He detested it, but these were her people and the old woman was entitled.

"Yes, ma'am," was all he said.

"They are in heaven right now," she said, with a certainty Charlie knew could only signify doubt or mental disease. "Jesus came and took Bill Junior to go and be with his little baby boy. He wanted that sweet little baby to have his daddy with him, to look after him."

"Yes, ma'am."

"Are you saved, Doctor Gants?"

He knew what she meant, he had heard that before too, but he never knew how to answer without being vicious, and her calling him doctor threw him for a second, too.

"Never mind." She dismissed the business of his salvation with a wave of her hand and Charlie noticed she was wearing gloves, the cheap brown cotton kind. "That's between you and your Maker, and I've never been one to preach. It's no skin off my nose either way."

Charlie stopped answering her and she did not appear to take any notice of it. She was talking to herself anyway, and Charlie understood that.

"Now, Brother Whitehead, he doesn't feel the way I do about that, and you can understand he wouldn't," she went on, bending over each of the graves to snatch away tendrils of grass from the freshly turned dirt. "Says it's a Christian's duty to witness. I've never seen it that way myself. Did you know . . ." She turned and pointed her garden trowel at him for emphasis. "That Jesus said that the reason he taught in parables was because he didn't want everybody to understand what he was saying?"

141

Charlie started to answer because she paused so long he thought she expected him to, but she went on before he could think of anything to say.

"The chosen few. That's what he meant by that. There's some of us chosen, and the rest . . ."

If she wanted Charlie to show any interest, he did not come through for her. He had other things on his mind. Mainly what was left in his mind of the night he had spent, a curiosity about what he would find if he struck off down the path on the other side of the cemetery and followed it through the stand of oaks he knew was there, if he would find the chapel, a crown of roses left discarded.

"Well, they're just on their own, that's all. It's a shame, but that's the way it is."

She straightened up and held her hand out toward Charlie.

"Ma'am?" he asked, wondering what she wanted him to do.

"Come here with me. Let me lean on you a little, if you don't mind."

"Yes, ma'am."

"Arthritis. Makes it misery for me going up and down these hills anymore."

Charlie took her arm and wondered if she wanted to go back now, but she turned away from the house and they took the path beyond and he knew they were going to the chapel.

It was a little more of a coincidence than Charlie was inclined to accept, and it occurred to him to wonder if the old woman had been out and about the night before. If it had been her shadow he saw at the window, then . . . That was ridiculous, he told himself, looking down at the old woman struggling up the hill at his side. Not as quick as the shadow was, not by a long shot.

When at last they came to the roses beside the little chapel, Charlie felt as if he had reached the end of a trek. The old woman took forever to cover the distance and Charlie wondered if she came out here often.

"This is our chapel, Doctor Gants," she said, her pride as obvious in her voice as her certainty that he had not been there before. "Built at a terrible expense by my great-granddaddy, in eighteen hundred and fifty-seven."

"Imagine," Charlie said, as if enthralled. He wanted to look inside.

142

"Before he ever built a decent house. Freighted the stone in himself. Family graveyard, family chapel. The land where you bury your people is the land where you belong. He didn't mean for our people to ever be put off this land. Not ever."

She seemed more animated now that she was in the clearing beside her chapel with her roses, and she tottered around without him, looking here and there at a bud or a bloom, muttering to them as if they were children. She started toward the chapel door, which stood open, and Charlie stepped forward to help.

"Is there something I can get for you, Mrs. McKendrick?" he offered.

"If you don't mind. There's a basket and some pruning shears just inside the door there. Thank you kindly."

Charlie stepped inside and took in the interior of the place with a sweeping look. It was as it had been the night before, except that it seemed smaller in daylight than he had imagined it. The early sun showed colors as it streamed in through the windows, one in the front above the door and one in each side near the middle of the chapel. The windows looked like stained glass, but Charlie made a note not to ask because he did not really care.

There was no sign that he and Jade had ever been there. The rose crown was gone and there was a smirking stillness in the place as if there had been no night at all.

He found the old woman's things by the door and took them to her.

"O-o-o-h, merciful Jesus on high!" she chanted as Charlie emerged from the chapel into the morning. "Merciful, merciful."

"What is it?" he asked.

"Just look at that. Just look!"

She pointed at one of the rose bushes and Charlie did not understand at first, until he saw that some of the branches had been cut, flowers taken. To make a crown of thorns, he thought to himself.

"That's just . . . Is there no . . . I swear."

"What is it?" Charlie could not understand the fuss. There were plenty of roses left, buds and blooms in every phase of flowering and dying. "What's the matter?"

"I wouldn't expect you to understand. Amber did this. I just know she did."

"What?"

"Cut all the roses off of one bush. She was forever doin' that. Can you imagine?"

"Not exactly," Charlie answered, truthfully this time. He did not know much about roses, but he could tell by running his thumb over the cut ends of the branches that these flowers had been cut recently, a hell of a lot more recently than Amber had died.

Charlie did not hear what the old woman said for a while after that. His head had begun to throb, the pain of the places on his head where the crown of thorns had been distracting him so that he could not hear her very well. He had other things on his mind.

CHAPTER TWENTY-THREE ■

OLD MRS. MCKENDRICK FUSSED ABOUT HER ROSES AND how thoughtless Amber was, taking so many flowers from one bush like that, without any sign that she understood what she was saying. But Charlie gave it a lot of thought. She was saying that Amber had cut the roses recently, within the last day or so. The fact that Amber had been in her grave so long did not seem to register with the old woman in the straw bonnet, but it did with Charlie, like an icy hand along his spine.

He commiserated with her about the wronged bush and finally she resigned herself that the damage was done, and then she did what she had come for. She gathered a basket of roses, no more than one or two from any bush, working her way all the way around the little chapel in the process. When her basket was full, she came again to the bush Amber had harvested and stood staring at it without saying anything more, her head moving from side to side and her tongue clucking between her teeth.

Ready to get on with it and then either to sleep or find something to eat, Charlie thought to make conversation, to take her mind off the damned bush.

144

"These are really beautiful," he said, meaning the roses she had gathered.

And they were, extraordinary. There were red roses and white ones, buds and young blossoms, so that once they were put out they would last awhile. And there were some of colors Charlie could not remember having seen before, shades of pink and yellow, even lavender, a few as deep a red as blood from a bad wound.

"They are my life," the old woman said, her eyes alight with such pride and passion that her seamed and tired old paunchy face seemed a mask, as if there were someone else within. Her voice trembled with tendrils of passion and deep conviction that Charlie had never heard when she spoke of her children, or to them. "My very life."

"I've never seen any like them."

"There are none like these," she said, her hand lingering over a few of the oddly colored ones. "These are my own hybrids. Originals."

Charlie was glad she felt so strongly about her roses, because she rambled on about them with such fervor that he was able to take the basket from her and lead her away from the chapel and back toward the graveyard.

"It'll soon be time to pick the hips," she confided in him. "A few more weeks, if frost comes like it ought to."

"I see," Charlie nodded, walking with the old woman on one arm and the flower basket on the other, not wanting her to suspect how surprised he was to learn that roses had hips.

There were holes like open mouths at each of the graves, which Charlie had not noticed before. These, it turned out, were pottery vases buried to their necks so Mrs. McKendrick could put out her freshly cut flowers. She did not ask him to help her as she toddled about the place, first filling a glass fruit jar with water from a spigot, then putting water in each of the vases. From a pocket in her apron she produced a tin of aspirins and she had to take off her gloves to work it open. One aspirin ground between her thumb and forefinger and dusted into each vase.

"Helps keep them fresh," she assured him.

"I see."

Charlie stood to one side and watched her labor over the graves. In each vase, first the baby's and then Bill Junior's, she placed, replaced, and fastidiously rearranged her roses. She seemed to have some pattern

145

in mind, or else there was an order somehow ordained that dictated which colors went where.

"Good morning."

Charlie turned to watch Jade approach, her long legs swinging effortlessly up the path. It was the first time he had seen her in jeans, her hair pulled up and back in a ponytail, a man's white dress shirt with the sleeves rolled up. He thought she looked fresh and natural, as if she belonged on the place.

"Good morning," Charlie answered.

The old woman did not say anything and did not look up from her work.

"I said good morning, Momma."

The tall blonde stopped beside Amber's grave and looked down at it, waiting for an answer.

"I heard you," the old woman said, still not looking up. "But I'm cross with you this morning, young lady."

"Whatever for?" Jade asked, looking from her mother to Charlie, her eyes clear and wide, giving her face a look of innocence.

Charlie returned the smile Jade aimed at him and looked from her wide and innocent eyes to her hands. But he saw nothing, no scratch or blemish on her long fingers, nothing to give her away as the weaver of a thorny crown.

"You know very well," Mrs. McKendrick lectured her. "If I've told you once, I've told you a thousand times. I'd really rather you didn't cut my roses, but if you must, at least please don't take them all from one bush. You know very well some of them simply cannot be replaced. I've spent years cross-pollinating, developing them. And you just come along and whack, whack, whack . . ."

Jade looked to Charlie with an eyebrow raised as if to ask him what her mother meant, and Charlie only answered with a smile.

"Momma, I don't . . ."

"Oh, don't give me that, Miss Amber McKendrick," the old woman cut her off, turning stiffly to point her trowel at her daughter. "I'm in no mood for it."

In the awkward silence that followed, Mrs. McKendrick finished and groaned to her feet, her hands on her hips as she finally straightened her back. Her work was done.

146

Charlie did not say anything, but he and Jade both saw that there were no flowers on Amber's grave.

"Lord only knows what'll become of my roses when I'm gone," Mrs. McKendrick lamented, looking approvingly at her work. "Lord only knows. That's the part about dying that'll be the hardest, I swear."

Her work finished, she abruptly turned and started off down the path back toward the house, as if she had forgotten or did not care that Charlie and Jade were there.

"Here, ma'am," Charlie offered. "I'll give you a hand."

"What?" she stopped and half-turned. "No, that's all right. Thank you just the same, Doctor."

She did not walk any better going back than she had coming out, but did not seem to care. Her head was cocked to one side and Charlie thought she was talking to herself.

"Momma . . ." Jade called out, but her mother did not seem to hear her.

"Don't let it . . ." Charlie began.

"What?"

"Don't . . . be upset. She's upset, it's natural."

"Thank you, Doctor. I'm all better now," Jade shot back, her innocent look darkening into something else.

"Okay, it's none of my business. Excuse me."

Charlie put up his hands to signal surrender and turned to go.

"I'm sorry," Jade said, and he stopped.

In the direction of the house Charlie could hear the sounds of people stirring. A door banged shut, there were voices. The day was brightening and the sun was burning off the haze of morning from the lake.

Who are you today, Charlie wondered. He studied her face and thought about challenging her. But he did not, because what he saw there was something in her eyes, a flicker of something unsaid, some scared and lurking pain. Who was she today?

"You . . . I wanted to talk to you," she said.

"That wasn't the impression I got," he smiled.

"I know."

He waited for her to collect her thoughts or to make up a story or whatever she was doing, without saying anything more. He wanted to

147

grab her and shake her, to make her admit the night before, but he did not. He would play her game, he decided.

"I don't know what you've heard about me," she began, then stopped to think some more. He did not say anything. "I mean, I suppose you've heard some talk, the family."

"Don't worry about it," Charlie said at last, when it seemed she would go no further. "You tell me."

"She didn't put any roses on Amber's grave," Jade said, looking down.

"We can fix that," Charlie said.

"What?"

"Come on."

He took her hand in his and led her away toward the chapel.

CHAPTER TWENTY-FOUR

IT WAS NOT THE SAME, of course, as it had been in moonlight and from here and there in the distance the bustle of life intruded. Charlie heard a pickup in the drive and a horse whinnied from the stable. Breakfast is late today, Charlie thought. He led Jade to the chapel and she said nothing until they were there, when he took her inside, slung her roughly past him toward the altar and stood between her and the door.

"What are you doing?" she asked then.

"Returning to the scene of the crime."

"What are you talking . . ."

"Knock off the bullshit, sweetheart. I'm in no mood for mind games."

"Let me out of here."

"In a minute. Talk to me."

"What are you going to do?"

"There's no telling," Charlie warned her, and he meant it. "I'm tired and hungry and just about fed up with you. Talk."

"I'll scream."

"No you won't."

"I will," she promised, backing away from him.

"You sound like you mean it. Like when you told me you were going to tell Poppa I'd been a bad boy." He moved toward her. "So scream."

She did not scream. She retreated until the altar was at her back, and she stared at him with a wild trapped look, but she made no sound at all.

"Okay, that's settled," Charlie said, pressing close to her. "Now tell me the truth."

"What do you mean?"

"The truth, goddammit. It's simple. It's easier than lying. Take a stab at it."

"I don't know . . . God, I don't know!"

"What the hell are you, a sleep walker?"

He could not tell then if she began to laugh or to cry, only that something broke in her and she slumped against the altar and covered her face with her hands. Her shoulders trembled and then shook violently. She crumpled to her knees on the floor and he stood over her, looking down at her and waiting.

Maybe she hoped it would have some effect on him, but he gave her no sign that it meant anything. He only waited, and at last she quieted and looked up.

"That's it, I'm a sleep walker," she said, smiling bitterly.

"Come on, come on."

"What happened last night, Charlie? What did we do?"

"You tell me."

"I wish the hell I could."

"I think you can."

"Did we get it on? Is that it? What, did we screw on the altar? Didn't we go skinny-dipping like last time? What?"

Jesus, Charlie thought, she's going to plead insanity. That's my line.

He talked tough to her some more and it was easy because of the way he felt, but it got him nowhere. And then because he was tired and because he did not know what else to do, he softened. He sat on the floor beside her. And he was tempted to tell her his story, because he thought he knew what she was trying to say. He looked at her and thought he saw the same things he had been through, the rooms with green walls and the pills in paper cups. But he did not tell her any of that.

"You can trust me," was all he said.

"Right."

"Talk. You'll feel better."

"Like hell I will."

"You won't feel worse."

She smiled without meaning it, a little sign of resignation and dread. And then, with a searching look into his eyes, she started to talk.

She talked about her mother and her sister, her twin Amber. Some of it did not make sense to Charlie, but he listened without interrupting. She told him about being young and foolish, about drugs and boys and then more drugs and men, about being sent away to a succession of doctors and clinics, and Charlie managed not to ask if she had spent any time with his Doctor Branville. Her family had money, she told him, as if he did not know, and said that after years of trying to cure her they had for the last few years been content to keep her out of sight. She had been "studying in Europe," she told him. She did not say what she had been studying, but Charlie thought he got the idea.

"She is dead, isn't she, Charlie?"

The question popped suddenly into the still shadowy air of the chapel and took Charlie by surprise. He did not answer, and Jade asked him again.

"You know she is," he assured her. "Amber drowned. Don't be . . ."

"Crazy? Easy for you to say, Charlie."

Yeah, Charlie thought. Easy.

"I . . . sometimes, I . . . it's as if I might not . . . exist. Charlie, I know how that sounds. I can't explain it. It's as if I were becoming Amber. I don't want to, I don't mean to, but . . ."

"You were Amber when you went for a swim the other night."

"Did I? I suppose so."

150

"You don't remember?"

"No. Yes, I do, but . . . like it's a dream. Christ, Charlie, I remember everything, whether it really happened or not. I wish I could make you understand."

Charlie thought he did understand. He knew about dreams that were real and times when it was the other way around, when things were inside out.

"You remember making love to me, then," he said.

"It was real," she answered, with a questioning undertone.

"Felt real to me," Charlie smiled.

"God," she said, burying her face in her hands again. "And the next time you saw me . . ."

"You nearly bit my head off."

"You must have thought . . ."

"Don't worry about what I thought. How much do you remember about last night?"

"Last night?"

"You don't remember," Charlie said, as the familiar tingle along his spine made him shudder ever so slightly. "You remember the first time, at the lake, but not . . ."

"Don't you play mind games, Charlie," Jade warned him. "I'm telling you the truth. Don't start screwing around with . . ."

"Take it easy. I was just asking."

"What happened last night?"

"Don't worry about it," he said, with his arm around her shoulder, hoping he sounded more reassuring than he felt. "There's nothing for you to worry about."

He held her and she turned toward him, her knees curled up and her head against his chest. She felt relaxed and soft against him, having decided to trust him. He thought she was not holding anything back from him, and he tried not to let her sense that she had not explained everything.

Looking down at her he caught her scent, the mingled essences of her hair and the curve of her throat, her faint unsettling musk pulsing in the warming stillness of the chapel, the lush and funereal breaths of a thousand roses. A dense and tingling languor settled over them and Charlie found himself mesmerized by the rise and fall of her breasts

151

beneath the open throat of her shirt. As if she felt the same way he did, she turned her face to his and her lips parted expectantly. They kissed, and she pressed herself against him until his hands on her shoulders forced her gently away.

"We should be getting back," he told her.

"Charlie . . ."

"Don't get things mixed up."

"Yeah," she murmured bitterly, biting her lower lip. "I understand."

"Meaning . . ."

"Meaning you don't want to get mixed up with a crazy lady. I understand."

"No, meaning I don't want to take advantage of you, that's all."

"Right."

"Sex and therapy may start out the same, but it's bad to mix them," Charlie said, thinking of the time he had slept with his shrink, Samantha Cartwright.

"You're not a psychiatrist, you're a horse doctor."

"Yeah, and you don't know what problems are until you've had some mare fall in love with you. I know what I'm talking about."

She was still angry and confused, but she laughed in spite of herself.

"I'm not some bloody mare," she told him.

"And I'm not your shrink, so . . ."

She kissed him again and he was glad, but he stopped her again.

". . . so next time . . ." he continued.

"Next time?"

"Yeah, if you feel the same way, next time . . ."

"We'll skip the therapy."

"If you want to."

"I'd rather you took advantage of me."

"Shut up," he said. "Come here."

He led her outside and insisted she help him cut some roses, being careful to take only one bud from each of half a dozen bushes. When they had enough, he turned back toward the graveyard and she followed.

"What are these for?" she asked.

152

"Amber."

"You're going to put flowers on her grave?"

"You are," he said.

"Oh?"

"It's what you do for dead people."

"Sounds like therapy."

"Do it anyway."

As they reached the cemetery, he turned toward her. "When your mother called you Amber, that was nothing to be upset about, you know. It's natural, with all the shock and upset . . ."

"No, she's always done that."

"Called you Amber?"

"Both of us, either of us. Whenever one of us did something wrong, she called that one Amber."

Charlie thought that over as he watched her arrange the flowers in Amber's vase.

"Was it you that cut the roses?" he asked.

"How the hell would I know?" she answered.

"Let me see your hands," he said.

"Why?"

"Humor me."

"But why . . ." she said, as she turned toward him, then, "Ouch! Goddammed thorns."

He saw blood on her fingers as she pressed them to her lips.

"Never mind," he told her.

CHAPTER TWENTY-FIVE ▰▰▰▰▰▰▰▰▰▰▰

WHEN CHARLIE AND JADE GOT BACK TO THE HOUSE IT was awake and they walked the last few yards in the welcome air of breakfast cooking. Charlie found Calvin at the table on the back porch working on a stack of pancakes and a pair of fried eggs.

"Morning." He beamed as Charlie came in.

"Good morning," Charlie answered.

With a secret touch on his hip, Jade brushed by Charlie and nodded good morning to Calvin on her way inside.

"You must have got up at the crack of dawn," Calvin said. He cocked an eyebrow and turned his head toward Jade as she disappeared through the door, smiling. "Anything in particular get you up?"

"Just a little flower-picking."

"Uh-huh. Hungry?"

"Famished."

"You're in luck. Molly's cranking it out in there."

Charlie went in and found the Goldmans eating at the little kitchen table. There was no sign of Jade. Molly was at the stove with a skillet full of eggs and there was a pot of coffee burbling on the counter, beside a platter of eggs and pancakes. Charlie spoke to everyone and helped himself.

"Have a seat," Simon Goldman offered, making room for him.

"No thanks," Charlie said. "Think I'll have mine on the veranda."

As he left for the porch, Charlie heard more voices and commotion behind him in the kitchen, but he was too interested in the food to worry about who it was. He settled in beside Calvin and ate without talking, until he was not hungry anymore. Calvin went inside and fetched him a second cup of coffee.

He was deciding whether to fill Calvin in on his long night or to wait until they were alone. The idea of a nap in the bunkhouse was becoming more compelling by the minute, and he was about to excuse himself when Poppa McKendrick stepped out on the porch.

"Good morning, men," he greeted them. "Bright-eyed and bushy-tailed, huh? That's good."

Charlie mumbled good morning and hoped this did not mean Poppa had plans for him. Calvin was enjoying Charlie's condition without knowing for sure what or why it was, and he answered McKendrick with more genuine enthusiasm.

"Where's my two grandsons?" McKendrick wanted to know. "Thought maybe they's out here with you."

"Haven't seen them," Calvin said, noticing that Charlie said nothing.

154

"Well, it's high time they were up and about. Molly!" McKendrick called back through the door. "Have you seen Jeff or Chip this morning?"

"No, sir. It's a little early for those two."

"The hell it is. Goldman, why don't you go up and rouse them for me? We've got work to do."

"Work?" Charlie asked.

"I guess!" McKendrick beamed. "Since I ran off all my hands, who do you think's going to see after this place?"

"Well . . ."

There was a considerable disturbance somewhere above them as the two boys heaped abuse on poor Simon Goldman for disturbing them.

"Shake a leg, you two!" McKendrick yelled up through the porch roof and any window that intervened. Charlie could see the old man relished the prospect of doing whatever work there was to be done.

"I guess Calvin and I could give you a hand," Charlie offered, trying to sound unenthusiastic without being obvious.

"Damned right," McKendrick said as he stomped back into the house to get things going. "I'm counting on it."

"Great," Charlie muttered.

Calvin laughed.

There was a lot of work to be done, and not much of it was fun. They fed the horses that stood in the stable stalls with their heads hung out the open windows impatiently, and then they shoveled the old hay and horse shit out of the stalls and fresh hay in. Calvin aggravated Charlie no end, singing as he worked.

"Calvin," Charlie told him at one point when they were more or less alone in one part of the stables. "If you don't stop singing 'Momma Don't Let Your Sons Grow Up to Be Cowboys,' I'm gonna take this horse-shit shovel and pound a hole in that goofy-looking cowboy hat with your goddamned head still in it!"

"Chill out, man. Be happy in your work. Put a song in your heart . . ."

"Shut up."

"Be a good buckaroo."

"What? Be a what?"

"You know, a rootin' tootin' buckaroo, like that."

"Have you lost your goddammed mind?"

"Pot calling the kettle black there, Charlie boy."

"You are black!"

"And which one of us used to wear the suit with all the belts in the back?"

"Okay, okay," Charlie answered, so tired and mad that he started laughing with Calvin. "But you don't see me ankle deep in horse shit singing, do you?"

"No, you're just ankle deep in horse shit."

"Jesus."

"Momma don't let your sons grow up . . ."

"Shut up. Just stop," Charlie begged. He was too tired for all this.

"Well, I'm just at a loss, Charles," Calvin said, his voice a passable imitation of Doctor Branville's. "I mean, what is my role here, if not comic relief?"

"What?"

"Step-and-Fetch-it, you know. Isn't that my role model?"

"Oh, for . . ."

"Because if it's anything more than that, I'm sure you would be more forthcoming, yes?"

"Stop talking like Branville, will you? You know I hate that."

"Thank you for sharing that with me," Calvin intoned. When he went on, it was in his own voice. "Now how about letting me in on what the hell's going on around here?"

"Hey, I'm in no mood for an ass-eating, pal. If you don't . . . don't forget, it was your idea to come along on this deal."

"To look after your interests. Which I can't do if you . . ."

"For Christ's sake, don't get temperamental on me. I just . . ." Charlie looked around to see if they were alone. McKendrick and his grandsons had left in one of the trucks with hay and feed for the pastured stock. "I was just waiting till we were by ourselves."

"Which we seem to be."

"Okay."

Charlie told him everything, where he had been and what he had

156

done all night, his chat with Mrs. McKendrick and what Jade had told him, the business with the roses and everything he could think of.

"Damn," Calvin mused when he had finished. "There's more nuts in this place than there was back at the Institute."

"Yeah. So what do you think of Jade?"

"Beautiful, crazy as a loon. What do you think?" Calvin answered.

"The same, I guess."

"Charlie, I . . ."

"What?"

"Think about it. Don't you think this is all getting a little heavier than you bargained for?"

"Probably. So?"

"So let's think about getting you out of here."

"I'm doing okay so far."

"Maybe. But when you lose it . . ."

"If I lose it."

". . . If you lose it, it'll come all at once. Doing okay part of the way won't be good enough if you don't make it all the way, if you don't come out the other end."

"I know. But I'm not ready to call it quits yet."

"Why not?"

"If I quit a loser . . ."

"Wait a minute . . ."

"Then what? I crawl into a shell and live with my eyes closed? I took on a job here, and I've damned sure not finished it yet."

"I just . . ."

"I know, and I appreciate it. But I'm okay."

"You know best, I guess."

"As long as you stop singing."

"Never."

Calvin was still singing when McKendrick made it back to the stables. They were through with the stalls and Charlie hoped that was it for the day. He noticed Jeff was not in the truck.

"Y'all about done?" McKendrick asked.

"Yeah," Charlie answered, noticing that Calvin stopped singing when the others were around. "All done."

"Well, y'all work slow enough, but it looks like you did all right."

157

"Where's Jeff?" Charlie asked.

"He's bringing one of the horses in." McKendrick stepped down out of the truck and looked back the way he had come. "Here he comes."

Charlie turned and saw Jeff astride a black horse, hell-bent for the barn. The boy let out a yell and flogged the horse with the loose end of the reins as he thundered across the pasture and flew past the truck. From the back of the truck Chip yelled encouragement.

"Damn," McKendrick muttered.

"What?" Charlie asked.

"I've asked him not to run her up here like that. He'll run her into something going like that. If he wants to run her . . ."

Jeff pulled the black mare up stiff-legged between the barn and the stable pens, setting her back on her haunches as she slid to a stop just short of a gate. Then he whirled her around and rode her back to the truck. He was bareback, and Charlie had to admit he looked like he knew what he was doing as far as riding her. But he thought the mare looked scared as she pranced and pawed the ground, her ears back and her eyes wide.

"What do you think of her, Doctor?" Jeff asked.

"Nice horse," Charlie nodded. "You might not run her up in here like that, though."

"Fast, ain't she?" Jeff grinned, ignoring his advice. "Know what she does in a quarter?"

"Tell me," Charlie said.

"Twenty-one flat."

"Bullshit," Charlie answered evenly.

"What do you mean?"

"I mean she's a good quick mare, but she doesn't do a quarter of a mile in world record time, not with a two hundred pounder like you on her."

McKendrick cast him an amused look.

"I meant her best time," Jeff shot back.

"Well, I'd have your stop watch checked if I were you," Charlie told him. "And I wouldn't run her so hard without a warm-up, either. Besides which, like I said, you ought not to run her up in here and make

158

that silly-assed sliding stop so short. You could blow a tendon that way."

"She can take it," Jeff insisted, the mare still fidgeting.

"You may think so, but she looks pretty scared to me. She's a good girl and she'll do anything you ask her to. So it's up to you to know better."

"Thanks for the advice," Jeff spat, looking from Charlie to McKendrick. "I'll remember that."

"You need to, if you aim to run her for any money."

"We don't race our horses," McKendrick cut in.

"You don't," Jeff announced. "I do."

"Well, then, you'd better take better care of your horses, Son. This one here and the one you let Bud Witcher take to the races. Because unless you win enough money to buy some more, they're all the stock you're ever going to have."

"Yeah, you'd better shape up, Jeff," Chip chimed in from the bed of the truck. "Or Poppa'll cut you out of the will and leave all his horses to my dad."

"Right," Jeff snickered. "The Star of David Ranch."

"Or maybe he'll let Uncle Chris have 'em."

"Better yet. He can ride 'em sidesaddle."

The two boys laughed heartily, much taken with themselves and still hung over from their long night. McKendrick ducked his head and Charlie could not be sure if this was because he was ashamed of his grandsons or to keep Charlie from seeing the blood in his eyes, his quiet rage.

"Why don't you take her out where you have a little more room and cool her down a little," Charlie suggested, meaning to break the silence that had gathered over them. "She's worth taking care of."

"Hey, you're the doctor," Jeff grinned mockingly.

Charlie watched the boy turn the horse back toward the pasture and ride her away at a slow walk, making a big show of patting her neck and her head between her ears, talking baby talk to her and in general being a smartass.

Chip jumped down from the truck and started toward the house.

"You through for the day, are you?" McKendrick called after him.

"Yep," the boy answered, then stopped and turned around. "Unless you plan to cut me out of the will, too."

"Go on." McKendrick dismissed him with a wave of his hand.

When the two boys were gone, McKendrick shook his head and turned to Charlie.

"I guess you read those books I gave you," he said.

"Yeah, I thumbed through them."

"You did all right."

Calvin eased away toward one of the stalls as if he had something to do there, and Charlie wished he had thought of that. He did not know what to do or say. He felt embarrassed for the old man. The boys were assholes, and there was nothing to say.

"Inherit my horses? I believe I'd sooner put a bullet in their heads," McKendrick said quietly.

Charlie sympathized, but could not help wondering if the old man meant the horses or the boys.

CHAPTER TWENTY-SIX

THE GOLDMANS WERE ARGUING QUIETLY AT THE DIN-
ner table that evening. Charlie had Jade on his mind. He had not seen her since that morning.

"I don't care," Simon Goldman insisted to his wife Ruth. "I don't want him going hunting."

"I agree," Chris chimed in as if he were entitled to a vote. "With all that's happened . . ."

"Chris, please," Mrs. Goldman cut him off.

"Well, I'm sorry, but that's how I feel. Like there hasn't been enough trouble . . ."

Chris held up his hands to make his point, then waved them down toward the Goldmans as if to show that he had done his best.

"Simon, he's bored to death sitting around this place. He's lost half a year out of his life . . ." Ruth began, leaning toward Simon so that she turned a shoulder to Chris.

"Such a life," Simon answered with a shrug. "Drinking and chasing girls. So there won't be any beer or coeds when he goes back?"

"You won't even try to understand," Ruth argued.

"I understand there's plenty for him to do here, he shouldn't be bored. He could be of some help to his grandfather, for example. I understand we are paying a fortune for him to go to SMU, he could take the trouble to go to class once in a while, he could read a book, even, it wouldn't kill him," Simon rejoined.

"We're paying a fortune. Always it's money," his wife said, shaking her head.

"No, this time it's guns. I don't want him schlepping around with a shotgun, him and Jeff traipsing all over with shotguns after some cockamamie birds to kill. For heaven's sake, with all the . . ."

"He's a young man, Simon. He's bored, he's not . . . always, you . . ."

Ruth McKendrick Goldman stopped scolding her husband when she realized that Charlie had come in, that he was standing in the doorway from the kitchen into the dining room. She turned to look at him and Charlie smiled awkwardly, then stepped aside as Molly bustled past him with a basket of fresh rolls for the table.

"Oh," said Mrs. Goldman with a smile. "Good evening, Doctor Gants."

"Good evening," he returned.

He had settled for a hot bath in the bunkhouse in lieu of a nap, and felt better if a little tired. The way he felt he could have skipped dinner and gone to bed, but he did not trust these people to get through the night without him.

There were just the four of them, Mister and Mrs. Goldman on one side of the table, in the same chairs they had occupied his first night on the ranch when they had all sat down together, and Chris in his assigned seat across the table. Charlie poured himself a cup of coffee and settled into the guest's chair, the one they had given him that first night. He could not help casting a glance across at the place where Bill Junior and his wife and the baby had sat. Only Chris seemed to notice, and when Charlie looked at him Chris smiled gently but said nothing.

161

"Are you a hunter, Doctor Gants?" Simon Goldman asked.

"Of what?" Charlie answered.

"In this particular case, of birds. Doves."

"The birds don't attack me, I don't attack them. Live and let live," Charlie said. He really meant it, but when he thought they were all staring at him, he smiled as if he were only trying to be witty.

"My sentiments exactly," Simon agreed.

"I suppose that settles it," Ruth put in. "What is this, a medical opinion?"

Charlie had not thought he was hungry, that he would just have some coffee and see who was at the table, but the smell of the food changed his mind and he was helping himself to roast beef and mashed potatoes as the Goldmans went on.

"I'm simply trying to make the point," Simon told his wife, "that this . . . hunting is . . . what's the word, inappropriate. That's all."

"Inappropriate for you maybe," Ruth retorted. "For me, too. But Chip is a young man. It's different."

"If he wants to shoot something, he could take a crack at some clay pigeons," Charlie offered. When he saw that the other three had turned to look at him curiously, he went on: "Skeet. If we don't have the gear on the place, I'd be happy to run into town and pick up what we'd need. He could blaze away to his heart's content, eliminate all the walking and when all is said and done, nothing has to die. It's the shooting that is all the fun, the rest, all that tramping around, cleaning the birds, that's just work. Unless somebody here's especially fond of chicken-fried dove?"

"I think that's a marvelous idea," Chris chimed in. "I really do."

"Me too," Mister Goldman voted.

"What's a marvelous idea?" Jade asked, appearing in the dining room door behind Charlie, coming from the parlor.

"Murdering skeet!" Chris announced.

"Murdering?" Jade asked, looking at Charlie.

"Not really murdering," Charlie assured her, trying to see into her eyes, looking for some kind of sign that she remembered, or she did not remember, who she was this time. "Skeet aren't alive anyway."

"I don't . . ."

"Jeff and Chip are dead set on going dove hunting when the season opens tomorrow," Chris hastened to bring Jade up to date. "Simon and

I think it's an atrocious idea, Ruth thinks Chip is entitled to a little entertainment, and Charlie has come up with a terrific compromise. Skeet."

"They're not alive?" Jade asked, looking at Charlie.

"Skeet is what you call it when you shoot clay pigeons. They're not really pigeons, just round targets, like plates. You throw them up in the air and shoot them."

"Oh. It sounds boring," she said.

"Well, it's not. You don't just throw them up, you have this thing, with a spring and . . . they're not easy to hit, and it's fun, it's not boring. Really."

"Oh."

Jade drifted around the corner of the table and brushed past Charlie's back to her assigned chair at the other end, at Momma's left hand, if Momma had been in her chair.

Now they were five.

"Dove hunting, huh?" Charlie asked. He did not give a damn if Chip and Jeff went hunting for each other, much less doves, but he wanted to hear them all talk a little, get a feel for them, see what kind of mood they all were in.

"Yes," Chris said, shaking his head with a shiver to make it clear he thought the whole notion barbaric.

"It's not that big a deal," Ruth Goldman assured him. "A little diversion for the two of them. I don't know why all the fuss."

"Well," Charlie offered, seeing that Simon had nothing more to say at that point. "It does seem a little, I don't know, inappropriate, given all that's happened. I guess that's how it seems to me, anyway."

Everybody looked as if they had something to say about that, but at that moment Papa and Momma made their entrance and everyone else turned to greet them instead of answering Charlie.

Momma looked fresh and rested. Poppa showed her to her chair at the end of the table nearest the kitchen, deposited her there with a kiss on her cheek and moved back along the table to his place at the other end, letting his hand fall on Charlie's shoulder as he went by. When Poppa was seated, he eyed them all.

"Where's the boys?" he asked.

"Upstairs, freshening up," Ruth said.

"It's supper time," the old man noted.

"They worked hard today," Ruth answered. "They're tired."

"It's not from any work they did today," the old man insisted. "Maybe they're working too hard on the night shift."

Charlie met the old man's knowing eyes and saw his little wink, but wondered if he was only kidding or if there was more to it.

"What are you talking about?" asked Ruth, quick to defend the boys.

"God a'mighty, sis," the old man laughed. "You ain't so old you've done forgot about night work, have you?"

The men laughed nervously, especially Simon Goldman, and Ruth curled her face into a good-natured reproof.

"Will," Momma said, her voice surprising Charlie because there was not only a tone of correction in it that sounded the way her daughter Ruth looked, but also a hint of old appetite and a lingering notion of the night and Poppa as a younger man.

"Go get 'em," Poppa ordered, in a mock-gruff tone. "We might as well all sit down to supper at the same time."

Ruth left to get the boys and Charlie felt again that he was intruding on a family. He noticed that the thought of these people as a family came and went, and he could not help looking at the empty chairs.

"Was Charlie any good today?" Jade asked.

Charlie turned to look at her as he heard Poppa ask, "I beg your pardon?"

"At the work. Was he any good at it?"

Charlie watched her turn her face to him and saw the impish and subtle smile tug at her lips, the twinkle in her eye. He decided it was a good sign.

"You could tell where he'd been, I guess," McKendrick answered.

Everybody smiled at that and Charlie supposed they had heard it before, that it might be the closest the old man came to saying anyone had done a good job at anything. He looked at Jade and the old man, wondering who knew what, and asked himself if maybe the only secrets around this table were the ones they were keeping from him.

"All right, all right!" Chip whined, banging through the dining room door alongside Jeff and just ahead of his mother, Ruth. When he

164

was in the dining room and for a moment the center of attention, he smirked at Jeff and announced: "Okay, we're here. You can start now."

Jeff and Chip giggled together, and Charlie tried not to wish they were dead. They're kids, he told himself. Assholes, but just kids. They'll grow out of it, they'll be real people some day. He was having trouble believing it.

The two young ones strutted to their seats and slumped down, eminently and obviously bored with the whole project of having dinner with the family. Charlie wondered if they had plans, if their plans included the two girls from the night before. These two may be up to back-to-back all-nighters, he thought, but I'm not.

There was quite a lot of family stuff, mostly good-natured and coded with three generations of collective memory and myth, so that Charlie felt much the outsider and did not ask anyone to explain any of it to him because he thought it was a fragile thing with this family in particular and by intruding he might ruin it for them.

They ate dinner and seemed in good spirits, and talked of the dove season and opening day and shotguns and dozens of other things that meant almost nothing to Charlie except that he could tell by the feeling they showed around the table that there was something there, and he wondered how Simon Goldman felt, and he watched him more than the others, and decided before it was all over that Simon had made himself a part of it as best he could and was happy with that. It made Charlie feel good for them.

In what seemed to Charlie a warm, almost glowing sense of family in spite of the arrogance and disrespect of the two young ones, Jeff and Chip, which even they seemed to be holding back in some sense of the thing. Poppa at one point when dinner was done and there was no longer any practical reason for them all to be there together, in the felt moment just before the first of them, whoever it might be, would scrape a chair away from the table and break the circle, looked down the length of the big table and smiled at Momma.

"This is good," he said. "The way things have been going, who knows?"

They all looked at him and then at Momma, at each other.

"Who knows," Poppa went on. "When we'll all sit down together again. Who knows if . . ." The old man halted in a feeling that came up out of him and stopped him from saying anything more for a moment, then went on: ". . . if all of us will ever sit down together here again."

That was that. The empty chairs around the table loomed up then, and the spell was broken. Charlie looked down at his plate and heard chairs, first one and then several, scraping away on the floor, the sounds of the family dissolving again, into their separateness and the night.

And suddenly Charlie knew. If the old man had had some inkling, or if he had only said that because of Bill Junior and the baby, whatever had made him say it, Charlie knew with a crystal certainty that thrilled and chilled him that this was the last time. The last time they would be together.

CHAPTER TWENTY-SEVEN

"**DON'T ANYBODY WANDER OFF,**" Poppa announced. "We're expecting company."

Charlie knew by the way all the rest of them reacted that the old man had not shared his secret with any of them.

"Who?" Momma demanded.

"Just company. I want everybody to be here."

"Aw, man," Jeff whined, sharing a look with Chip, who looked down at his watch. "How long do we have to wait?"

"Not long," Poppa answered. "They're running a little late, as a matter of fact. I expected them in time to have supper with us."

Whatever they all thought of it, or might have expected, none of them insisted on leaving, any more than some murmured bitching by Chip and Jeff, which made Charlie think they did have plans with the two girls from the night before.

"There they come," Poppa said, looking out through a parlor window from the kitchen door.

Charlie heard the sounds of the car screeching to a sliding stop on the gravel out front and guessed by the sound of it without looking out that it was the lawyer Childress. He was right. The tall thin man appeared on the porch as Poppa pushed the screen door open to welcome him.

But that was not all. Charlie stepped back and felt a warm blush across his face when he saw the woman who had come from town with the lawyer.

"Poppa, let me introduce Doctor Samantha Cartwright. Sam, Mister McKendrick."

Poppa took Sam's hand when she offered it and told her how welcome she was to his ranch. Sam smiled delightfully and assured him that Mister Childress had told her all about Poppa, how she was so happy to meet him, and like that. She did not look past Poppa at Charlie, and Charlie stood rooted to the parlor floor, saying nothing.

The family moved toward the front door, exchanging looks and eyeing Sam. They all wondered what was up, and so did Charlie.

"Let's all find a place and sit down," Poppa offered, with one hand on Sam's arm and the other extended to show that he meant for everyone to take a seat in the parlor.

Charlie watched Sam as she looked from one to the other of them and finally looked at him. She smiled, but Charlie did not. As everyone shuffled and chose a place to sit, Sam slipped away from Poppa and came toward Charlie. She was still smiling when she reached out to him and put her hand on his shoulder.

"Can't you say hello?" she asked.

"Hello."

"How are you?" she insisted. When Charlie said nothing, she added, "I understand there's been trouble."

"Do you?" he asked, his mind racing. "I wouldn't have thought it would have made the Dallas papers."

"You look good," Sam went on, not caring to answer the question he had really asked. "A little drawn. Have you been sleeping well?"

"What are you doing here?" Charlie demanded softly, smiling, so the others, some of whom were watching him, would not see how he felt.

"I'm here to help you," she said, with a look on her face that seemed to say she meant it. "I was . . . concerned about you."

"Yeah, I . . ." Charlie began, but Poppa called them all to a conference.

"I've got an announcement to make," Poppa began. "To all of you, Mister Childress here included. I asked him out this evening to take care of a little legal business, but I didn't tell him what it was. This here is Miss, uh, Doctor Samantha Cartwright. She's a friend and associate of Doctor Gants, and she'll be staying with us for a while to give him a hand. Now, about this legal matter . . ."

Charlie had shown Sam to a seat on the sofa and was standing behind her. He looked down at her as she smiled at each of the faces the McKendricks turned toward her, then she looked up at Charlie as if she thought he would be relieved or grateful that she and Childress apparently had not told McKendrick that she was Charlie's shrink. Charlie did not feel grateful. He felt something else entirely.

"I've given this a lot of thought," Poppa said. He was standing near the entrance area, facing the family where they sat or slumped, in the case of the two young ones, on and around Momma's plastic-wrapped good furniture. "I never had put much stock in this business about a curse. I've heard that foolishness all my life, how there's an old Indian buried under the big tree, and, well . . . that's all it is, foolishness. A man makes his own luck."

"What does that have to do with . . ." Chris interrupted, but Poppa waved him off.

"I'll get around to it, Chris. Just hear me out." Poppa pursed his lips in thought, ran his hand across his face, and then went on. "On the other hand, there's been a right smart of trouble, more than I can lay to bad luck. Momma, if you'd rather not sit through this . . ."

"Go ahead, Poppa," was all the old woman said. She sat with her hands folded in her lap, her shoulders drawn up a little, as if expecting a blow.

"All right. Amber, the baby, and then Bill Junior. It's too much. And I might as well tell you, I've been to see the sheriff."

"The sheriff?" Ruth asked, exchanging looks with her husband Simon.

"Yep, and he don't think Bill Junior hung hisself."

168

All of them had something to say then, talking at once, twisting in their seats.

"Meaning what?" Chris asked. "That it was murder?"

"Yeah," Poppa answered. "And he's got some evidence to back that up. He'll be by tomorrow early to ask some questions, too, so I don't want anybody wandering off. Y'all hear me, you two?"

This was aimed at Jeff and Chip, and they both nodded.

"And I think it's a good idea if both of you stayed in tonight, too."

The two boys did not like the sound of that, and Charlie thought they were as surprised as he was that the old man seemed to know they had been out the night before.

"Do you two understand me?" Poppa insisted.

"Yes, sir," Jeff agreed glumly. Chip nodded again.

"Good. Now, in light of this about Bill Junior, I've had to consider something I'm afraid I've been trying to put out of my mind. Something . . . pretty awful."

He stopped to think again, and no one interrupted him.

"It's pretty clear," he went on, "that if there's been any dirty work going on, it's been for a reason. And I'm afraid that means that whoever's behind it . . . might be one of us."

More squirming and jumbled talking. Charlie heard mostly protests that this was unthinkable, but he also thought he heard one or two say they knew it.

"If that's what it is," Poppa continued, as the others stopped talking to listen. "It's bound to be about money, about this place and what it's worth. I reckon it's about the money, being's I don't guess any of you care about the place. Jeff," the old man fixed a saddened gaze on the boy. "I'd hoped you might, but there's no point in that. If you got this place, you'd make a race track out of it, or sell it like the rest of them, for whatever it'd bring. Ain't that right?"

"Once you're dead, old man, what the hell do you care?" Jeff shot back.

"Jeff!" Ruth cried.

"Show a little respect, Jeff," Simon admonished.

Poppa looked at Charlie and raised an eyebrow as if to say it was a shame. Charlie nodded.

"So . . ." Poppa said. "Until we get this settled, I've decided to do something about it. That's why I've asked Mister Childress out here tonight. I'm gonna change my will."

Poppa waited for them to raise hell about that, but to Charlie's surprise there was not much said this time, just a lot of looks exchanged and few mutterings. This was serious, and there was a lot of thinking going on in the room.

"The way it stands now, if I die, there's provisions for Momma to live here the rest of her life, and the estate is to be divided, share and share alike, among our surviving heirs. If she goes first, which she won't . . ." Poppa and Momma exchanged smiles. "I take this house and the original little spot of land around it and y'all split up the rest. Mister Childress, I'll tell you right now, officially, in front of everybody how I want the new will to read. Charlie, Doctor Cartwright, y'all are witnesses, too."

Sam and Charlie nodded, both wishing he had not involved them.

"If I die first, the same goes for Momma: She keeps the original little home place for the rest of her life. Then it goes to . . . you may have some ideas about this, Childress, but I was thinking maybe Paris Junior College or East Texas State, somebody that'll use it the way I'd like to see it used. Everything else, all the other land, mineral rights, everything of any value, goes to the school we decide on as soon as I'm buried. None of you gets any of it." Poppa turned to Childress. "You know what I want. Put restrictions on it about how they're to use the land and the money it brings, make sure they keep up the cemetery, such as that."

"Yes," Childress answered. He had begun to take notes. "You could put it in trust, the heirs as trustees."

"With you as executor or whatever you call it, overseer," Poppa agreed.

"Wait a goddamned minute," Jeff broke in, advancing toward the old man. "I've worked my butt off around here, are you telling me all that comes to nothing?"

"No, Jeff. Them two horses you're hell-bent on racing, they're yours. And all of you'll get something. A . . . what do you call it, Childress?"

170

"Uh . . . a stipend, a remembrance?"

"Yeah, a stipend. Twenty thousand dollars apiece."

"Twenty thousand?" Ruth wondered aloud.

"That's right, so you can pay off that German car you nagged your husband into buying whether he could afford the payments or not. Is that all right with you, Goldman?"

"It's your money," Simon Goldman answered evenly. But Charlie sensed that what Simon was holding back was different from the rest. Charlie thought that Simon might have been relieved somehow, might have been choking back a belly laugh. The others were not in a laughing mood. "I don't care what you do with it."

"Good," Poppa said, smiling at him.

"You don't think you're overreacting a bit, Poppa?" Chris asked, managing to sound more concerned about his father than about the money.

For Charlie's part, he was wondering about the money. Twenty thousand was a hell of a lot of money in his book, and these people were acting like it was a very poor consolation prize. Childress had said McKendrick was rich, but Charlie was having to redefine the term.

"Maybe, I hope so. But here's the way I look at it: God help us, if somebody here is behind any killing, it's gotta be so they can get a bigger share of the inheritance. If there's no inheritance, maybe . . ."

"No more killing," Chris finished his thought.

"Yep."

"Jesus," Chris muttered, looking around the room as if he were seeing his family for the first time. "I can't believe . . ."

"I'd rather not myself," Poppa agreed. "But I don't want to take the chance. There's already been more than enough . . . trouble. Oh, and another thing. The twenty thousand apiece, that's fixed, no matter how many there are of you. You got that, Childress?"

The lawyer nodding, writing on a legal pad in his lap. As if they were more offended at the idea they might kill each other off for their stipends than anything he had said before, Ruth and Jeff and Chip exploded, screaming to be heard over the din they all made at the old man. Charlie noticed Jade, who sat on the arm of a chair, looking down. She shook her head slowly from side to side.

Chapter TWENTY-EIGHT ▬▬▬

AFTER EVERYONE HAD GIVEN UP PROTESTING AND complaining to Poppa, they all went their separate ways, still fuming or shaking their heads or dealing with the news in their own ways. The last thing Poppa had told them had been that he would change the will back so that his survivors would get their full shares if and when the killer, whoever it was, was found out or came forward. The next to the last thing he had told them was that the sheriff was coming out early the next morning and would want to talk to everybody. He had stressed *everybody*, adding that he would not be surprised if, in light of his new will, some of them decided to leave. He told them not to, until the sheriff came.

As the others scattered, Poppa turned to Lawyer Childress to say something, and Charlie stepped between them. He asked McKendrick if he could have a word, and he and the old man went into the hallway, where they would not be overheard.

"What is it, Charlie?" the old man asked.

"You're putting yourself on the spot here, don't you think?"

"Could be. You think if it's one of the kids they might try to—to stop me before I could change the will?"

"Damned right. So I'm going to stick close to you . . ."

"No, you ain't," the old man cut him off. "That'd just scare them off."

"What did you have in mind?" Charlie asked.

By way of an answer, the old man pulled back one side of the cardigan sweater he was wearing to show Charlie the butt of a revolver tucked into his belt.

"I don't think this is a good idea," Charlie said.

"Maybe not, but it's better than just waiting. No offense, Charlie,

I know you're doing your best. But if any of 'em wants that money bad enough to come after me, I'll be a-waiting."

"Okay, but why don't I camp outside your door anyway, just for . . ."

"Nope."

"Calvin, then. He could . . ."

"It'd just screw things up, Charlie. You go about your business, and I'll see to myself. I mean that."

There was no use in arguing with the old man, who turned away and motioned for the lawyer to join him in the den. In the angry sulking house, Charlie found himself alone in the parlor with Sam.

"Come here," he told her, and led her by the arm out the back of the house, down the porch steps and down the path toward the big tree. When they were far enough from the house that they were beyond the rectangles of light cast by its windows, he turned on her.

"What the hell are you doing here?" he demanded.

"I told you, I was concerned about you and I came to see how you were holding up."

"And?"

"And what?"

"Come on, come on, don't con me. Out of the blue, you just wondered how I was doing?"

"It had been a while and I hadn't heard from you, Charlie."

"The hell you hadn't. What did Calvin tell you?"

"Don't . . ."

"What did he tell you?" Charlie put his hands on her arms and shook her, not nearly as hard as he wanted to.

"Nothing. He said . . . You're hurting me."

"You're damned right I am."

"He told me about the baby who died, and the suicide. The hanging . . ."

"What else?"

"Noth . . . he said you were doing all right."

"I don't believe you, Sam. If he said that, what are you doing here?"

"Calvin is . . . look, goddamn it, let go of me and we'll talk. You're hurting me."

173

"I'm sorry," Charlie said, letting go of her.

"Thank you." Sam rubbed her arms and stepped back from him. "Calvin is not a doctor, and he's not the most clinical person in the world."

"So?"

"So, he's a friend of yours."

"Like hell."

"Charlie, he . . . . Never mind. I didn't feel comfortable with what he was telling me. A baby died. You woke up one morning and found a dead man hanging from a banister. How's your head, by the way?"

"That's the sixty-four-thousand-dollar question, isn't it?"

"Don't be arch, Charlie. I mean . . ."

"You mean the bump. You think you already know about the inside, don't you?"

"Up to a point, yes."

"Terrific."

"If you're about through venting your hostilities, Charlie, I'd like to know how you've been. Any dreams? Any . . ."

"Any ghosts? No, Sam, you're the first one. You're the only ghost from my past I've run into so far."

"What's that supposed to mean?"

"You're the shrink, Sam, figure it out."

"I have already. I'd hoped you might have."

"What's that supposed to mean?"

"Never mind. Let's stick to current affairs . . ."

"Fine. What did you tell Childress?"

"That you'd sent for me."

"Jesus Christ!"

"That you thought I could be of some help. Not to you personally, Charlie, I was careful not to give him that idea. I told him there were family members you wanted my opinion on."

"Jesus H. . . ."

"I'm telling you, Charlie, I didn't give Childress any reason to think you weren't holding up. You've got to trust me . . ."

"Never again."

"It's the sexual thing, isn't it?" she said with an incredulous shake of her head that reminded Charlie of Jade in the parlor, shaking her head at the news of her father's changing the will. "You're obsessed with it, aren't you?"

"Let's not discuss it, okay?"

"Of course not, Charlie, don't bring it out into the open, don't resolve it. You'd much prefer to nurse it like a festering wound, wouldn't you?"

"Shut up."

"We slept together. Once. Would you like an apology? Would that help? Okay, Charlie, I'm sorry it happened."

"It wasn't ethical of you," Charlie said, hearing himself sound like a petulant child. "Either I was a client or something else. You don't make love to clients."

"So turn me in, Charlie. File a complaint with the board. But for the record, we didn't make love, we simply fucked!"

She said it pretty loud, and about at the same time Charlie heard the screen door slam at the back of the house. He turned to see Jade standing on the back porch looking out into the night. He and Sam were beyond the light and he did not think Jade could see them, but he knew how sound carried at night. He and Sam waited without saying anything more until finally Jade finished the cigarette she was smoking and threw the butt into the yard. When she went back inside, the screen door slamming again behind her, Charlie turned to Sam.

"Branville sent you here, didn't he?" Charlie demanded of Sam, not wanting to answer any questions she had about Jade or any of the rest of it.

"You flatter yourself," Sam laughed. "You're a dead end as far as he's concerned. If you'd produced, you'd still be there, and we'd have a grant."

"Produced?"

"Never mind."

"What do you mean, produced?"

"Perhaps you've forgotten having it explained to you a number of times. Once more: Doctor Branville was interested in you initially because he thought you might be exceptional in a way he has a professional interest in . . ."

"Yeah, ESP or something."

175

"Something like that. Only you weren't. You were just thoroughly fucked up in the head, a basket case. When we took you into the Institute, in case you've forgotten that too, you were in a wheelchair, drooling on your pajamas and sliding back and forth into some kind of spookhouse in your mind."

"All right, all right."

"You feel so used and abused, don't you, Charlie? Poor man, the mean shrink took you to bed and then didn't love you anymore. It's been a little less one-sided than that, if you can get over your hang-up with me. We put your head back together, Charlie, and it didn't cost you a dime."

"Send me a bill."

"You couldn't afford it."

"So repossess me."

"You shut up, and listen to me for a minute. I'm here on my own time, for my own reasons. I may be able to help you. I'm certainly not going to do anything to hurt you."

"You showed up, didn't you? I may have a relapse."

"Nice try, Charlie, but I give guilt trips, I don't take them."

He turned away from her and kicked something that might have been a fallen limb on the ground. Seeing her again had stirred things up for him, but he was not what he would have expected. He did not feel broken-hearted or anything like that, he was just angry as hell that she had popped up again. Maybe that was progress.

"I've had a long day, Charlie. Two hours on the road after half a day at work, and that lawyer drives like a maniac. If you don't want to fill me in on what's going on around here, I don't see any point in wasting my time, so I'll just turn in."

"Where?" Charlie asked, turning back to look at her. He had not thought about it, but had assumed she would go back to town with the lawyer.

"They're going to put me up at the house. They said there was a room available."

"That's right, there is." Charlie laughed this time.

"What's funny?"

"Nothing. It's the room where the baby died. The dead son's room."

"Oh."

"Maybe it's your turn to see ghosts."

"I doubt it."

"Me too. You're not the type."

"Whatever that means. Good night, Charlie."

"Wait a minute."

"What?"

He looked at her, silhouetted against the lights from the house, her face in shadows.

"It's okay."

"What is?" she asked.

"That you came."

"I know."

"Of course you do, I forgot you know everything."

"Apparently not, I don't know how to take you sometimes." She stood looking at him for a moment. "I'm glad you think it's okay."

"Me too, but I'm not sure I understand it."

"One step at a time."

"Right."

"So do you want to tell me about it?"

"What?"

"Everything, what's been going on around here. Do you have a suspect?"

"A lot of them. We'll talk tomorrow."

"All right. Good night."

"Good night. And, uh . . ." she stopped and looked back at him. "You probably ought to lock your door when you go to bed."

"I will. You too."

"Right."

He watched her return to the house and tried to put everything about her out of his mind. He had enough trouble trying to get a handle on things with the McKendricks. He did not need any old business to throw him off.

Sam looked back in his direction from the lighted back porch, one hand shielding her eyes against the overhead light. She shrugged as if to say to Charlie that she could not see him from there, for what that was worth, and went inside.

It did not work, trying to put Sam and all the rest of that business out of his mind. He was mad, and he wanted to hit something. He had another long night ahead of him, and he wished he had told Sam about his last couple of days, his sleepless night playing guardian angel to Jeff and Chip and their girlfriends at the lake. She thought she had put in a rough day! But he was too mad to think about anything except it kept popping up in his mind like some kind of cork, the way he felt and all the reasons why, trying to figure it out. Before he could focus on the night ahead, he had a score to settle.

There was a light in the bunkhouse window and Charlie knew he had been right about why Calvin had not showed up for dinner. He had taken a nap after the hard day's work in the barn and had slept through it. As he passed the uncurtained window and looked inside, Charlie saw Calvin, sitting on the side of his bunk looking at his wristwatch. Time to get up, pal, Charlie thought.

Calvin looked up with a grin when Charlie came in the door.

"Hey, man, I slept through mealtime."

"I guess you did," Charlie said.

"Hope there's some leftovers, I'm starved."

Charlie did not answer.

"It's amazing what a little honest labor will do for a man's appetite, ain't it?"

Calvin was busy putting his watch on his wrist and did not look up at Charlie until he sensed there was something wrong.

"What?" he asked, looking up at Charlie, his smile fading as if he suspected bad news.

"Get up," Charlie said.

"What's going on?"

"Just get up."

Calvin rose to his feet with a puzzled look.

"Charlie, what's the matter with you?"

"Nothing. I just need to vent a little hostility."

"Say what?" Calvin asked.

Charlie swung at Calvin's nose, dead center in his suddenly suspicious face, not at all bothered that it was not fair. But Calvin was quick and almost got out of the way. He ducked his head and his left arm shot up to block the blow. Charlie got enough of a punch in that his fist caromed off Calvin's temple and drove him back, off balance, across the bunk and onto the floor on the other side.

Calvin put his hand on the bed and drew himself up to a crouch, looking across the bed at Charlie with a wary stare.

"Sam says hello," Charlie told him.

CHAPTER TWENTY-NINE

"**FEEL BETTER?**" Calvin asked.

"Some."

"Good. You plan to do any more of that?"

"Maybe."

"Okay, but I ought to warn you, Charlie. While I believe in therapy of all kinds, I can't help thinking that getting my ass whipped is beyond the call of duty."

"You've warned me."

"Then you won't mind if I put up a little fight?"

"Whatever."

"Good. Long as we understand each other."

"That's a laugh. You goddamned spy. Snitch."

"That's me, dirty sonofabitch that I am. Sneaking off every chance I get, telling Doctor Sam how well you're doing. Wouldn't blame you if you shot me, Charlie."

"Why did you do it?"

"Dumb question, man."

"Humor me."

"Because she asked me to."

"Great."

"She's the doctor."

"Right."

"I think you're in pretty good shape, you think you're in pretty good shape. At least, I think you do. But she thinks she needs to keep tabs on you. That's all it is."

"Why?"

"Probably some sinister plot, Charlie. It couldn't be that she just wants to make sure you're doing all right. That couldn't be it, could it?"

Charlie did not say anything.

"Nah, that couldn't be it. Must be a sinister plot."

Calvin ran a hand over the side of his head and Charlie thought there was a little swelling there. The two men looked at each other without saying anything more for a minute or so.

"So, Charlie, what d'you say?" Calvin asked finally. "Is there gonna be a second round here, or is the therapy session over?"

Charlie did not answer.

"Because if it is, I'd really like to check out the leftover situation before they turn out the lights in the big house. I'm nervous about prowling around in their kitchen once they're all turned in. They might shoot me for a burglar, forgetting for the moment that they have a black guest on the place."

"I guess I'm through, unless you want some pay-back."

"I'm not a vindictive man, Charlie. Besides, I'm not sure I didn't have that coming. To tell you the truth, I'm glad the woman is on the place. She can do her own stuff, firsthand. I didn't care much for . . ."

"Skip it. I don't care."

Calvin nodded his head and got to his feet. Nothing else was said between them as Charlie watched him leave and walk to the big house. When he was gone, Charlie looked around the bunkhouse and eyed his own bed longingly. But he had things to do, and he made himself go out into the night.

He looked the house over and then turned away, walking in the direction of the big tree and the lake beyond. When he had gone up the trail far enough that he knew he was out of sight and had gone far enough up the hill toward the tree that he would have a good view of the house, he stopped.

From where he stood, he could see the back of the house and all of one side, as well as the cars and trucks where they were parked. Satisfied that no one could get far from the house without his seeing them, he hunted around for a good spot and settled in. He sat on the

180

ground and put his back against a tree that was big enough to hold his weight, not too big to look around by turning his head, without having to shift position and make any noise.

He was not sure what time it was, but he could not shake the feeling that something was afoot. Poppa's announcement had stirred everyone up and the sheriff was coming out early in the morning. Time was running out for someone. He would rather have been inside protecting Poppa from his heirs, but there was no use worrying about that. Poppa wanted it his way, and Charlie could only hope the old man knew what he was doing.

Charlie had not been on his stand long when he heard voices from the front of the house and first a car door and then the front door of the house slamming. With a roar of its engine and the distant clatter of spun gravel, lawyer Childress's big Lincoln fishtailed out the long drive and swung onto the road on its way back to town.

And then nothing. The night settled in around him with its furtive sounds and the cool touch of a breeze off the lake. Charlie sat watching and thinking until after a while here and there first one window and then another blinked dark, until at last the house was asleep. Just before the last light went out, he saw Calvin make his way across the porch and then the yard to the bunkhouse. He was rubbing his belly with one hand, picking his teeth with the other. Good for him, Charlie thought.

CHAPTER THIRTY

"YOU'RE OUT LATE."

Charlie's head snapped up at the sound of the voice beside him and he cursed himself.

"I fell asleep," he said aloud.

"Kind of," the voice answered.

Charlie looked to his right at the old Indian sitting beside him.

"Where did you come from?" Charlie demanded.

181

"What difference does it make?"

A wolf howl curled up out of the darkness to Charlie's left and sounded so close that Charlie imagined for a moment that he could smell the beast.

"Jesus!"

"I beg your pardon?" the old Indian said.

"Didn't you hear that, that frigging wolf is so close I can smell his breath!"

"Coyote," said the old man and in the moonlight Charlie saw a smile on the dark face beside him.

"Goddamned timber wolf," Charlie insisted.

"No more wolves, just old Coyote. He can sound like a wolf if he wants to."

"Yeah, right."

"He's a good ways off," the old man assured him.

"If you say so."

"Is this the night?" the old man asked.

"I beg your pardon?"

"Never mind."

"No, what did you say? The night for what?"

"I guess maybe not. You are out late again."

Charlie did not say anything. He wanted to be sure he was not dreaming any of this. He did not think he was.

"Ever seen one of these?" the Indian asked, handing Charlie something.

"What is it?" Charlie asked. He held the thing out from the shadows that clung to his tree, into a patch of moonlight. It was two sticks joined at one end with rawhide thongs. It might have been some kind of crude nutcracker, if you put a walnut between the two sticks and squeezed them together, the rawhide joint keeping pressure on. He could see that the sticks were bowed a little, as if something big had been squeezed between them. The inside edges of the sticks were scraped and rough. "What is it?" he asked again.

"Who knows?" the Indian answered.

"Where did you get it?"

"From the lake."

The sticks were damp and the rawhide, when Charlie examined it as best he could in the poor light, was sodden.

"What is it for, do you know that?" Charlie insisted.

The Indian shrugged his shoulders.

"I thought maybe you would know," he said, looking away from Charlie as if he were somehow disappointed in him.

"Me? How am I supposed to . . ."

"You're supposed to be the one. I think you are."

"The one for what? What one?"

"Who knows?"

They sat together without talking, listening to the sounds of the night and especially the coyotes calling back and forth. Charlie squeezed his eyes shut and then opened them wide. He looked around at the trees and shadows, at the thing in his hands. At the old man, who was still there beside him. It was not a dream.

"Who are you?" Charlie asked.

"My name, you mean?"

"Does it matter?"

"I don't think so. You wouldn't know it, anyway. It says . . ." The old man halted, looked down and then away before he turned back to Charlie and continued. "I am supposed to know things."

"What things?"

"Good question. About the coyote, things like that."

"Where the hell are you from?"

"Here. I am from here."

"I'm not . . . you are real, aren't you? I'm not imagining all this?" Not if you can ask that, Charlie told himself, you never asked the dead captain that when he came to you in your dreams, did you?

"I think I am real," was the old man's answer.

"I don't know . . ." Charlie said. "You remind me of somebody."

"Who is that?"

"A guy I used to know. He was a policeman, a captain, only . . ."

"What?"

"Only he was dead. I could see him but nobody else could. If he was a ghost or if I was crazy, well . . . let's just say there was some question about the whole thing."

"I remind you of him?"

183

"Yeah, in a way. Except of course, you're real." Charlie reassured himself with his hand on the old Indian's shoulder, his solid, bony shoulder. "Don't get the wrong idea, old man, I'm not crazy. Not anymore, anyway. I just talk this way sometimes when I have a lot on my mind."

"I think you are the one," the Indian said, looking at him.

"Again with that," Charlie yapped. "The one what?"

"Who knows?" the old man shrugged again.

"You're supposed to know things," Charlie reminded him.

"Yes, it's too bad about that."

"Okay, fine. I'm confused. Are you happy?"

"No."

The simple deep finality of that no went through Charlie like a cold hand on his heart and he tried to see the old man better, to look into his eyes in the darkness. But the old man was not there anymore.

A coyote howled mournfully, a little closer than before.

CHAPTER THIRTY-ONE

CHARLIE FLOPPED THE STICK AND RAWHIDE CONTRAP-tion against his leg and looked from side to side, hoping to see or hear the old man going away. He might have convinced himself that any one of the dozens, hundreds of small noises in the dark woods was that, but he did not want to. The old man was simply and instantly gone.

It occurred to Charlie again that he might be dreaming, and he was so tired after the long night before without sleep that he was able to imagine that he was in his bed at the Institute after all, that everything that had happened since he left had only been a dream, some long extended time-warped fantasy. But he shook himself awake and looked around him at the trees and underbrush, at the big house down the hill with all its windows dark, and he knew it would not be that easy.

He blinked his eyes hard a few times and opened them wide.

Something was up, he told himself, something is in the wind tonight. Don't fall asleep at your post, pal. It would have been better if he had someone with him, and he thought of Jade and of Calvin. Of the two, he would have preferred Jade, but he knew she very well might distract him more than sleep. Besides, he did not want her in harm's way, he wanted to protect her, and he was not at all sure that being with him tonight was safe. Calvin, on the other hand, Charlie would not have minded putting at risk. He was still mad at Calvin, but not the way he had been at first.

The old man, the old Indian, Charlie put out of his mind. Okay, he told himself, the guy knows his way around the woods, he comes and goes and I can't keep up with him. Don't get spooked over it. You know a spook when you see one, don't you, Charlie boy?

Satisfied that he was awake, he turned his attention to the questions that had accumulated during his stay at the McKendrick ranch. It was his heartfelt conviction, one of the few he retained, that simple greed was one of the two real motives when it came to murder. Love was the other one, but it did not seem to apply in this case. From his experience as a homicide investigator he had long ago learned to laugh at the horrific monsters and ghouls people invented to scare themselves with. He knew the vilest monster imaginable was nothing more than a blank space upon which we felt safe in projecting the evil within us. And he knew that all the evil in the world was accounted for by greed and love. It was greed this time, he felt sure. Greed for the fortune Poppa McKendrick had kept and husbanded from the land his ancestors took from the Indians. It all traced back to the land, Charlie thought. What was that saying he had heard somewhere, "Behind every great fortune lies a great crime"? He could not remember where he had heard it or about whose fortune it had been said, but he thought there was some truth in it. Whatever McKendrick was worth, in cash, blooded horses, oil or whatever else, it all traced back to the first McKendrick, or the first . . . whoever it was that Momma descended from. They came and they took the land, and that was where it all started. Now someone had lost patience with the process, the inheriting business. They were trying to bump ahead in line, whoever they were, and they wanted it all. They wanted it now, and they would stop at nothing to have it. He could not help thinking that in their way whoever was behind whatever was going on was a throwback to the first of them who took the land from the Indians. Isn't that weird, Charlie asked himself, alone beside his tree in the dark woods. I suppose their great-greats would be proud of them, in a way.

He thought about Jeff and Chip. In that order, and much more of Jeff than Chip. Jeff, who lost his father to a far-off war and his mother to who knew what. Probably run off from this place, or bought off, gone back to her own family and left her son behind. Sons are a primary value to a man . . . and woman, too, for that matter . . . as, how had Chris put it that night in his father's den? As stewards, links between the past and the future. Poor Chris, he really did not figure into his father's scheme of things. A stump on the family tree, or whatever the old man had said. Chip was an asshole, what happens when decent people try to give a kid everything. But Charlie honestly did not think there was enough fiber in the boy of any kind to imagine or concoct a plan that required . . . what murder demands, much less carry it out. He'd join, Charlie thought, he'd go along, if somebody showed him the way. Yeah, Charlie told himself, Chip would be a prime recruit for a lynch mob, especially if he was drunk, but a murderer? Hardly. Jeff, on the other hand, showed a sign or two that Charlie had learned to heed. His way with the horses, his tone with Poppa McKendrick, even just the way he carried himself. Charlie had seen all of it before, and he knew better than to underestimate Jeff. Still . . . Charlie made himself imagine the baby, Bill Junior's baby, asleep in his bed in the room upstairs in the big house down the hill. As if he were the murderer, Charlie imagined how it must have been, easing the door silently open, creeping across the floor to the crib, looking down at the sleeping, helpless face . . . Without meaning to at all, Charlie thought about his own daughter, Elizabeth. Little Bit. What in the world am I doing here, Charlie asked himself. What in the wide, wide . . .

Ta-phooom!

Charlie's head snapped toward the sound, the two-count muffled rolling repercussion he recognized immediately as a gunshot. Off to his right somewhere, behind the outbuildings, between the big house and the lake, someone had fired a gun. A shotgun maybe, Charlie told himself, listening as the reverberations of it rolled across the lake behind him and back again. How far off?

186

The way sounds carry in the lakeside woods at night, it might have been miles away, but Charlie did not think so. Something about it, the pulse of the sound like the waves that lap up the muddy bank of the dark lake, the clear first syllable of the discharge, made him think it was not very far away at all. Charlie pushed himself against the tree, to his feet, and started off toward the sound. At least, he moved away in the direction he decided the shot had come from.

He jogged down the trail toward the house until the underbrush thinned out, then cut to his right at angles to the trail, keeping the bunkhouse's looming dark solidity on his left for a landmark. Beyond the bunkhouse, toward the woods' thinnest arm where the trees and brush thinned out into pasture except for one long finger that ran along the fence row over a low hill away from the house behind the barns and corrals, peering ahead as he went as if he thought he might see something that would make the night shooting all right, that would explain it somehow.

Charlie could almost see beyond the woods, he could almost see into the pasture and the fence row that ran beyond the trees themselves, and was about to stop and convince himself that it was all right, that someone somewhere, a stockman worried about his animals, had only shot at a coyote or some other predator, when he heard it.

At almost the same time he heard another coyote howl, somewhere well beyond him in the direction he was going, out in the thin edge of the woods around the lake, as if to say, "Take care, there's a hunter out tonight."

But this other thing he heard was not the coyote or any other animals that belonged in the woods at night. It was the huff and puff of someone running, the jostle and rustle of something human coming his way. But before he could react, the shadows that splayed themselves before him, that ebbed and flowed and gathered and melted away as he jogged along, yielded up a solid human form and Charlie and the other collided, ran together without either of them able to anticipate it, and with a mingled "Oooomph!" and a muttered curse, they caromed off each other into the groundling shadows.

For two or three heartbeats Charlie lay still, holding his breath so that he could hear everything, his mouth open so that even the ragged in and out of his own lungs, the air drawn up and down his throat, would not distract him. And he did hear, in the silence of his self-suspension, the hurried but purposeful scurrying of malice.

Charlie saw moonlight cool and straight, fastidiously straight, glimmer on what he knew could only be the long barrel of a gun, and part of him noted ironically the effect: the slow-motion, disbelieving special reality by which he knew that he was facing death again. He threw himself as hard as he could across the space that separated him and the scurrying gunman, and felt diagonally across his chest the hard rattling machinery of the gun as he wrapped his arms around the figure and drove with his legs like a football player to overcome the would-be killer and drive him down. And down they went in a heap, the other first beneath him and then twisting free, Charlie clambering to keep his hold and hold himself inside the deadly radius of the gun.

Whump! The sound and shock cojoined to loosen Charlie's grip as the hardwood butt of the gun drove once, twice against his ribs. When he twisted in hopes the next blow would land in a new place, the other shoved loose and Charlie felt him rising to his feet. Looking up in darkness, Charlie could only make out a purposeful mass among the deferential shades of night and underbrush. He lunged to close the distance again and in the sharpened sense of deathness heard the whistling arc of the gun descending. His head exploded with the dullish thud and brilliant sparks of impact as the other swung the butt of his gun down hard at Charlie's head.

Charlie fell back and rolled to one side, with pretensions of doing something more, until the fast-running tide of blackness caught him and tugged him back upon the ground. He forced his eyes wide open, or thought he did, the world tightening above him into smaller and smaller circles of murky light. From somewhere far above him he heard grinding carbon steel and clanking resonant doom, the "rack-rack" of a pump shotgun's forearm being worked to load a round into the chamber. Jesus Christ, he heard himself thinking, a shotgun. There won't be enough left to . . .

188

CHAPTER THIRTY-TWO

THE TREES ABOVE HIM MOANED IN THE DARKLING breeze. Or else it was Charlie who moaned, and opened his eyes to wonder where he was. The left side of his head lay open like a gaping wound, and every creature who scurried through the woods at night had nibbled at his brain. Or maybe not.

Charlie made his left arm retract by willing it to respond. That done with great effort, his hand explored the left side of his face and reported no gaping wound, only a mushy bulbous lump. He tried at first to bend at the waist and lift his head into a sitting position. This hurt dreadfully, and he sank back onto the ground. His mind ran up and down from side to side, wondering, until he suddenly remembered and shot awake with a start, his hands held out in front of his face, to find that the gunman was gone. He wiped his eyes clear of either blood or tears and assured himself there was no shotgun muzzle staring down at him. And then at last he rolled himself to one side and pushed with his elbow to lift his head gingerly. That hurt too, but he held himself that way until the worst of it had passed and then in stages he worked his way up until after what seemed a very long time he was on his feet. Shaky and dizzy, but ambulatory.

Off somewhere he heard voices he could not make out, sounding curious and alarmed. He saw rectangular eyes of light opening upon the mystery of the night, and that was how he figured out where he was, and he made his unsteady way back to the house.

When he had gone more than halfway he heard off to his left a voice he remembered, and turned his head, noting in some part of his mind that it was curious the way his field of vision had been reduced, to see Calvin running toward him.

"Jesus H. Christ, Charlie, are you all right?" Calvin demanded, his voice painfully loud and near.

189

"Probably," Charlie answered. "Don't shout."

"What . . ." Calvin began, still shouting, then lowered his voice. "What happened?"

"I . . . I'm not sure," Charlie answered truthfully.

"What are you doing with that?" Calvin asked, careful to modulate his voice.

"What?" Charlie asked, annoyed.

"This!" Calvin rejoined, taking the shotgun from Charlie's dangling hand. "What are you doing with this?"

Charlie could not remember picking up the gun or how else he might have come into possession of it. He looked down at it, his attention having been drawn by Calvin to it, and wondered at it himself. He put both hands on it and took it back. Curious, he depressed the slide release and worked the forearm back and forth. To his surprise, a loaded shell clanked out and struck him on the chest. Like a dazzled altarboy, Charlie repeated the ritual three or four more times and after one more loaded shell (he could tell by the weight of it, the way it stung his chest and the sound it made when it hit the ground at his feet) the rest of it was futile. The gun was empty after that.

"It works," Charlie mused aloud.

"Right," Calvin agreed. "So what . . ."

"But if it works, if it's not jammed or . . . Then why didn't he . . ."

"What?"

"I don't understand why he didn't go ahead and kill me. The gun didn't jam or . . ."

"Who, Charlie?"

"I don't . . . Where's Poppa?"

"In the house, I guess," Calvin answered, the innocence on his face that a man can only muster when awakened from untroubled sleep.

"Goddamnit!" Charlie roared and bolted toward the house.

He charged the last few yards and up the steps, across the porch and shoved his way past Chris McKendrick, followed closely by Simon Goldman, through the door and kitchen toward the stairs, yelling all the while: "Where's Poppa?" No one answered him, as Chris and Simon stepped aside to let him pass and looked at each other with eyebrows raised.

190

Up the stairs he bounded, screaming and his head roaring. Somewhere deep inside him the question twittered like a dying star, something about the validity of wills unsigned, but Charlie's head was full of pain and fury, and had no room for any of that.

"Come on, come on!" the voices rose up the stairs behind him.

Charlie looked back to see Chris and Simon charging up the stairs behind him, overtaking him. They shoved up toward him together, driving him back against a wall between two doors, both of them clambering for the shotgun. He kicked off the wall against them, breaking their reaching hands free of the gun, and shoved them hard, bringing the gun up hard to work it free and in the process driving the biting edge of the shotgun butt, the pointy lip where it fits against your chest, an inch or two into Chris's sternum, which put him out of it and sent him clambering down the stairs, his hands outspread to catch a banister newel if he could.

"Get off me!" Charlie demanded, his voice reverberating inside his own battered head. "Back off, goddamnit. I know what I'm doing!"

He turned to move down the hall toward Poppa's room, and happened to catch in a corner of his eye a glimpse of Ruth, her face a contortion in which he imagined he saw not only terror but something about her husband. Her face appeared in the crack between her door and the facing, and was gone with a slam and the clattering of her locking the door with a key.

Down the hall, which pitched and yawed only about as much as a boat the size of the kitchen table downstairs would do in the Gulf of Mexico when a storm blew up, Charlie made his way, the shotgun banging off the wall on his left as he reached out to steady himself to keep from falling.

He made the door to Poppa's room and only then remembered that he had in his ritualistic curiosity unloaded the shotgun, which he nevertheless presented in suitably threatening fashion for the benefit of whatever he found on the other side of the door. He was after a struggle finally balanced well enough to raise one foot and kick in the door when, to his surprise, it opened and Poppa McKendrick looked out.

"Charlie?" the old man asked, his eyes traveling from Charlie's bloodied face to the shotgun muzzle leveled at him. "Are you all right?"

Before Charlie could answer, or for that matter decipher from his muddled recollections and premonitions an answer, there was in the hallway to his right the padding of feet and then a clear and calm-voiced notice given:

"Doctor Gants, lower the gun to the floor."

Charlie looked in the direction of the voice and saw Simon Goldman standing in the hallway between the banister where Bill Junior's body had been strung and the door where Charlie a moment before had seen Mrs. Goldman's face. Simon was in a perfectly acceptable version of the kind of shooting stance one sees on TV every evening in prime time when the cop shows are on.

"I don't want to hurt you," Simon cautioned.

Curious thing to say, Charlie thought, as the troublesome remote and detached part of him also noted that the German-made Walther semiautomatic pistol in Simon's hand was a curious choice as well, given the man's background.

"Hold on, everybody hold on, now," Poppa McKendrick ordered, stepping out of his room far enough to shove the barrel of the shotgun Charlie held toward the roof and away from everybody, at the same time putting himself between Simon Goldman and Charlie. "Everybody just hold the hell on!"

Seeing that McKendrick was unharmed and apparently unthreatened, Charlie lost interest in the shotgun and took it with his left hand near the receiver, raising the barrel to the roof so that it no longer endangered or alarmed anyone, meaning to show Simon Goldman that everything was all right.

"Poppa, step back . . ." Goldman began, but said no more after that, being unaccustomed to ordering the old man around.

"Put that thing down," McKendrick ordered Goldman. "And make sure the safety's on, if it has one."

"Poppa . . ." Goldman tried once more.

"Do as I say," the old man insisted. "Put that thing down, Simon. Everything's all right."

Charlie did not know if it registered with Simon Goldman or not, but that was the first time he could remember McKendrick calling his son-in-law by anything but his last name.

"Charlie," McKendrick whistled in honest admiration. "You've got quite a lump on your head there."

192

"I guess so," was all Charlie managed to say.

"There's a first aid kit down in the kitchen. Come on, and we'll see what we can do for it."

"That's all right, I just . . ."

Charlie did not argue very hard with the old man, who insisted that they go downstairs and do something about Charlie's head. Charlie was more interested in Simon Goldman and what he did with the Walther. He was relieved to see that Simon did as McKendrick wished. He first lowered the mean-looking little pistol, then thumbed the safety on and took it into the room he shared with his wife. Goldman did not come out, and Charlie wondered about that, but let himself be led down the stairs by old McKendrick. On the way, they collected the inadvertently wounded Chris McKendrick and the three of them, Charlie, Chris, and the old man, ended up seated at the kitchen table, where they were joined by Calvin, who had followed Charlie into the house at a safe enough distance that he had fallen in step behind Simon and Chris as they had charged up the stairs. He had taken Chris's tumble down the stairs to mean that he was most needed down there and had not ventured any further. He already had the first aid kit out trying to do something for Chris when Charlie and old man McKendrick came down.

They did all the first aid they knew to do on the ones that needed it, and Charlie apologized profusely to Chris and by his proxy to the absent Simon Goldman, and tried his best to explain what he had run into in the woods outside. After that, there seemed nothing else to do except that Poppa McKendrick break out a bottle of his whiskey, and they drank to each other's health. Charlie was relieved that McKendrick was safe, amazed that he himself was still alive; if Calvin took note that this was the first time in centuries that a black man was invited to drink in the McKendrick house, his appreciation of the bourbon itself precluded any exposition.

Before the bottle was uncapped, though, Charlie insisted on a head count. Leaving the recuperating Chris downstairs with the sympathetic Calvin, he and Poppa McKendrick checked downstairs and upstairs, the latter involving a room-to-room knocking and talking exercise that left Charlie exhausted. The Goldmans were accounted for, and Charlie and Poppa found Jade's room empty, but accounted for that in short order when they knocked at Samantha Cartwright's door.

193

Sam opened the door at the first knock and from the hall Charlie and Poppa looked past her into her room and saw Jade perched on the side of the bed.

"Is everyone okay?" Sam asked.

"Fine," Charlie answered before Poppa could say anything.

"We heard some commotion," Sam said, looking at Charlie.

"Yeah, a little uproar," Poppa admitted. "You girls doing all right?"

"Fine," Jade answered from her perch on the bed.

"It didn't sound like the kind of brouhaha women would get into," Sam offered, looking pointedly at Charlie.

"You kids bunking together tonight?" Charlie asked.

"In case you're afraid of the dark, Charlie," Sam shot back. "If you'd like to sleep in the house, I'm sure Jade wouldn't mind if you took her room."

"Just asking," Charlie snapped, not failing to notice how Jade giggled at that. "Night."

"Good night, Charlie." Sam smiled. As Charlie and Poppa turned to go, Sam snagged his sleeve and drew him near to whisper: "You know I'm here if you need me, Charlie."

"Fuck you," Charlie whispered, smiling tenderly.

They made the rounds, Charlie and Poppa, and concluded that, surprising only to Charlie, who despite his exhausted condition imagined that he had kept a close watch on things, Jeff and Chip were missing but that everyone else was accounted for. Poppa did not seem upset that his grandsons were out and about. He said that despite his advanced age and subsequent conservatism he could still remember the call of the wild. Poppa led Charlie back to the kitchen and companionship.

Charlie and Poppa and Calvin and Chris drank, first in nothing more than relief that no more damage had been done, and then in earnest that Charlie had come so close and survived some death-dealing scrap he could not describe to suit any of the rest of them, and finally to the warm and ebullient sense of goodwill that comes from the bottle itself on a dark night after trouble.

They finished their own capacity for goodwill and thanksgiving before they finished the bottle, and Poppa replaced the cap with the announcement that they all should go to bed.

All but Charlie agreed, and Calvin pleaded that Charlie belonged in bed in the bunkhouse until he awoke of his own free will.

"Go ahead," Charlie insisted. "Y'all go on to bed. But I'm telling you, Poppa's the logical one, the next target, and I'm going to keep an eye on him."

"The hell you are," Calvin put in. "You can't keep both eyes open. Look at you."

"Whatever." Charlie refused to submit. "I'll hunker down in the hall by his door, if I have to."

"Okay, okay," McKendrick himself put in. "I'll round up some blankets and you can sleep in the damned old hall, if that's all that'll do you."

"Done." Charlie smiled like a survivor.

"And I suppose you think you'll be up till morning," Calvin said.

"If I can, I will," Charlie answered.

"'If I can, I will,'" Calvin mimicked him. "If you had any goddamned sense, you'da come got me tonight, and you wouldn't'a had to go one on one with some dude with a shotgun. All right, Charles, you win. You and me, we'll make a nest outside the old man's . . . Mister McKendrick's door, and you and me'll guard him till daylight. How's that?"

"Whatever," Charlie said, feeling he should not encourage Calvin to risk it.

"Fine," Calvin retorted. "You're welcome."

And that was what they did, Poppa and Charlie and Calvin arranging blankets Momma dug out of some closet deep inside the room she shared with Poppa, half a dozen hand-made blankets and patchwork quilts so the two of them would be warm.

From the crack of his closing door, Poppa whispered to Charlie, "Just be careful with that damned shotgun, will you, Charlie?"

"Don't worry," Charlie encouraged him. "It's not loaded."

"It ain't? Then what the devil good is it?" McKendrick demanded. "Go downstairs and look in the drawers under the gun rack in my den. That's one of my guns and there's shells aplenty for it."

"That's all right," Charlie assured him. "Good night."

Charlie, like most policemen who have been around long enough to know, believed absolutely in the omnipotent totem of "rack-rack."

Calvin began a stream of conversation as soon as McKendrick's door snugged closed, and kept it up as if his own voice were a totem in itself to ward off not only evil spirits but the propensity of the night to produce a threat, until after half an hour or so Charlie noted first the slurring, staggering rhythm of his speech and then the lapses. And then there was silence in the corridor except that Calvin snored.

Charlie listened for a time to the wordless incessant murmur from behind the door where Sam and Jade, he knew, discussed him. Dissected him. And then even that fell into silence. At last Charlie was alone in the hall and the soon to be ended night.

And that was when his dream began.

CHAPTER THIRTY-THREE

THE OLD MAN LOWERED HIMSELF INTO A SQUAT BESIDE Charlie and nodded at him.

Charlie knew at once that he was dreaming this time and he made himself wake up. Except that it did not work, he tried to wake up and dreamed that he did, but could not really break through the warm close fog of sleep that lay over him.

The old man was talking to Charlie, but in an odd way. Charlie understood what he was saying without actually hearing his voice somehow. The old man was telling him about a coyote.

"Coyote was the clever one," the old man told him. "In the first place, when the people first came up out of the ground to live in the world and before they went off in different ways and made all the different tribes, death was not like it is now. When you died, your spirit left, but then the people all would come together in the medicine lodge and pray your spirit back. Nobody stayed dead that way. The trouble was, the place got crowded because nobody stayed dead and babies

196

came. There was not enough game for everybody to eat and we had not learned to plant seeds for food at that time. So one time when somebody died, Coyote went into the medicine lodge with the others to pray the dead one back. Coyote stayed close to the door of the lodge, though, and when he heard the spirit coming he shut the door and did not let the spirit in. Ever since, people stay dead."

"Leave me alone," Charlie said.

"It is said that this is why Coyote lives the way he does now, always hiding and running, looking over his shoulder. This is why he talks at night, howling at the spirits."

"Who cares?" Charlie demanded, trying to make himself wake up.

"And that is why our spirits do not come back to us. Now they go far away, up into the sky at night. When a spirit gets to the right place then he turns around and looks down on the people. We see them, all the spirits, and we call them stars."

"Why are you telling me all this?"

"I thought you might be interested."

"I'm not."

"That's funny," the old man said. "I didn't think I would be mistaken about this."

The old man sat thinking for a while and Charlie relaxed. It's only a dream, he told himself. He would be awake soon and probably would not remember any of this. It was all right as long as the old man did not talk.

"But if you die before you are ready, then you cannot find your way up into the sky."

"I told you I'm not . . ."

"I thought I would tell you some more and maybe you will change your mind."

"No, I . . ."

"Take me for instance. I was the shaman for my people, the keeper of our legends and our medicine. When I died, I had not finished passing all this on to the young man who was going to take my place. After that, the white people took our land and our people were sent away. They were sent into a strange place and they did not have the medicine to show them who they were. They were lost after that."

"You're a ghost, right?" Charlie asked.

"I suppose so."

"Terrific. Here we go again."

"What do you mean?"

"I've done this before. Dreamed about a ghost before."

"That explains it, I guess. I knew there was something about you."

"Yeah, and I wound up in a nuthouse over it. People said I was crazy."

"They didn't understand."

"Yes, they did," Charlie said. "They were right, I was crazy. But I'm not anymore, and I don't believe in ghosts."

"A trapped fish must swim deeper to be free again," the old man intoned solemnly.

"What the hell is that supposed to mean?"

"Guess you don't know much about fish traps. Once a fish is in the trap, if he tries to fight it, he is done for. If he goes the way the trap lets him go, deeper, he can get out."

"Meaning?"

"Meaning you shouldn't fight me so hard. Listen to me, and stop trying to shut me out. Maybe you can get out of your trap that way."

"Wake up, Charlie. Jesus . . ." Charlie said, trying to wake himself up and end the dream.

"It is a funny thing if you think about it," the old man went on. "I have been waiting a long time to go up into the sky where I belong, but it never happens. Every night I hope maybe this time I will find my way, but . . ."

"So what do you have to do?" Charlie asked, having decided to humor the old man in the hope he would go away. "How do you get things straightened out?"

"Don't know," the old man admitted. "That's the funny part."

"Give me a break," Charlie muttered. "What kind of a ghost are you, anyway?"

"Don't know."

"Well you're sure as hell not like the other one. He knew what he wanted and he wouldn't leave me alone until he got it. He didn't give me a moment's peace until we solved his murder. How the hell am I supposed to get rid of you if you don't even know what you need?"

198

"That's a good question," the old man said, nodding. He did not have an answer, he just nodded.

I'm making this whole thing up, Charlie told himself. It was the lack of sleep, the run-in with the gunman, and probably seeing Sam again. It's all caught up with me, and I'm making this guy up.

"What about the curse?" Charlie asked the old man.

"What?"

"The curse you put on this place, this family. Don't you have to see the curse come true or something, isn't that what you're waiting for?"

"I didn't put a curse on anybody. Why would I?"

"Because they killed you and stole your people's land, for god's sake."

"No. They brought their curse with them. It is in their blood."

"You've lost me."

"It is in their blood to take things, to gather up things. When there comes an end to the things they can take, they kill each other over the things they have. That is their curse."

Charlie thought about that and remembered Poppa McKendrick's ideas about his family, the way he talked about children and grandchildren as if they were breeding stock. He wondered if generations of breeding for the traits McKendrick prized might not produce here and there a mutant capable of murder.

"Maybe I was wrong about you," the old man admitted. "Talking to you does not seem to be helping."

"I know," Charlie agreed. Then, seeing the sad look on the old man's face, he added, "I'm sorry."

"Me too. I am going now."

"Good."

"I will give you a gift."

"That's not necessary, just . . ."

But the old man was gone again, as suddenly as he had disappeared from Charlie's side in the dark woods. Charlie dreamed that he looked about for the old man's gift but found nothing and slipped back into dreamless sleep.

After only a heartbeat's dark and untroubled rest, Charlie opened his eyes and looked down at himself sleeping on the floor outside McKendrick's room. Feeling tight and warm as he imagined a balloon

199

would feel, he rose effortlessly above himself until the ceiling was at his back and he expected to bump against it the way a balloon would. But he did not, he only went farther up, until he was free in the night sky and the roof of the big house fell away beneath him. He could see the dark shimmering lake beyond the trees and like a darting swift he suddenly was there, skimming over the low waves with their burden of moonlight and buried secrets.

Up again, straight up into the dark and starry sky he shot, unimaginably fast and effortlessly until the moon looked close enough to touch. Then over and down again, screaming toward the lake below. His mind raced ahead and memories scudded past like clouds and then impossibly it was not night any more and he found himself beneath a gray and somber cloud that stretched as far as he could see and he knew where he was. Below him he saw the blue roof and white steeple of a little country church beside a road and the cemetery behind the church, the cars parked and the two dozen mourners huddled around a new grave, their hats pulled down and their shoulders set against the cold drizzling rain. He circled lower and lower, until he could make them out. His mother was there, his aunts and uncles, and there beside the casket listening as the preacher assured them all that Charlie's father had gone to heaven he saw himself. He circled lazily, enthralled at the scene, and looked down at himself standing there, holding his daughter's hand and now looking up into the sky. He had become the circling hawk he remembered watching at his father's funeral.

Back up he climbed and through the low and doleful cloud into the night sky beyond and driven by the wings of his mind into another night then down low to skim over the tops of the trees around the McKendricks's cemetery on the low hill, tipping over onto one wing to dodge the big tree where the shaman lay buried and circling to find the shore of the lake. He looked down at the dark water and it was alive with the pulse and splash of a swimmer. He circled, watching, as the swimmer with the glimmering moonlit hair made her way toward shore. Her strokes were strong and rhythmical. Charlie came to rest upon a tree branch above the place where the blond girl emerged from the water and strode toward the shore. When she stopped suddenly and looked down at her leg, Charlie knew what that meant, and he tried to do something, but could not. He could only watch. The girl looked around at the night and said something to the big tree that loomed above the others not far away as if it too were watching. And then, with a violent yank, she fell back and could not scream because the water rushed into her mouth.

Down from the tree Charlie came without understanding how and into the water, beneath the surface where he could see the girl struggling and being dragged farther and farther away from shore toward the deep tree-lined channel in the middle of the lake. Charlie saw everything, but could do nothing to help her and she died.

When he had seen it all, he rose again and followed his mind inside the big house to another night and watched the baby die. He saw and could not save Bill Junior after that, and then he knew almost everything, for all the good it did. He could not change anything.

It was almost over, he sensed, night was ending and with it the old man's gift. He had to go back now, but before he did he hurried to the place out behind the house and the time hours before when he had fought the gunman. From there he hurried back to the place and time where the shot was fired, the shot he had heard from his hiding place, and then his time was up and he barely made it back before McKendrick's door opened and he woke up.

CHAPTER THIRTY-FOUR ▮

"MORNING, CHARLIE," McKendrick greeted him, looking down at him through his open door. "Mind if I . . ."

But Charlie did not answer. He pushed himself to his feet and ran along the hall and down the stairs, stopping halfway down to yell back at McKendrick to call the sheriff's office and tell them to send an ambulance quick. Then he was gone, out through the kitchen and across the back porch. McKendrick watched him go and stood wondering, not understanding what he meant.

"What the hell . . ." McKendrick mumbled.

Calvin stirred, awakened by the noise Charlie made.

"What's up?" he asked McKendrick, one eye open.

"What?" McKendrick asked in return, looking down at Calvin as if he could not remember why he was there. Calvin was the first black man ever to have slept in the McKendrick house, and the old man had the notion that too much was happening too fast. "Damned if I know," he answered finally. "Charlie just jumped up and ran out of here hollering for me to call the sheriff for an ambulance."

"Why?"

McKendrick shrugged his shoulders and held his hands out wide to say he had no idea.

Calvin pulled himself stiffly into a sitting position and yawned himself awake.

"Did I miss something?" he asked McKendrick.

"If you did, I did," the old man answered. "I opened my door and woke him up and he jumped up and tore out of here."

"Might have had a nightmare," Calvin thought aloud, and did not say anything more about it, wondering if Charlie might have started having those dreams again. "Go ahead and call the sheriff, I'll go see what's up."

"Sheriff's due out here this morning anyway," McKendrick reminded him.

"What time is it?" Calvin asked.

"Midmorning."

"Like hell," Calvin yawned again. "The sun's not even up good yet."

"Six o'clock," McKendrick insisted. "Halfway between midnight and noon."

"Okay," Calvin relented. "If Charlie said we need an ambulance, go ahead and call for one. We can disregard it if . . ."

Calvin did not finish his thought as he pushed himself to his feet with sounds of his joints popping. He had been about to say they could disregard the ambulance if it turned out that they did not need it because all that had happened was that Charlie had gone crazy again.

"All right, I guess," McKendrick said, then muttered something more as he turned and went back into his room toward the telephone on his night table.

Calvin heard Mrs. McKendrick asking her husband what was going on and as he started down the hall toward the stairs he realized his left leg was asleep because he had slept with it curled under him somehow. He shook the leg and rubbed it with both hands and then stopped in front of the door of the room McKendrick had assigned to Samantha Cartwright. He was trying to decide whether he should wake her or not when he turned at the sound of another door opening to find Sam and Jade looking out through the open door of Jade's room.

"Good morning," Calvin greeted them.

"What's all the noise about?" Jade asked.

"Not sure," Calvin answered her, looking at Sam with one eyebrow cocked to make sure she understood what he was afraid of. "Charlie woke up hollering about an ambulance and ran out of the house. I'm on my way to see what it's about now."

"Shit," Sam muttered. "Did he have . . ."

"A nightmare maybe," Calvin cut in. "Or could be he heard something . . ."

"Right." Sam shook her head and ran a hand through her hair. She pulled her robe on as she stepped out into the hall and made her way toward her own room. "I'll get dressed and be right down."

"Okay," Calvin said.

"I asked her to bunk in with me," Jade explained to Calvin, who did not care one way or the other. "I didn't feel like being by myself."

Calvin smiled and nodded to show her he understood or did not care or whatever, and then hobbled down the stairs on his tingling leg, thinking it would be too much to ask that there would be a pot of coffee on in the kitchen.

There was no coffee made and nothing handy to eat, so Calvin pushed on through the kitchen and out the back into the yard, where he came up short and wondered where Charlie had gone.

"Charlie!" he called out. "Where are you, man?"

No answer at first, then he heard Charlie calling and set out toward his voice, into the woods behind the bunkhouse. He had gone far enough that he could not be seen from the house and was thinking he might ought to wait for Sam to catch up when he heard a noise in the underbrush and Charlie appeared.

"We got an ambulance coming?" Charlie asked, breathing hard.

"Yeah, McKendrick called the sheriff. What's up, man?"

"Come here," Charlie answered, turning to lead Calvin deeper into the woods, along a narrow path that ran off at an angle from the way Calvin had come, away from the house and off to his left, toward the far end of the lake. "I don't think it's any use . . ."

Calvin did not ask what Charlie meant by that because he was busy following him and did not think Charlie could hear him anyway and then suddenly he saw the fence appear, a four-strand barbed wire job that ran along a straight line of creosoted posts and separated the pasture from the woods along the lake. Coming alongside Charlie, who had stopped in the trail, he saw what was left of Chip Goldman.

The boy lay sprawled on the ground on the near side of the fence, his arms thrown up beside his ruined head. His feet were near the fence, one hunting boot lying atop the bottom strand of wire. His head lay in the direction of the house. He was on his back.

"J-e-e-e-zus," Calvin whispered.

Charlie pointed toward the fence and then Calvin saw the shotgun. It was leaning against the second strand of wire from the top, its muzzle angled up, its butt resting on the ground on the other side of the fence.

"He must have crossed the fence and then tried to pull the gun through after him. Stupid kid, he had it loaded and the safety off, and he snagged the trigger on the barbed wire, right?"

"Maybe," Charlie said, looking at the shotgun on the fence. "Where's the other gun?"

"Where you left it, leaning against the wall by Poppa's door."

"Okay, here's what you do. Go back to the house. Tell Poppa to call the sheriff back, reduce the ambulance to code one and get word to the sheriff what we have here. Then . . ." Charlie put his hand on Calvin's arm and gripped it hard to make sure he was listening. "Then you go and stand over that shotgun. Don't let anybody touch it. When the sheriff comes, make sure he gets it and that he treats it like evidence, you understand?"

Calvin understood, but he was mesmerized by the body. He held up one hand to block his view of the boy's face, where the shotgun pellets had shredded the flesh into an oozing pulp, and was struck by the silly idea that the rest of him was still okay. From the neck down, the kid did not appear to have a scratch on him. For whatever good that does, he thought.

204

"Understand?" Charlie repeated.

"Yeah, reduce the ambulance to code one and guard the gun. I got it."

"Get going."

"Right." Calvin turned to go, still fascinated and horrified by the sight of the corpse. He started back up the trail toward the house, then stopped and turned back to Charlie. "Only . . ."

"What?"

"How did you know about this?"

"What difference does it make?"

"None, Charlie. Except that you woke up from a sound sleep knowing this . . . was out here. I don't understand . . ."

"Neither do I. Now get a move on, will you?"

"Right."

Calvin ran back along the trail and when he heard Samantha calling him he did not bother to answer her because he was almost clear of the brush and she saw him when he came out into the yard.

"Where is he?" she asked.

"Through there, there's a trail not far in, follow it to your left, you can't miss him," Calvin rattled, his breath ragged with the running and with the possibilities he did not want to think about. He caught Sam's arm as she turned to go and added, "It's Chip, the Goldmans' kid. He got his head blown off. You might . . ."

"Where are you going?"

"Charlie's orders."

"Okay," Sam answered him as she pulled away and disappeared into the underbrush.

Calvin went inside and found the house alive with questions and everyone sleepy-eyed and upset.

"What's going on out there?" Simon Goldman demanded of Calvin as he came in the door.

"You folks just take it easy and stay in the house until the sheriff comes," Calvin answered, glad at least that it was not his job to tell the man about his son.

"But what's all the ruckus about?" Goldman insisted.

"Put on a pot of coffee, why don't you?" Calvin told him. "We'll all get a chance to ask questions in a little while."

Nothing Calvin said satisfied Goldman, but there was nothing he could do about that, and he pushed past the man and up the stairs. At the landing he met Mrs. Goldman coming out of Chip's room.

"He's not in there," she said to Calvin. "Is Chip downstairs?"

"No, ma'am."

"Well, where is he then, do you know?"

"No, ma'am," Calvin lied.

Chris joined them on the landing to announce that Jeff was gone too and to ask what was going on. Calvin said he did not know and eased past them toward Poppa's room. Behind him he heard Ruth Goldman asking Chris or anyone in earshot if her son Chip was in some kind of trouble and Chris assuring her that everything was all right.

The gun was still there, leaning against the wall beside Poppa's door, and Calvin wished he could take it and leave the house to get away from the Goldmans and the questions, but he was not sure that was what Charlie had meant for him to do. He had said to keep an eye on it and tell the sheriff to treat it like evidence. He figured that meant it should not be moved, as nutty as that sounded, since Charlie had lugged it around the night before.

Poppa's door opened and McKendrick appeared, dressed but unshaven. Beyond him Calvin saw Mrs. McKendrick pulling on a robe.

"What is it?" Poppa asked.

"Charlie said to call the sheriff back, tell them to reduce the ambulance to code one and tell them . . ."

"What?"

"Jesus, man, I hate this," Calvin muttered.

"Spit it out, boy."

The boy thing registered, but Calvin had more on his mind.

"Chip is dead," he said artlessly.

"What? What are you saying?"

"Chip's dead."

"What are you talking about? How?"

"Gunshot. Charlie found him out back, by the fence."

The old man was still fighting it, not wanting to understand what Calvin had told him, and Calvin knew how that was. He had seen it before, and he knew what came next. Mrs. McKendrick would scream like a bomb falling and then the whole house would go hysterical around him.

"S-s-s-h, Mister McKendrick." Calvin motioned with an upraised palm to the old man, his other hand reaching out to hold McKendrick close so they would not be overheard. "Let's don't get everybody upset just yet, okay? I think we probably need to keep everyone inside the house until the sheriff gets here."

"Wha . . . oh, yeah, I guess you're right." Poppa nodded, his eyes wide and his jaw slack.

"What is it, Poppa?" Mrs. McKendrick asked, shuffling toward them in her slippers and a pink robe with roses down the lapels. "What's wrong?"

"We . . . we're not sure just yet, sugar. Having a little trouble locating the boys."

"What?"

"Don't upset yourself, Momma," McKendrick said soothingly, recovering himself a little. He put his arm around her shoulders. "Why don't you go down and get breakfast started, seeing as Molly's running late coming in. There you go."

The old man sent his wife padding off down the hall toward the stairs with a gentle push and turned back to Calvin.

"What was that you said about the ambulance?"

"Charlie said reduce it to code one."

"I don't . . ."

"It means tell them there's no hurry."

CHAPTER THIRTY-FIVE

WHATEVER CODE THEY RAN, it was not long before the sheriff's people were on the scene. A marked unit arrived first, with two young deputies who took charge of things as soon as they could get anything out of the Goldmans and the others in the house. Everything was confusion and a lot of questions until finally Calvin called down from his post at the shotgun to tell one of the deputies what was going on. The deputy was no more eager than Calvin to break the news to Chip's parents, and he left his junior partner with Calvin and followed Calvin's directions to the body, where he found Charlie and Samantha arguing.

"Then please tell me how in the hell you knew . . ." the deputy heard Sam scream before he came into view of the body.

"It doesn't matter!" Charlie rejoined.

"The hell it doesn't! Why won't you tell me, then?"

"I don't need this crap, Sam. This is not the time . . ."

"It is the time, Charlie. Don't forget . . ."

They stopped arguing when they saw the deputy.

"Morning, officer," Charlie said, turning toward the lawman.

"Morning," the deputy answered, looking from Charlie to Sam and back, his right hand hanging loose alongside his holstered revolver, just in case. "What do we have here?"

Charlie stepped aside and pointed at the body.

"Oh," the deputy said. "What do you know about it?"

"Just what you see," Charlie said, raising both hands as if to say help yourself.

The deputy, a lanky dark-haired man with nervous eyes, moved around Charlie and stood beside the body, looking at everything, the wounds, the gun, the whole thing.

"Are you the one who called?" he asked Charlie.

"I asked Mister McKendrick to call."

"It came out at first as a code three ambulance call."

"Right."

"You found him . . . like this, and you didn't know he was dead already?"

"I . . . called before I found him," Charlie said, thinking it had not taken long for them to get to the sixty-four-thousand-dollar question.

"I don't understand," the deputy said, looking from Charlie to Sam.

"Neither do I," Sam muttered.

"Officer, I don't want to be rude or uncooperative . . ." Charlie began.

"Good," said the deputy.

208

". . . but if it's all right with you, I'd like to wait for the sheriff."

"Oh?"

"Yeah. It's kind of a long story, and I'd rather just tell it once."

"Oh. Shame it doesn't work that way."

"No?"

"Not exactly. The way it works is you tell it to me while it's fresh on your mind. Later you tell it to the sheriff. And probably a couple more times after that. Then you put it in writing and you sign it."

"Yeah, I know . . ."

"That way, we make sure you don't leave anything out."

"That way, you catch me if I screw up and forget to tell it the same way every time. I understand that . . ."

"I tell you what, while we're chatting, you want to just put your hands on top of your head and turn slowly until I tell you to stop?"

"Look . . ." Charlie began.

"I asked you nice," the deputy said.

"Okay, okay," Charlie grumbled, following the deputy's instructions until he had been frisked, pretty thoroughly and very carefully. He felt it when the deputy tugged something out of his hip pocket, but it did not register at first what it was.

"Would you like to tell me what this is?" the deputy asked, holding up the two sticks bound together at one end with rawhide that the old Indian had given him.

"Yeah, that's part of the story, too. I forgot I had that on me."

"Okay. You don't mind if I hang on to this for the time being, do you?" the deputy asked.

"Not at all. I want you to have it."

"Thank you."

"You're welcome."

"Now," the deputy said when he was through. "How about telling me what you know about this."

"Uh . . . his name is Chip Goldman. He's Mister McKendrick's grandson, his daughter's son. As far as I know, he was last seen around dinnertime yesterday."

"When you say dinnertime," the deputy put in, "do you mean noon or evening?"

"Evening," Charlie said. "Suppertime, I guess you'd say."

"Go on."

"That's it, really. I found him this morning."

"Yeah," the deputy said. "Right after you put in the call for an ambulance."

"Uh-huh."

"You can see how confusing that is, can't you, sir?" the deputy asked. "How you happened to call for an ambulance before you knew anybody needed one."

"Yeah, that's the part of the story I'd rather . . ."

"Officer, I am a psychologist, a therapist," Sam stepped in to announce. "And this man is my client . . ."

"That's a lie," Charlie spat at her.

"Take it easy," the deputy cautioned Charlie. "It'll work better if you two take turns talking."

"My name is Samantha Cartwright. I am on staff at the Branville Institute in Dallas, where Mister Gants here has been a patient for several weeks."

"Inpatient or out?" the deputy asked.

"In," Sam said.

"What kind of commitment?"

"This has nothing to do with anything!" Charlie exploded.

"Take it easy, Mister . . ."

"Gants," Sam said, and then she spelled it for the deputy, who did not take his eyes off Charlie long enough to get out his notebook and write it down.

Charlie heard more cars coming in around the house and he was almost glad the sheriff and the others were coming. This was not working out at all so far. Car doors slammed and he heard voices. The deputy spoke into the handheld radio he wore in a carrier on his belt and gave the others directions to the body.

Sam wanted to tell the deputy everything, but he was through listening. The suits were on the scene now, and he had all the writing he needed to do. The investigator would take it from here. He just kept his eye on Charlie until the others came.

There were two investigators, a couple of middle-aged guys in what Charlie thought of as dress jeans and white dress shirts, no ties. Each of them carried what looked like tackle boxes that Charlie knew were full

210

of crime-scene search equipment and supplies. When they saw the dead boy on the ground, both of them pushed back their straw cowboy hats and made faces. They had a job ahead of them.

The uniformed deputy filled the two investigators in on what he knew, talking softly so that Charlie could not make it all out, and all three of them looked him over pretty carefully. Then one of the investigators said something to the deputy and he asked Charlie and Sam to come with him. He ushered them out of the woods into the backyard of the house and invited Charlie to have a seat in his squad car. In the backseat, behind the cage. Charlie tried to tell the deputy that would not be necessary, that he wanted to talk to the sheriff, but the deputy insisted. Charlie was not surprised when the car door closed behind him to see that he was locked in. There were no handles on the inside of the doors.

Charlie sat in the deputy's car and watched Sam talk to the uniformed deputy, who appeared to be writing everything she said into his notebook. He could not hear her well enough to make it out, but he had a good idea what she was telling him. He heard a screen door slam and looked up toward the house to see Calvin and the other uniformed deputy coming down the steps, Calvin in front. The deputy had the shotgun action open, and was carrying it with two fingers through the trigger guard, so that it hung upside down along his leg and jiggled as he walked.

Calvin saw Charlie in the police car and raised his eyebrows as if to ask what was going on. Charlie shook his head.

The sheriff arrived about that time and let Charlie out of the deputy's car, but not before he and Sam and the deputy had huddled up for a conference that Charlie thought lasted a hell of a long time. As the three of them talked, Sam doing most of the talking, they looked in Charlie's direction from time to time, and Charlie saw Sam nodding her head again and again. Charlie looked at Calvin, who stood leaning against the porch steps unattended, and he was mad at him all over again for dragging Sam into this.

Finally it was Charlie's turn. The sheriff opened the car door and motioned for him to step out. But before he could say anything, one of the investigators came hiking out of the brush with the shotgun that had been leaning on the fence near the body. It had a tag on it now and

211

Charlie thought he could make out dusting powder on it where they had looked for fingerprints. The investigator conferred briefly with the sheriff and then called for the deputy, the junior man, to bring him the other shotgun, the one Charlie had left in the house. The investigator, carrying the gun gingerly the same way the deputy had, turned and went back into the woods, after putting the first shotgun into the trunk of one of the unmarked police cars and making sure the trunk lid was closed tight.

"All right, Mister Gants," the sheriff said upon rejoining Charlie, the deputy and Sam beside the car. "What do you have to say for yourself?"

"For starters, I can imagine what she's been telling you, and I want you to know I am not crazy."

"Meaning I suppose that you think Doctor Cartwright's been telling us you were?"

"Didn't she?"

"What else?"

"Well . . . the thing is, see, the snag here is just that I knew about Chip before I actually went down there and found him. I knew he had been shot, I mean. That's what's got everybody looking at me sideways, right?"

"But you can explain that, can't you?" the sheriff asked.

"Yeah, but I don't think you'll believe me. See . . ."

"Wait a second," the sheriff interrupted him. "Bob, have you Mirandized Mister Gants?"

"No, sir," the deputy answered. "No formal custody or suspicion."

"Then why did you lock me in your car?" Charlie demanded.

"He might have thought you were loony, Gants," the sheriff answered for his deputy. "Doesn't mean he suspected you of killing the boy, necessarily."

"Am I under arrest right now?" Charlie asked.

"Nobody's going to be allowed to leave here until we have statements from them, including you. This little discrepancy of yours, about knowing the boy was shot before you could have known, that's the kind of thing that we like to say engenders suspicion. And that's why I'm going to read you your rights. Anything wrong with that?"

"Probably not, but you needn't bother. I know the drill."

"Of course you do, being an ex-policeman yourself, an ex-homicide investigator at that."

"Terrific," Charlie hissed at Sam. "You told him everything you knew, didn't you?"

"Most of which wasn't news," the sheriff said. "I've been looking into you right along, Gants. And once I got past that Aggie doctor bullshit, you weren't very hard to find out about. You got your name in the paper too many times."

"Okay, fine. I'm glad that's cleared up anyway. Now, I . . . ."

"Not so fast, Gants," the sheriff warned him. "I haven't read you your rights yet. Now you listen . . ."

The sheriff pulled his badge case out of the shirt pocket where the flap with his badge on it hung down outside the pocket. He took a laminated card from inside the case and read Charlie his rights.

Charlie had no choice but to wait for the sheriff to finish and did not pay much attention when still another car drove up. So he was surprised to hear the voice of Lawyer Childress just as the sheriff finished reading the card.

"What in the world's going on here?" the lawyer demanded. "Sheriff, is this some kind of training exercise, or did I just overhear you . . ."

"Morning, Childress," the sheriff smiled at the lawyer. "Gants, I guess you're going to tell me this is a coincidence, your lawyer turning up out of the blue like this."

"He's not my lawyer," Charlie said.

"Not so hasty there, Charlie," Childress put in. "What's going on here?"

Before Charlie or the sheriff could answer, a keening wail went up from inside the big house that sounded like a soul tumbling into hell. Then another, two women joined their long and cutting screams into a chilling chord that caromed off the walls of the house and the woods and carried echoing across the lake beyond.

"I guess Poppa told them," Charlie said.

"Better him than me," the sheriff muttered.

"Told them what?" Childress asked, his eyes wide at the sounds from the house. "Sheriff, what the hell is going on here?"

213

The sheriff told him in a few words about Chip and where things stood.

"I'd better go in and see if I can be of any help," Childress said when the sheriff was through, looking down absently at the briefcase in his hand. "Good lord."

The lawyer started toward the house, then turned back toward Charlie.

"Sheriff," he asked. "May I have a word with Charlie?"

"He can hear you from there," the sheriff said, meaning that he did not want Charlie to go off with the lawyer as he had indicated. "Tell him anything you like."

"I have a right to confer with my client," the lawyer said.

"No you don't. He has a right to a lawyer, you don't have a right to him. You know better than that," the sheriff said.

"What is he charged with?"

"Nothing yet."

"Then why?"

"You want to talk to him or not, Childress?"

"Charlie, I'm not sure it would be proper for me as the attorney for Amber McKendrick and the family to represent you as well, but I am prepared to advise you until you can get a lawyer that it'd probably be best if you didn't say anything."

"Thanks," Charlie said.

The lawyer turned and hurried up the steps into the house, where the women's crying went on unabated.

"So, like I was saying," Charlie began once the lawyer was inside. "The way I knew about Chip's being shot is simple, it just doesn't make any sense . . ."

"You don't aim to follow your lawyer's advice, I take it," the sheriff broke in to make sure they kept the record straight.

"It'd be good advice if I were guilty of anything," Charlie replied. "Now do you want to hear this or not?"

"Go right ahead."

"Okay. Last night I had a dream . . ."

Sam made a sound, like a snort, full of vindication and I-told-you-so, to show she had been right all along. Charlie had had a relapse.

Charlie did not bother to argue with her anymore. He just told the sheriff the whole thing, about the old Indian and his gift, the flying dream that let him come and go in time and everything he saw in his dream. When he had told it all, Charlie ended by saying, "And that's it. I saw Chip in my dream. I saw him shot. And I was so sure it was real when I woke up I told them to call an ambulance. I didn't know he was dead."

"Well, you're right about one thing," the sheriff said. "I don't think much of your story."

"Whatever. It's the only story I've got."

"Uh-huh. Well tell me, Charlie, while you were doing all that flying around backwards and forwards in time and everything, did you happen to see anything of the other boy?"

"What?"

"Jeff McKendrick. We counted heads and he's not accounted for."

"No, I don't know where he is. He slips out sometimes, I know, to pick up girls. I don't . . ."

"If you do know, you might as well tell us, Gants. We're fixing to get up a search as soon as we're done with the scene, and if you can save us the trouble, it wouldn't hurt anything."

"Is his pickup here?" Charlie asked, looking around in the driveway full of cars.

"No," the sheriff answered. "How about it?"

"I don't know anything about him, I told you. He'll probably turn up."

"Probably."

"Never mind about Jeff for now," Charlie said. "What about the rest of it?"

"The murders you saw in your dream, you mean?"

"Yeah. Amber and the baby, neither of them was an accident. And Bill Junior didn't hang himself. They were all murdered."

"Y'all excuse us," the sheriff announced to Samantha and his two deputies, throwing a look toward Calvin who was still leaning on the porch waiting to be questioned to make sure he included everybody. "Bob, y'all take Mister . . ."

"Rakestraw," Calvin volunteered. "Calvin Rakestraw."

"Y'all take Mister Rakestraw into the bunkhouse over there and take his statement."

"Sheriff," Sam began, eager to make sure he understood Charlie's condition. "I want . . ."

"Miss Cartwright. Excuse me, Doctor Cartwright, you are a mental health professional, aren't you?"

"Yes, I'm a psychologist."

"Then I believe you are most needed right at this moment inside there where all that hollering is going on. Would you mind?"

"What? No, of course not."

Sam went inside, looking back at Charlie and the sheriff as she went.

When they were alone in the yard, the sheriff fixed Charlie with a long and steady look before he said anything more. Then he held up the two bound sticks his deputy had taken out of Charlie's hip pocket. He held one stick in his hand and flopped the other back and forth. Charlie waited to see what the other man had in mind.

"Now tell me the rest of it, Charlie."

Chapter Thirty-Six

"THE REST OF IT?" Charlie asked.

"You know, don't you?" The sheriff leaned in close and his eyes drilled into Charlie's. "You know who the killer is."

"Yes, I think I do."

"You saw it in your dream?"

"Not exactly, but I think I've got it worked out."

The sheriff took a minute to think that over, and Charlie did not feel up to trying to explain about the dream anymore. In his dream the murders had been done in darkness, the dark murky water of the lake, the baby's room, downstairs in the dark house at night when the drunk had been hanged. And he had seen the victims best, not the murderer. But he thought he was right about the killer anyway.

"Okay," the sheriff said. "Who?"

"It won't help without any evidence."

"You tell me who it is and we'll get evidence, one way or the other."

"You almost sound like you believe me, Sheriff. Mind telling me why?"

"Prob'ly I just want to. I don't have anything else. Too, there's the business with the two guns . . ."

"The shotguns, yeah," Charlie cut in. "I think I've got that part figured out."

"Sure 'nough?" the sheriff cocked his head.

"I think so. The one you found at the fence I would guess had a spent shell in the chamber but probably hadn't been fired. The other one, the one I took in the house last night had been fired. I unloaded it out in the woods, don't know if y'all found the shells yet or not. And I'm guessing you didn't find any usable prints on either gun, except maybe some of mine on the second gun. Chris and Goldman got hold of it last night trying to get it away from me, they probably just left smudges. Is that about right?"

"About. There were a couple of prints on the second gun. Of course, we haven't had a chance to compare yours yet, but they're probably yours."

"Yeah, that's what I thought."

"You want to be careful, Charlie, you don't talk yourself into engendering some more suspicion on yourself."

"No, it just makes sense if you think about it. Chip's death wasn't supposed to look like an accident. It was supposed to look like a murder disguised as an accident. Clumsily."

"Why?"

"So the real killer could take care of two birds with one stone. Kill Chip and put the rap on somebody else by planting the murder weapon on them, somehow. Only I stumbled along and screwed up the plan. If it had worked, two more heirs would have been eliminated and Poppa wouldn't change his will because the killer had been found out."

"Nice theory."

"Yeah, but . . ."

Charlie and the sheriff turned at the sound of a truck pulling in behind them and saw Jeff McKendrick park and ease himself gingerly out of the cab. He was none too steady on his feet as he made his way between the sheriff's cars in the direction of the back porch.

"Come here, boy," the sheriff called out.

"Yes, sir?" Jeff answereed when he had come close enough that he did not have to raise his voice to be heard. "What's going on here?"

"Where have you been?" the sheriff demanded, ignoring the boy's question.

"Out," was all Jeff said.

"Do better," the sheriff said flatly. "This is serious business."

"I been passed out drunk for a while. Really."

"Whereabouts?" the sheriff asked.

"In my truck."

"Don't piss me off, boy. I've got a lot on my mind." The sheriff was losing patience.

"What's going on here?" Jeff looked worried.

"You answer me first. And cut the bullshit."

"Okay, lighten up. I was, uh . . . up at the boat landing on the lake."

"This lake here?" the sheriff asked, pointing with his thumb at the lake behind the house.

"No, Womack's Lake. Me and a girl . . . You don't need to know her name, do you?"

"Matter of fact, I do. What become of her?"

"To tell you the truth, I ain't sure. I got pretty drunk and must have nodded off. I expect she lit out afoot. She had to get home before her daddy got up to go to work."

"Uh-huh. What about Chip?"

"What about him?"

"He wasn't with you?"

"No. Why, what's happened to Chip?"

"How come he didn't go with you?"

"I don't know. I asked him if he was up for some partying, but he said he had something to do."

"What was that?" the sheriff asked.

"He didn't say," Jeff answered.

"Okay, I tell you what. You go over there to the bunkhouse. There's a couple of deputies in there taking Mister Rakestraw's statement. You tell them I said for them to take yours, too. You got that?"

"Yes, sir. So what's this about?"

"Chip turned up dead this morning."

"How?"

"We're looking into it."

"Goddamn," Jeff muttered, looking at Charlie.

"Go on, boy," the sheriff said. As Jeff walked away, he added, "And don't forget to give the deputy that girl's name, hear?"

Jeff nodded and went into the bunkhouse.

"What do you think?" Charlie asked the sheriff.

"Sounds like something he'd do. You'd think if he was in on a killing he'd made up a better story."

"Yeah, but I'd sure like to know what Chip had to do last night that he thought was more important than . . ."

Charlie stopped when he saw one of the investigators walking toward them. The sheriff turned around to see what he wanted.

"Sheriff, do you want me to print 'em all here or are we going to take 'em back to the office?"

"Go ahead and print Mister Gants here. There's no hurry on the rest of them. We can ask them to give their statements and prints later on, when they've calmed down some."

"Okay." The investigator nodded. "Mister Gants, step over here if you will."

The investigator set his box on the ground beside the police car and took out a printed fingerprint form and a couple of pads in cellophane wrappers. He worked quickly and efficiently and he had a set of prints in a couple of minutes. Then he filled in the spaces on the top of the form, asking Charlie for his date of birth, full name, and address. The address question stumped Charlie, since he had not thought about finding a place to stay since leaving the Institute. He thought about it for a minute and then gave his mother's address in Sulphur Springs. The investigator put everything back in his box.

"How much longer will you need at the scene?" the sheriff asked his man.

"Not long. Here's the JP now."

They turned to watch the car drive in, and the investigator went to meet the Justice of the Peace who would view the body and make a preliminary ruling. As the two of them started back into the woods, the

219

investigator waved at the two attendants who were sitting in the ambulance to come along. They would be bringing the dead boy out soon.

When they were alone again, the sheriff turned to Charlie.

"Who is it?" he asked.

Charlie told him, and explained his reasons. The sheriff listened thoughtfully, then pushed back his hat and whistled softly.

"Damn, man . . ." the sheriff began.

The slamming of the screen door on the back porch interrupted him, with a howling scream that came after and the tumbling thuds of clumsy footsteps down the steps into the yard.

"You sonofabitch!"

It was Simon Goldman, and Charlie turned in time to see the little Walther pistol jump twice in his right hand. The two rounds whistled past Charlie's head as the popping sounds of the shots followed. Charlie and the sheriff jumped away from each other, each of them diving to the ground and rolling. Charlie rolled away from the police car where they had been standing, across an uncovered two or three yards of ground to the protection on one of the other sheriff's cars. Two more pops and Charlie heard the slugs whining off the ground around him.

As Charlie rolled up into a crouch behind the fender of the car, he heard yelling from the house and doors slamming.

"Simon, don't!" someone screamed, and Charlie recognized Ruth Goldman's voice. "For God's sake," she pleaded.

"Yeah, Simon. Listen to her," Charlie yelled. "Think about what you're doing."

"You killed my boy!" Goldman answered, walking toward Charlie with the gun extended at arm's length in front of him.

Charlie backed down the length of the car, and scurried around its front as Goldman reached the rear of the car and pointed his gun down toward the place where Charlie had been.

"Hold it right there, Mister Goldman!" the sheriff warned.

Charlie did not risk raising his head to look, but he heard the sounds of men running toward the gunshots, and the voices of the deputies as they came.

"Goddamnit, Goldman, I'll have to kill you if you don't drop that gun!" the sheriff yelled, and Charlie started to move around the front of

220

the car, looking underneath it for Goldman's feet, trying to see where he was.

"Now!" Goldman whispered, suddenly looming over the hood of the car.

Charlie looked up into the barrel of the automatic, into Goldman's twisted face behind the sights. Charlie raised one arm, started to say something, and then Goldman's head flew back with an oath and a crunch, the pistol jerked upward and fired again, and then Goldman disappeared beneath the fender of the car. Charlie rushed around the car to see Calvin lying atop Goldman, the older man breathless and sobbing on the ground. Charlie saw the pistol lying on the ground and picked it up.

"Calvin?" Charlie said. "What in hell . . . ?"

"Lost my head, Charlie. Won't happen again."

"You . . ."

"Goddamn, man, I nearly shot you," the sheriff swore as he came running up. "Roll over, Rakestraw. I've got him."

Calvin pushed himself away and the sheriff knelt over Goldman and put handcuffs on him.

"Calvin, I don't believe it," Charlie said. "Are you okay?"

"Uh-huh. You?"

"I'm fine, thanks to you."

The two deputies and the investigators converged on them and from the house, now that the shooting was over, the rest of the family boiled out into the yard, everyone talking at once. Ruth tried to throw herself on her husband, but the lawmen kept her away.

Poppa McKendrick found Charlie and Calvin.

"Are you two all right?" he asked.

"Yeah," Charlie assured him. "Did you see what Calvin did?"

"Craziest damned stunt I ever saw," McKendrick said. "He came out of the bunkhouse on a dead run. I bet he leapt twenty foot across there, hit old Goldman square in the back. Never saw anything like it."

"Me either," Charlie agreed. "I owe you one, man."

"Damned sure do," Calvin said. "I don't know what got into me."

"I tell you, the sheriff was about this far from shooting Goldman," McKendrick said, holding up his thumb and index finger just a knife's edge apart. "You saved one of them's life for damned sure."

The yard was full of people, the family members milling around with Momma and Ruth Goldman crying and Jade trying to calm Momma down. Chris had Ruth by her shoulders, struggling to keep her back out of the deputies' way. The sheriff had Goldman put into a squad car and Lawyer Childress took the sheriff by the arm and led him off to one side.

"Sheriff, what do you plan to do with poor old Simon there?" the lawyer asked.

"I plan to put his poor old butt in jail, naturally."

"Oh, come now . . ."

"Attempted murder."

"Sheriff . . ."

"Charlie, you sure you're all right?" the sheriff asked, looking beyond the lawyer.

"Yeah, I'm okay."

"Well, step over here a minute and let me take a look at you anyway," the sheriff insisted. "You know how it is, you can overlook something in the excitement."

"Sheriff, I really must point out . . ." Childress interjected.

"What?" the sheriff demanded.

"It's obvious, the man's son was just found shot to death. Naturally, he thought Charlie here was responsible."

"Naturally?" the sheriff asked.

"Of course. From the house he saw your deputy put Charlie in the squad car, you were interrogating him. Charlie came storming into the house last night minutes after everyone heard a shot fired, carrying a shotgun, blood all over his face. What else was he to think?"

"That we were conducting an investigation, that we were going to handle it, that's what he was supposed to think," the sheriff shot back. "Are you going to stand there and tell me . . ."

". . . that Simon Goldman temporarily lost control of himself due to his emotional condition. He's not responsible for his actions."

"That'll sound good in court, counselor. For now, he's bound for the county jail."

"I'll get a writ," the lawyer said.

"And I'll get a lunacy warrant," the sheriff shot back.

"If that's the way you want it, I'll see you back in town," Childress said as if it were a threat. Then he said a hasty but concerned good-bye to Poppa McKendrick. He was explaining things as best he could to Momma when the sheriff drew Charlie close to him.

"I'm going to try something here, Charlie. Might put you on the spot. Are you game?" the sheriff whispered.

Charlie nodded and the sheriff turned to face the yard full of people. With his hands raised he called for their attention.

"Listen, y'all. Listen." When they all had turned toward him and were quiet, except that Momma and Ruth kept crying, he made an announcement. "This is not the way we normally do these things, but this here is not your normal situation. Now Mister Goldman here just tried to kill Charlie because he thought he knew what happened out here, and I want to set the record straight before anybody else gets hurt."

Charlie stood watching the sheriff and the faces of the people in the yard.

"Chip Goldman was not murdered, he committed suicide. He left a note."

Momma and Ruth fell silent and Poppa looked from the sheriff to Charlie.

"Chip was behind these killings. Bill Junior and the baby. He said that in the note. So, to set the record straight, this business is finished. I don't want anybody trying to take things into their own hands, and that's why I'm telling y'all now. I'm sorry if this is hard, but I don't know how else to do it."

The word suicide ran through what was left of the McKendrick clan and took the edge off them, dulled the voices of the mourning women and left the men silent. The uniformed deputies drove away toward town with Goldman and the sheriff found and conferred with the justice of the peace, who pursed his lips and nodded at whatever the sheriff said. Jade led her mother back inside the house and Ruth let Chris lead her that way. Sam went to Charlie and Calvin to see for herself that neither of them was shot. The justice got in his car and left and not long after that the two attendants appeared carrying the remains of Chip Goldman in a plastic bag on a stretcher between them. When they were out of the tangled brush of the woods, they lowered the stretcher's legs and trundled their load the last few feet to the waiting ambulance. When they had driven out the drive onto the road and the investigators with their boxes repacked were ready to leave, the sheriff stopped to have a word with Charlie.

But before the sheriff could say what he had to say, Childress reappeared from the house, having gone inside with Poppa to confer.

"Sheriff, I hope you'll reconsider filing charges now that the heat of moment . . ."

"Childress, I'm not filing on him because I got excited. He tried to kill a man."

"There's no point in arguing, then."

"Not until we get in front of a judge."

"Fine," Childress almost whispered, his teeth clenched.

"Excuse me," Sam interjected. "Maybe I can be of some help here."

"Oh?" asked the lawyer.

"As an expert witness, to Simon's emotional state."

"Well, I suppose that would help . . ."

"Let me get my purse and I'll ride with you," she said.

"Sam . . ." Charlie reached out to stop her.

"Charlie, I'm sorry the poor man tried to shoot you, but he's no more responsible for his actions than . . ."

Charlie knew what she meant, no more responsible than he was sometimes. He did not say anything more.

"Oh, but listen," Childress said to Sam. "I'm not sure I can bring you back. I'd hoped to get by here early this morning and get on the road. I have a meeting in Dallas this afternoon that would be a nightmare to reschedule. Can you find a way back, do you think?"

"Calvin can take her and bring her back," Charlie offered. "You wouldn't mind, would you?"

"Mind leaving this place? Not much." Calvin smiled.

"I could drive myself, Charlie," Sam said.

"It's no trouble," Calvin insisted, "I could use a little time off."

"All right, then, " she agreed. "I'll just be a minute."

When the sheriff and Childress had gone to their cars and Sam into the house, Charlie walked Calvin to his Mercury and looked over his shoulder to make sure there was no one to overhear what he said.

224

"Calvin," he said. "Whatever you do, don't bring Sam back here tonight."

"Huh?"

"I mean it. Both of you stay in town tonight. I don't care how you do it, just do it."

Calvin would have liked to ask a few questions, but Sam came out of the house all ready to go.

Charlie stood in the emptying yard and watched Childress and Calvin drive away. The sheriff was the last to leave.

"Be careful now, you hear?" the sheriff called to Charlie as he pulled away.

Charlie waved and watched them leave, then turned to go into the house. He stopped on the porch at the sound of thunder rumbling in the distance and looked up at the sky. Dark clouds were rolling in over the lake and he saw a flicker of lightning.

CHAPTER THIRTY-SEVEN

CHARLIE THOUGHT THE HOUSE SEEMED LIKE A FU-neral home as he listened to his footsteps on the kitchen floor. No one was about downstairs and there was the awkward hush of mourning in the place. He guessed that Momma and Ruth had been taken to their rooms, that Poppa and Chris and Jade were seeing to them, and he wondered if Poppa would mind if he got into the whiskey. He decided he would risk it.

In the den he found the bottle they had not quite finished the night before and poured what was left into a heavy glass. He tugged the curtain open on the window behind the couch and looked out at the sky above the lake.

"Help yourself," Poppa said as he stepped inside the door.

"Hope you don't mind," Charlie apologized as he turned to face the old man.

"I don't. Had the same idea myself."

McKendrick went to the bar and broke the seal on a fresh bottle, made himself a drink like Charlie's, undiluted. Charlie waited to see what the old man would say.

"Mighty early in the day to be drinking the hard stuff," the old man said without expression on his face or in his voice.

"Not if you've been up all night," Charlie offered.

"You've been up most of two nights, haven't you?"

"Yeah."

"Well, I guess you can get some sleep now," Poppa said without looking at Charlie, as he slumped into a chair.

"I guess."

"You got anything to say to me, Charlie?"

"Like what?"

"I don't know. Something that'd make it all make sense." He wiped his eyes with a hand and drank his whiskey. "I . . . don't know."

"How's Momma doing?" Charlie asked, not wanting to lie to the old man.

"She's doing. I gave her her medicine. The doctor said he'll be out in a little bit."

"Medicine?" Charlie asked.

"Heart."

"How bad?"

"It ain't killed her yet," the old man said.

"I'm sorry."

"Me too."

"That's why you were so sure you'd outlive her the other night when you were talking about the will."

"I sure need to. I hate to think about that old woman left to her kids. What's left of them."

"You look healthy enough. You'll probably outlive the bunch of them."

"Shows all you know."

"What do you mean?" Charlie asked.

"Cancer."

"Goddamnit."

226

"That's what I said."

"Isn't there anything they can do?"

"Some," the old man said. "But I don't aim for them to. I'll play out my string here."

"But . . ."

"Six months here beats a year in a hospital in Houston or somewhere."

"I . . . I don't know what to say."

"Nothing to say, Charlie. That's just how it is."

"Who knows about this?" Charlie asked.

"None of the kids. Just the doctor and Childress."

They sat and drank for a while, each lost in his thoughts.

"The worst of it . . ." McKendrick began, as if he had been thinking how to make Charlie understand something important. "Is that it all ends with me. I wouldn't mind so much if . . . there was somebody to keep it going."

"There's Jeff," Charlie said.

"It'd be nice to think so. But you and I both know he . . . he's not the kind to pass anything on. He'll just use it all up and there's the end of it."

"People change . . ."

"The hell they do," the old man said with a bitter chuckle as he finished his drink.

"What about Jade?" Charlie asked.

"Jade." The old man poured himself another drink and offered to do the same for Charlie, who stopped him before he refilled the glass completely. "There's a case for you. Strange girl."

"I guess I haven't seen it," Charlie said, remembering the things she had told him, how she had changed from night to morning.

"No, she's been on pretty good behavior lately. Don't know what she was up to when we called her home for Amber's funeral. She's got her own world off there somewhere, overseas."

"Yeah."

"Did I hear my name?" Jade asked, stepping into the room.

"Might have," Poppa said. "Join us?"

"Sure," Jade answered, with a look at Charlie, as if she was surprised at the invitation. She made a drink, a moderate one with ice

227

and water to soften the blow of the whiskey, and then settled on the couch between the two men in the chairs. "Am I interrupting anything?"

"No, sugar," McKendrick said sadly. "Just trying to figure out what it all means."

"I gave up on that a long time ago," she said, sounding wistful.

"Did you get Ruth to bed?" Charlie asked.

"Yes. I gave her one of my Valiums. She's sleeping."

"One of yours?" Charlie asked.

"Yes. I'm high-strung." She smiled back.

"I didn't know that was a medical condition," Charlie said.

"Depends on your doctor," she said, still smiling.

"Doctors," McKendrick snorted.

"Here you all are," Chris said, sticking his head through the door. "May I join you?"

"Help yourself," McKendrick said with a wave of his hand.

Charlie thought the old man was slurring his words after a couple of drinks. They were strong drinks, but Charlie wondered if he had not taken some medicine, too.

Chris declined McKendrick's offer of whiskey but found a bottle of white wine in the little refrigerator and poured himself a glass of that.

They sat in the den with the curtains open on the window and consoled each other in silence, each drinking and lost in thought, and Charlie watched through the window as the storm moved in.

CHAPTER THIRTY-EIGHT

CHARLIE'S HEAD SNAPPED BACK AND HE OPENED HIS eye to see the old Indian squatting beside him on the floor of the den. Charlie did not realize he had fallen asleep until it registered in his mind that the others had left the room and someone had put a quilt over him.

Thunder rumbled over the house like a drum roll, and Charlie saw

228

through a gap in the curtains someone had pulled closed that the sky outside was darker than before.

"I'm glad you're here," Charlie said to the Indian, who only grunted noncommittally. "I need your gift again."

The old Indian laughed quietly. "Do you know about lightning?" he asked.

"What?"

"In the beginning, lightning lived upon the earth, but he was too powerful and he had a bad temper. When he was angry he would lash out and kill someone and afterward he would be sorry. The chiefs sat in council and banished him . . ."

"Never mind about that," Charlie interrupted. "I need the gift."

"That's pretty funny," the old man said. "But when lightning was sent away, monsters came up out of the earth and fed on the people. Finally they let lightning come back if he promised to kill the monsters and not to harm the people anymore. And that is what he did."

"Who cares?" Charlie almost shouted before he caught himself, not wanting to attract any attention. "What about the gift, the dream?"

"It was a dream this time?" the old Indian asked.

"Yes, of course it was. You know that, I dreamed I could fly. I was a hawk, and then I changed into something else. I could go back and forth in time and I saw things that had happened . . ."

"Ah, the gift was good then. I am glad."

"And now I need it again," Charlie whispered, rising out of his chair toward the old man. "I need to dream the dream again, so I can be sure of what I saw."

"You weren't paying attention the first time? That's too bad."

"I was . . ." Charlie stopped to collect himself to keep from shouting. "I was paying attention, but . . . look, is there some problem, why can't you just let me have the dream again and be done with it?"

"I don't think it works like that," the old man said.

"What . . ."

"I make a gift. It just . . . what it is comes from you, I think. And it is not easy to do."

"One gift to a customer, is that what you're telling me? Goddamn you . . ."

"My medicine is good, but it has been a long time after all . . ."

"Oh, for Christ's sake!" Charlie rose from his chair and shook the quilt to the floor. This was insane, he told himself. If you're going to conjure up ghosts, Charlie, you ought to do a better job. "What are you doing here anyway," he demanded of the old Indian. "I thought you only came around at night."

"It is night."

"What?"

Charlie pulled the curtains open and looked out the window to see darkness over the woods, the darker shadows of the trees lined against the black night sky by a flickering tongue of lightning on the horizon, more thunder following after.

"Christ, what time is it?" Charlie asked, but it was too dark in the room to see his watch.

In the downstairs darkness a phone rang. Charlie stumbled against his chair in his hurry to answer it on the kitchen extension.

"Yeah?" he said.

"Charlie?" he recognized the sheriff's voice.

"It's me. What's up?"

"Sound like you just woke up."

"I did."

"You're kidding."

"All right, all right, Sheriff. What?"

"Nothing, don't look like it's panning out."

"What do you mean?"

"How long you been asleep, Charlie?"

"I'm not sure."

"Great." Charlie heard the sheriff cursing almost far enough away from the mouthpiece of the phone to avoid hurting his feelings. "Okay, let's see . . . the doctor went out to the ranch to see to Momma and he brought Ruth back to town with him. Ruth, Samantha, and Calvin all got rooms out here at the motel for the night. Ruth wanted to stay close to Simon, who is overnighting at the hospital for mental evaluation, and Calvin convinced Sam they didn't want to risk those roads in a storm."

"Good," Charlie said, doubting that Calvin could convince Sam of anything.

"And Lawyer Childress was last seen hauling ass south on highway 24 heading for his meeting in Dallas. Did I leave anybody out?"

"I don't know," Charlie said, his head spinning. He tried to shake himself awake.

"That should leave Momma, Poppa, Jade, and Chris out there with you. Jeff too, if he hasn't run off again."

"Okay."

"Maybe I ought to send somebody out there," the sheriff offered.

"Why?" Charlie asked, thinking he had heard the screen door close softly on the back porch.

"Keep an eye on things," the sheriff said.

"You mean keep an eye on me. I don't think that'll be necessary, thanks anyway."

Charlie hung up the phone and looked around the corner to see if anyone was stirring upstairs. All the doors to the rooms were closed and he did not hear anything. He went through the kitchen and out onto the porch in time to see a figure disappearing up the trail in the direction of the big tree. In a tremorous wink of lightning, he saw the long blond hair.

"Jade," he whispered, not wanting to call out for her for fear of stirring the house. With a last look back inside to see if anyone was there, he hurried down the steps into the yard and followed her into the night.

CHAPTER THIRTY-NINE ▰▰▰▰▰▰▰▰▰

THE RAIN HAD SLACKENED FOR THE MOMENT, but there was a chill to it, and Charlie wished he had taken time to grab a jacket on his way out of the house, or the quilt from the den. Except for the peekaboo strobes of the lightning, the night was hopelessly dark, and he soon lost sight of Jade. He had taken the trail that led to the big tree when a movement off to his right, frozen in the brief glare of a lightning bolt that sounded as if it might have struck nearby, caught his eye. There she was, moving toward the low hill. She was not going to the big tree or the lake, she was headed for the cemetery. What the hell, he thought to himself.

He cut across and reached the cemetery trail, stumbling along as much by feel and memory as by anything he was able to see. Up the brow of the hill and he found himself among the tombstones that loomed and sparkled in another lightning flash. No Jade. Then he knew where she was going and he hurried on.

Charlie came to the little chapel and saw the door was open. Without calling her name, he went inside.

"I knew you'd come," he heard her say before he was able to see anything in the dark innards of the chapel.

"Did you?" he asked.

"Yes."

He could feel her near him, her rain-soaked hair and body steaming within arm's reach.

"What are you doing here?" he asked, blinking his eyes and trying very hard to see.

"Listen," she whispered.

The rain had picked up again in a freshening wind; it drove against the roof and the stone walls.

"Like drums," she said. "Look."

He followed her movement with his eyes and ears, and when the next lightning bolt filled the little sanctuary it bled the reds and yellows of the stained glass windows over the woman, who stood in the distorted angles the windows cast across the floor and the altar behind her. Charlie thought he saw her hot eyes glimmer like a cat's.

"I love it," she whispered. "Don't you, Charlie?"

"Well . . ."

"Don't you feel it?" she insisted.

He could make her out now, between the lightning bolts, as his eyes grew more accustomed to the darkness and she moved from side to side. She *was* like some kind of cat, he thought.

"Come here, Charlie," she purred. "Come on, Charlie."

She was reaching out to him and he did not move away. Her hands found him, her fingers working up his chest like snakes, over his shoulders, up either side of his throat until they grasped his face between them and she bent him down to her. Her lips met his, open and warm like a wound, and she kissed him. Her tongue worked into his mouth and she sucked him down into her, her body arched against his. His hands reached out and closed around her, followed the ridge of her spine down to the swelling of her haunches.

"Come on, Charlie," she whispered with her warm breath in his ear. "Come on."

"I . . . uh . . ." Charlie sputtered, his words smothered in her kisses. He pulled his lips away. "I shouldn't be here. I ought to keep an eye on things at the house."

"It's over, Charlie," she murmured, and Charlie could see her smile in the dark. "All over. You heard what the sheriff said." She kissed him, slowly and hungrily. "You don't have to stand guard anymore."

"Yeah," Charlie said. "But . . ."

She pulled away, backing away from him up the aisle toward the altar.

"Remember?" she said, with a naughty laugh. "Come on, Charlie. You remember."

Thunder rumbled over the little church and more lightning lit the scene, painting the woman blood red and glistening gold as Charlie watched her lower her robe to the floor. She stood in the dancing glow of lightning, nude, her arms outstretched toward him, imploring him.

"Charlie . . ." Her voice trailed off and was lost in a thunder bolt.

What was it the old Indian said about lightning, Charlie wondered. It kills our monsters?

And then the chapel was dark again and he could not see her anymore. He called to her and raised his foot to take a step toward her, but froze at the frigid kiss of steel on the nape of his neck.

"Don't do anything stupid," a voice hissed in his ear.

"Right," Charlie answered, not moving.

"Put your hands on top of your head," the voice told him. He obeyed.

With a heavy click the chapel filled with a greenish light and Charlie looked down at the camp lantern on the floor.

"There, that's better," the voice behind Charlie announced.

Charlie was looking at Jade, who stood a few feet in front of him, by the altar. Her mouth was open and her eyes were wide, but she did not try to cover herself, she just stood looking dumbfounded. Charlie could not help thinking she looked like a statue, she was so perfectly still.

From behind Charlie a hand reached out to pat him down, while the barrel of the gun remained in place at the base of his skull.

"Now kneel down, if you don't mind," the voice said.

"Kneel?" Charlie asked.

"That's right, as if in prayer. Do it."

Charlie lowered himself to one knee, his hands still on his head.

"Good," said the voice.

Charlie hoped he had not missed his chance. When he could feel the pistol touching him, he had a chance of taking it. Now it was just somewhere behind him. He hoped the man behind him would move in close again before he was through.

"Sit down," the voice said, this time talking to Jade. "That's right, there on the altar where I can see you."

When Jade and Charlie were where he wanted them, the voice took on a self-satisfied tone.

"Now, that's comfy, isn't it?"

"Childress, you know this isn't going to work," Charlie said.

"You don't even sound surprised," the lawyer said in an aggrieved voice. "I suppose you've known all along."

"Not long enough," Charlie said.

"No, not nearly long enough, I'm betting. That was a smart-assed thing you put the sheriff up to, that business about Chip leaving a suicide note."

"Actually, that was his idea."

"You're too modest. You knew that by saying that you'd smoke the killer out, didn't you?"

"Something like that."

"Because only the killer would know for sure it was a lie."

Charlie did not want to help him out too much, he was more interested in dragging things out.

"It was like putting me on notice, Charlie, that you were on to me. You knew it was me, didn't you?"

234

"Yeah."

"How?"

"You wouldn't believe me."

"Try me."

"It came to me in a dream."

"Don't be cute, Charlie. I'm serious."

"Me too. It's a trick I learned from an old dead Indian."

"What?"

"Never mind. What about the woman?"

"Don't be noble, Charlie. You've got your own problems."

"You're a reasonable man, Childress. We can work something out, can't we?"

"What happens to her depends on you, Charlie."

"How's that?"

"Level with me and maybe she doesn't get hurt. If you try to con me, I'll make you watch her die. Fair enough?"

"Like I said, you're reasonable. What do you want to know?"

"How you figured out it was me. And no bullshit about dead Indians."

"It stands to reason, if you don't believe Amber and the baby were accidents, or that Bill Junior was a suicide."

"How so?"

"Easier for somebody on the outside to do the dirty work. An outsider would never be missed on the ranch, wouldn't have to worry about slipping in and out of rooms without being heard, waking somebody up. Except for the baby, maybe. Anybody could have done that."

"That's thin. What else?"

"When you and I scrimmaged in the woods last night, it had to be you. I knew that after I thought about it."

"Yeah, that's what I thought," the lawyer said.

"Or Jeff. He's about your size."

"What?"

"But if it was Jeff, that would mean Chip was in it, too."

"Which would explain why Jeff had to kill him."

"Simpler is better, Childress. You don't cut somebody in on murder unless you have to. One man who knew his way around the place was all it took."

"You're guessing, Charlie."

"Not really. You'd have done better to have settled for a little less. You didn't have to knock off the whole damned family. For that matter, an original share would have been plenty, before any of the killing started."

"That's another thing. What makes you think I'm in the will at all?"

"You don't have to be. You're a lawyer, McKendrick's executor. If a million dollars goes through your hands, half a million sticks to your palms."

"With that family watching me like hawks? You've got to be kidding. They'd hire an army of accountants and auditors. They wouldn't trust anyone."

"And that's where you screwed up, Counselor. When Poppa made his announcement last night about the new will, everybody on the place knew that put him on the bull's eye. Hell, one reason he did it was he hoped whoever the killer was would try to take him out next. Either that, or whoever it was would try to take you out, to give them more time before the new will was drawn up. But he was safe with you, wasn't he. You wanted him to change the will. His leaving all his money to an institution with you holding the purse strings, that would have played right into your hands. You were the only one who wouldn't have lost out."

"I see . . ."

"Matter of fact, if you'd really been smart, you'd have tried to talk Poppa into a deal like that in the first place . . ."

"Everybody's a critic," the lawyer snapped. "What else?"

"That's about it. If we had enough to make a case, the sheriff would have arrested you already."

"That's what I thought. You aren't holding back on me, are you, Charlie?"

"Perish the thought. Except . . ."

"Except what, goddamnit!"

"There's your boat winch out in the channel."

"What? How do you know about that . . . ?"

"This old Indian . . ."

"Enough of that! You're stalling."

236

"That's how you killed Amber, isn't it? If I'm making all this up about the old Indian, how do I know how you killed her? I saw you, that's how. In a dream. You were in the lake, waiting for her when she went swimming there. Waiting in the black cold water for her. You were all decked out in your scuba gear, the same gear I saw in the photograph on the wall in your office. You're a diver. You waited for her, I don't know how long. I don't know if she came the first night, or if you waited more than once . . . But you knew her, you knew she liked to swim there alone at night. Poppa had warned her not to, but she was hard-headed. You told me that yourself when you came to see me at the Institute. You followed her when she swam back toward shore. You swam up behind her and you slipped your little homemade vise around her ankle. She must have thought at first she had stumbled into a root branch. Before she could get loose you had the two sticks closed around her ankle and the rawhide loop slipped up to close it. That was when you used your boat winch. You had a line run from the winch out in the channel to the vise. Once you had it on her, all you had to do was pull your end of the line and it worked off the winch to tug her out into deep water. When you'd got her out a ways, it pulled her under. She didn't have a chance, you had leverage and she couldn't get free. She'd have been a handful for you if you'd just tried to wrestle her under, but you weren't taking any chances, were you?"

"You've a hell of an imagination, Charlie," Childress said.

"You cranked her out, Counselor, and when you were sure she was drowned you slipped off the vise and that was that. But you didn't take the time to retrieve your winch, did you? It's still out there, anchored to a tree in the channel where you left it. Why was that? Lose your head, or were you just bushed from the effort?"

"They searched, they dragged the lake," Childress protested.

"Looking for a body. Oh, they'll find the winch all right. Of course, I imagine you can explain . . ."

"I lost that winch off my boat trailer, somebody stole it . . ."

"That you lost the winch or somebody stole it, right."

"And . . . uh, I haven't bothered to report it because . . ."

"Because you've had so much on your mind."

"Exactly, I've had too much on my mind."

"So that's not a problem."

"Of course not."

"And you thought you'd gotten rid of the vise thing, too. That was a solid touch. When they found her body, naturally they thought the marks it left on her ankle were from the trees and crap underwater. No reason to suspect foul play."

"How did you find it?"

"The Indian. The sheriff has it now."

"It doesn't prove anything. Neither does the boat winch."

"Not by themselves, but it all adds up, doesn't it?"

"Not enough."

"I know," Charlie admitted. "That's why we had to set a trap for you."

"What?"

"A trap. We had to set you up, get you worried enough to show your hand. And you did."

"You aren't serious," Childress insisted.

Charlie looked at Jade, who was fidgeting, her eyes on Childress or maybe on the door behind him.

"Yeah, I am."

"So where's the sheriff?" Childress demanded.

"Timing's always a problem with these things. He's running a little late, I guess."

"You're impossible."

"But he's coming. You'll never get off the place."

"The hell I won't. I haven't even been here. I was in a meeting that broke up a couple of hours ago. Right now I'm in my hotel room with a Do Not Disturb sign on my door and instructions that no calls are to be forwarded. And that's where I'll be in the morning when they call to tell me they found you dead."

"Yeah, I guess that could work. I suppose you know your way around out here well enough to have your car stashed somewhere. You probably have a route worked out, back roads and everything, where nobody'll see you."

"You're damned right I do."

"Okay, sounds pretty good. Only . . ."

"Only what?"

"Only what's supposed to happen to me? How do I turn up dead?"

238

"Now, you can figure that out, Charlie."

"Suicide's the only thing I come up with."

"Exactly. As a matter of fact, the subject came up this afternoon and I don't think Doctor Cartwright would have any trouble buying it. And she's your doctor."

"Not anymore."

"Don't quibble. It was some cop's suicide that put you over the brink in the first place, wasn't it?"

"Yeah, only that was murder too."

"Close enough."

"You're probably right," Charlie admitted. "What about Jade?"

"Poor Jade will disappear."

"That's it?"

"Why not? She's done it before."

"I don't know, Counselor . . ."

"It's not your problem, Charlie. You don't have any problems anymore. Your time is about up."

Charlie heard Childress's feet scrape on the stone floor as he moved closer. Good man, Charlie thought. If you're going to sell this as suicide, you'll have to get in real close.

Childress stopped, and when he spoke again his voice was close behind Charlie, close enough that Charlie knew the gun was almost within his reach.

"Don't you have any questions, Charlie?"

"Uh, no, I can't think of any."

"Don't you wonder why I brought you into all this? I can't believe that's not driving you crazy. No offense."

"Nah, I guess you thought I'd stir up some ghosts or something, cloud the issue with a lot of stuff about the Indian curse. At best I'd be a distraction, at worst, no threat. And it made you look like you were doing all you could to get to the bottom of things."

"Good, Charlie. Very good. And that's about the way it worked out, isn't it? Your old dead Indian and all that."

"Looks like it."

"Good-bye, Charlie," Childress whispered, so close Charlie felt his breath.

The slug would come from the right side, Charlie knew, so it would look like he had shot himself. High, around the temple. He could not see the muzzle of the gun, but he had to chance it. Time had run out. He dropped his head and twisted to one side, his right hand spread open and arcing back over his right ear.

A fireball lit the room and roared like a cannon, Charlie's ears ringing as he turned, the heel of his right hand striking metal as the slug caromed off the stone floor and into the wall behind him. In the ringing, dizzy instant before the next shot fired he heard the clattering of the empty shell on the stone floor. He pushed off with both feet, turning back toward the gun as he reached for it with his right hand. Childress cursed and threw his left arm across Charlie's throat to keep him away. The dead black eye of the muzzle of the gun loomed in Charlie's face for an instant and he saw Childress's finger tightening on the trigger. He yanked the gun up and over with the fingertips of his right hand as it belched fire again and roared, blinding him. A stained glass panel shattered overhead and shards of colored glass showered down on the two men. Charlie closed on the gun again, his hand searching frantically. Childress got his left arm around Charlie's neck and tried to throw him, but Charlie braced himself, knowing he had to stay as close to the gun as he could. He found the flat cool metal again as Childress groaned with the strain of trying to break his neck or twist himself free. It was a big gun, with plenty of barrel, and Charlie put everything he had into clamping his right hand down hard over the top of the slide.

Charlie heard Jade squeal and scamper past toward the door at the same time Childress finally managed to break Charlie's balance and throw him. With his left arm, Charlie held tight to Childress, his right hand staying on the gun in spite of the other man's twisting it from side to side. Childress bent low and got leverage on him, and over they went, crashing over a pew, spilling the rough wooden bench on top of them as they crashed to the floor and the gun barked again. Charlie screamed as he felt the slide kick back, the sharp metal edge ripping his palm, and the bench behind him exploded in a shower of splinters as the slug slammed into the pew. For all he could do, Charlie could not manage to keep his grip on the gun. The slide bit into the flesh of his palm and the recoil yanked the gun up and away. He clambered after it, his wounded hand reaching out for it, as Childress kicked free of him and crawled away.

240

"Now!" he cried. "Now you crazy sonofabitch, I've got you!"

Charlie lunged for the gun again as the lawyer pumped it toward him and pulled the trigger. Nothing. Charlie took the kicks Childress aimed at him to keep him off as he used his left hand to pull the slide back and clear the jam. Charlie's hand had kept the spent shell from ejecting, had jammed it in the port. Now the slide clanked home with the heavy certain sound that Charlie knew meant it would work this time. Charlie saw the gun rock forward, blue steel in the darkness of the chapel, a strobe of lightning like a sheet thrown over the two of them. In the eerie and oddly comforting disassociation that always came when he met death reached out, Charlie saw the lightning flash as if it were frozen and lasted a long time. He saw the muzzle of the gun cranking down out of Childress's left hand with the slide clanking home, the right hand of the killer punching forward, the bore of the gun driving toward his eyes, and Charlie's left hand reaching, closing from beneath the gun, driving it up. His bloody right hand lashed out and he saw his blood daubed up Childress's left cheek, toward his eye, and Childress's head jerked back, a disgusted look on his face. Charlie watched his own left hand drive up in the leisure of the distended half-second before the hammer fell, taking the barrel of the gun up with it, and then the fourth shot boomed, muffled and smelling of burnt powder and flesh, as Charlie drove himself up under his twisting hand and shoved the barrel of the gun toward Childress's head so that when the lawyer's finger pulled the trigger the muzzle blast swallowed his face with its disgusted look. Childress's mouth flew open with an inhuman sound like an echo of the slug that had drilled itself into his brain, and then collapsed in a heap.

Dark again, and Charlie's desperate breathing, heart pounding in his ears from the struggle, his ears ringing hopelessly with the thunder and lightning of the big gun, and now the only sound was the falling rain again.

Charlie pushed himself off the dying lawyer and looked around for Jade, hoping she had not been hit. He looked toward the door, the way she had run when the fight started, and saw her there.

"Are you all right?" he asked.

She did not answer.

"Jade?"

Backlit in lightning through the door, with the stained glass streamers on her face, he saw that she had clutched in both hands the garden shears her mother kept in the basket by the chapel door. Her face was wild and her eyes were . . . Charlie shifted the gun in his hand and called her name again.

"Charlie?" she answered this time. "Oh my god, Charlie, I thought . . ."

She fell in a heap on her knees in the aisle between the pews and Charlie put his arm around her shoulders. She cried, and then he stood and tugged her to her feet. She stood staring down at the dead man until Charlie found her robe and put it over her shoulders.

"Let's go," he said to her.

She did not answer, only laid her head on his shoulder and let him lead her out the chapel door to the path that led back to the big house, through the cemetery and down the little hill.

"What's that?" she cried, and he felt her go rigid against him.

Charlie heard voices and saw lights at the back of the house, like fireflies flittering up and down the back steps, from side to side.

"Over here!" Charlie called, and the fireflies turned on him and Jade, bathing them in the brittle glare of flashlights. Charlie looked at the woman, then up at the sky. The rain was slackening and the lightning was moving off.

"Who is it?" she demanded, shrinking behind Charlie.

"Take it easy," he assured her. "It's the cavalry. We've been rescued."

CHAPTER FORTY

IT WAS THE SHERIFF AND A COUPLE OF HIS MEN AND Charlie told them in a few words what they needed to know. He handed the bloody gun over to the sheriff and took Jade inside.

She was a wreck, all tears and wet hair, and he led her through the kitchen, where Poppa and Chris stood with their faces full of questions. He took her upstairs to her room.

"You'd better get into something warm and dry," he told her, then he went down the stairs to see Poppa and explain everything.

Before he could say anything, Poppa held up a hand.

"I swear, Charlie, you're making a drinking man out of me," he said, and marched off in the direction of his den.

Chris sat down at the table when Charlie did, each of them taking their regular seats out of habit. He did not ask Charlie any questions, waiting until Poppa came back.

Charlie heard the old man coming, the clinking of glasses, and thought he would not mind a drink, just as the back door opened and Sam and Calvin came in shaking themselves dry.

"Charlie," Sam began, looking relieved. But then she saw his mangled hand. "What on earth . . ."

"Nothing to worry about," Charlie assured her, his eyes on the bottle of whiskey McKendrick set on the table in front of him.

"What did you get ahold of, man?" Calvin asked.

"Got it caught in some machinery," Charlie smiled up at him. "Nothing serious."

"Get out the first aid kit," McKendrick said and Chris did. "There might be something left in there that'll help."

"Thank you," Sam said as she set to work.

McKendrick poured a drink for everybody that wanted one, and only Sam passed. She was busy with Charlie's hand. Chris apparently thought it occasion enough to have whiskey like the others.

"All right, Son," McKendrick said, leaning toward Charlie across the table. "Tell us."

Charlie looked from one end of the table to the other, at the empty chairs. They are like tombstones, he thought.

"Let's wait, if you don't mind," he said. "Till everybody's here and then I'll only have to say everything once."

"Who else?" the old man asked.

"Who else what?" asked the sheriff as he came in the back door.

"There," McKendrick said. "That's everybody."

"Jade's not here," Charlie reminded him.

"She looked pretty used up, boy," McKendrick said. "I don't imagine . . ."

"She'll be down in a minute," Charlie assured him.

There were some looks exchanged and Charlie poured a drink for Jade, who appeared in the door a moment later, in a long terry-cloth bathrobe with her hair done up in a towel.

"Y'all excuse my appearance, please," she said. "But I thought I heard a cork being popped down here."

"Here you go." Charlie handed her her drink as she passed behind him on her way to her regular chair.

They all heard the sound and turned and saw Jeff leading Momma through the door from the stairs. The sound was Momma, making a soft and tremulous hum inside her throat without moving her lips, a low and expectant moaning that would break out into the banshee keening he had heard the night the baby died, Charlie knew, when he was through talking. Poppa rose and put his arm around her shoulders and led her to his chair. She sat there warily, and Poppa stood behind her. Jeff did not take his chair, but slumped against the doorframe and looked at Charlie.

"Okay, Charlie. Full house, now let's have it," McKendrick said.

"All right with you, Sheriff?" Charlie asked.

The sheriff nodded.

He told them everything, in order as best he could, from the time of Amber's visit to the Institute to that night in the chapel. He told them how he came to suspect Childress to begin with, and then he told them about the Indian, the old shaman of the tree. He tried to describe his dream, the gift that the old man had not been able to duplicate. And he went a little beyond that to try to explain to them how he had felt something from his first day at the ranch. He tried to make them understand, but as he looked from one face to the other around the table he knew he could not. Finally he could not think of anything else to say.

"So that's it," he said in closing. "I can't expect you to believe in dead Indians, but . . . uh, you know, na kusinah."

"What?" Sam was the first to ask.

"Na kusinah. It's Caddoan, means 'that is all.' "

"And how would you know that?" she asked.

"Never mind."

"Well, I'll just be goddamned," old McKendrick said. "I'll be goddamned."

"There is more," Charlie said.

"What?" McKendrick asked.

"Could I see you for a second, Sheriff?"

Charlie rose and the sheriff followed him from the kitchen past Jeff in the doorway into the parlor where they exchanged a brief whisper before returning.

"We're listening, Charlie, for Christ's sake," Sam said.

"Childress didn't kill the baby. He was in the den with witnesses. And that means . . ."

"Holy . . ." McKendrick blurted. "There was somebody in it with him."

"I'm afraid so," Charlie said. "One of the heirs. Childress would have done all right for himself managing the trust, but that was Poppa's idea, and it came late in the game. When it started, Childress was in on an heir's share. It had to be that way."

"Killed that little baby," McKendrick whispered, his voice cracking.

"Yeah," Charlie said. "That was the worst of it. How anybody could live with that . . ."

"Jesus," Chris said. "I'd hoped the baby was an accident, whatever else. To think . . ."

Silence fell over them, except for Poppa's muttered oaths, Momma's unbroken hum and the clink of ice in their drinks. Charlie took the folded sheet of paper out of his shirt pocket. He studied his scrawled notes before he went on.

"And I know who," Charlie said, not as if he were boasting, but with a tired sadness in his voice, a reluctant resignation.

"Who?" McKendrick demanded.

"I've tried to keep track of things," Charlie went on, looking at the piece of paper. "Mainly where everybody was at the time of each killing, hoping there would be some kind of pattern . . ."

"So who is it?" Chris demanded.

"Most of you had alibis for some of the murders, not for the others. That's how it is with innocent people, they don't know when they'll need alibis. But there is one person who had alibi witnesses for every murder except one, except for the killing of the baby. One who made sure that when something happened she had a witness. Like a roommate."

With that Charlie looked at Sam, and he saw it register on her face like a blow. She turned and looked at Jade. "You!" she cried.

"What?" Jade protested. "You're crazy."

"Probably, but I'm also right," Charlie answered.

"I don't have to listen to this!" Jade screamed, rising.

"You damned sure ain't leaving," the sheriff said, taking a step toward her. "That's about enough melodrama, ain't it, Charlie? We got the damned statement."

"I guess you're right," Charlie said.

"What statement?" Jade asked, crumbling a little. "What are you talking about?"

"May I, Sheriff?" Charlie held out his hand and the sheriff handed him the notebook from his pocket. There was a ballpoint pen marking a certain page. "Thank you."

From the yard the turning red lights of the ambulance lit the kitchen as it growled in low gear around the corner with the dead lawyer aboard on its way to the morgue.

"If your friend Childress were still with us," Charlie said, "he could explain something called a dying declaration. It's a legal thing. A statement given by a man who knows he's dying that shows his own guilt in a crime is admissible in court against anybody else that statement names as a conspirator. Did I get that about right, Sheriff?"

"That's the way they taught it when I went to school, Charlie."

"This," Charlie said, opening the sheriff's notebook to the marked page, "is Mister Childress's dying declaration." He took his time reading it, then looked at Jade and smiled an evil smile. "And it's all here. What do you say to that?"

"No, no," Jade screamed, shaking her head violently and backing away from the table into a corner. "No, it's a lie!"

The sheriff reached inside his rain coat and pulled out his badge case. He jammed his index finger inside the case and tugged out his laminated Miranda card.

"Miss McKendrick, you have the right to remain silent and not make any statement at all and any statement you make—"

246

"No, no," she screamed again, crying now, her head dashing from side to side, her hair spilling out from the unwinding towel.

"No-o-o-o!"

"—may be used against you at your trial. Any statement you make may be used as evidence against you in court—"

"Make him stop, Daddy," she begged, crying, her arms flung out toward the old man.

"You killed that baby," the old man said.

Jade howled like a cornered animal, her teeth bared at them as if she would fall on them like a mad dog.

"You have the right to have a lawyer present to advise you prior to and during any—"

"It . . . was . . . all . . . *his idea!*" she screamed, the last sound of the last word swirling up through the house like a banshee, and then she fell to her knees on the floor in a sobbing mass. "And he told on me!"

She said that last part in a voice that sounded like a child, a naughty little girl with her lip stuck out. The sheriff lifted her off the floor and put handcuffs on her. He dragged her out onto the porch and called a deputy to take her away. She turned to look over her shoulder at Charlie.

"You believe me, don't, you Charlie? He made me do it."

The sheriff and Sam both turned toward him for his answer.

"Maybe," Charlie said to Jade. "People use crazies sometimes." His eyes met Sam's. "I figure either he roped you in so he'd have you to blame it on if things went wrong—"

"Yes," Jade cried, nodding her head. "That was it . . ."

"Or else the whole thing was your idea. You wouldn't be hard to fall in love with, kid. And a man'll do terrible things in that condition. More so than for money, I believe."

Jade's eyes narrowed from hopeful saucers to venomous slits, but she said nothing more and the sheriff took her away. And then it was over.

Charlie looked around the table at the faces of the survivors and thought he had not done them all much good. Momma erupted finally into her brokenhearted aria, and Jeff and Chris tried to comfort her.

"Could I see that, Charlie?" Sam asked.

She pointed to the sheriff's notebook and Charlie handed it to her.

"It's Childress's dying declaration, all right," he told her. "I wouldn't lie about it."

"So I see."

Sam looked at the marked page, traced with blood and splattered with rain. There was one line to the statement. "Fuck you," it said. That was all.

"He wasn't in much shape to talk, but they said he did get that across before he died," Charlie explained.

"You were bluffing," Sam said.

"All the way."

EPILOGUE

THE RAIN HAD STOPPED AND THE SKY WAS CLEARING
and Charlie was ready to go. He did not want to stay at the McKendrick
ranch any longer. He stood in the trail near the big tree and looked up
at it. He had been waiting a good while.

"Okay," he said at last. "Don't bother saying good-bye."

Behind him at the rear of the big house Calvin honked his horn
impatiently. Charlie turned to go and there he was, the old man standing
in the trail behind him.

"Well," Charlie said.

"Yes," answered the Indian.

"Is it tonight? Is this the night you . . ."

"I hope so," the old man said, with a little shiver. "It feels like it."

"So, when . . . never mind. Listen, I'll keep my eye on you,"
Charlie said. The Indian's face showed his puzzlement. "In the stars.
When you take your place, I'll keep my eye on you."

"You are funny," the old man said, shaking his head. "With so
many stars, how would you find me with your eyes?"

"I'll just pick one. One that's not too goddamned bright."

"Yes." The Indian smiled. "That might work."

"Right. Well, I'm leaving now."

"Good-bye, Charlie."

"Good-bye . . . " Charlie stopped and stepped toward the old
man. "You didn't tell me your name."

"It is Ouin Anet Chouve."

"Big name," Charlie said. "What did you say it means?"

" 'Man Who Knows.' It makes me laugh, too."

Charlie was laughing a little at that, but he shook the old man's
hand, wincing because it still hurt where Childress's gun had bitten him.

249

"I don't know where you came from, if I dreamed you up or if you're . . . Anyway, good-bye."

"Yes," the old man said.

Charlie walked back to the yard behind the house and opened the door of Calvin's car. He turned to look back toward the tree, but of course the old man was not there anymore. Charlie got in the car and Calvin drove them away. Charlie did not think about the Indian anymore for a while. He was looking forward to seeing his daughter again after being away so long.